To Fred, I
hope you [enjoy this]
as much as [I did writing]
it.

Stephen R Dyson
USN Ret.

DREAMCATCHER

Stephen R. Dyson

AuthorHouse™
1663 Liberty Drive
Bloomington, IN 47403
www.authorhouse.com
Phone: 1-800-839-8640

© 2011 Stephen R. Dyson. All rights reserved.

No part of this book may be reproduced, stored in a retrieval system, or transmitted by any means without the written permission of the author.

First published by AuthorHouse 5/17/2011

ISBN: 978-1-4567-6064-9 (sc)
ISBN: 978-1-4567-6065-6 (e)

Library of Congress Control Number: 2011907394

Printed in the United States of America

Any people depicted in stock imagery provided by Thinkstock are models, and such images are being used for illustrative purposes only.
Certain stock imagery © Thinkstock.

This book is printed on acid-free paper.

Because of the dynamic nature of the Internet, any web addresses or links contained in this book may have changed since publication and may no longer be valid. The views expressed in this work are solely those of the author and do not necessarily reflect the views of the publisher, and the publisher hereby disclaims any responsibility for them.

To My Wife

She inspires me to do things far beyond my own inclinations. The story parallels our lives and even though it is fiction, there is truth that we have lived and experienced in one form or another. I have always said that I was the luckiest man on earth, experiencing the total love and devotion of not one but two women. When most men never find it once.
The name Dreamcatcher came to me as the book took on a life of it's own, enabling me to share my innermost thoughts with the person I most admire, and could have only dreamed of, Terry.

1

It is hard to look at yourself in the mirror and know that your very existence is pointless.

Seven years ago, his graying hair had still been mostly curls of red and no matter how hard he tried, he could not comb it completely straight, so he kept it short instead. His neatly trimmed beard showed very few if any gray hairs. Nevertheless, he had felt tired and old when he retired from the US Navy Aviation. It seems so long ago. I have been lost ever since, he thought. Well, that was not exactly true. I feel like I have been off the track since I came back from that war. It is now eighteen years of living a screwed up life.

No, not in the military…that had been the only sane thing in his years. Just in my personal life. "Hell, I don't even feel alive anymore, all I do is exist".

September 1987, and Stony Dawson, was on Hwy 17 driving north from Orlando, Fl. He was returning home from the yearly visit his children. He always drove this trip because he and his late wife had taken this route back home many times when the children were babies. He was heading to his mother's home in Springfield, Mo. As he passed NAS Jacksonville, his mind slipped back to 1980, and the last time he had seen the main gate.

The time ticked by and so did the miles as he reflected back on his life. He felt these past years were a disaster. He knew he had not done well since his beloved wife, Marilyn, died in 1971. That damned Viet Nam war had screwed up his entire world, everything, as he had known it was forever changed. When Marilyn died that had been the last straw. If I had gotten killed in that crap hole, Marilyn might not have passed on and the kids would have had their mother to rear them, not me.

She left him with five children to parent by himself. Child rearing was a lost art to Stony.

He came to the intersection of I-75 and US 82 at Tipton, Ga. taking the familiar turn, his thoughts went back to the kids. The visit with the children and his grandchildren had not turned out bad at all, this year. Now that they had their own families and own problems, they did not blame him so much for the trouble in their lives. Maybe we are all getting older, and more tolerant, he thought. He had kept his promise to Marilyn, which was to stay in the Navy and keep the kids together until they were ready to be on their own. He had accomplished that, not well, but he had kept his promise.

As Stony drove north on old US 82, the blackness of the night and the passing patches of fog reminded him of the turmoil of his life after his wife had died. He had missed her so much, still did. He caught himself searching the crowds because of a glimpse of someone that looked like her. Then realization would set in and he knew he would never see her again, not in this life. Often times crying himself to sleep at nights when the loneliness so completely flooded his inner soul. That painful experience would not go away, even after all these years.

All the plans they had made for their lives, the children's

experiences, school, plays, proms, and eventually marriages, the grandchildren they would revel in, middle age, and the final 'rocking chair days' would never be shared with the one, the only one he had ever wanted to grow old with.

The Viet Nam war had made him old before his time, but he had raised the children and kept them all together. Tears rolled down his cheeks. He hoped 'Pris', (the nickname he had called his beloved Marilyn) would be proud of his efforts. Looking back now, he was not sure he had really done any of them a favor. Parenting had been a task he had only endured, never embraced. He was not close to the children, or for that matter, any of his family. He could only say… he had kept his promise. That had been his total concentration getting through this life. A promise was a promise and meant to be kept.

Stony pulled off the road at Eufala, Al and into an all-night diner's parking lot, pulling his car into a space at the outer edge of the lot. God, how time flies when you are having fun, he laughed at his own private joke as he got out of the car and stretched his legs. He rubbed his face vigorously with his hands, trying to hide the effects of his sadness and melancholy. He walked around in the parking lot trying to get in some sort of casual attitude, before he entered the restaurant. It was important for people to think he had everything under control. If they only knew, he had not controlled anything in his life for a long time. He was getting weary of trying to give the appearance that life was good and that he was handling it well.

The night air was thick, heavy and he could swear that he could smell the crappie, which would be bedding close to the bank's edge in Lake Eufala. One of his most favored activities was fishing and the last seven years he had had little time to even think about it, let alone actually do it. Now that all the children were married off, and beginning lives of their own, maybe he could find the time to fish, and hunt, and generally anything that involved being outdoors. God, he hoped so, spending time in nature was something that could help replenish the soul. Maybe after this trip is over, I can do just that, he thought as he entered the restaurant's door.

He bantered lightly with the waitress while eating his meal. Then Stony requested his thermos be refilled with coffee and then exited the building, making his way across the lot. Filling his lungs with the fresh scent of the Alabama countryside one last time, he got behind the wheel, swung the car back onto the highway and proceeded on the journey that would eventually lead him home to Arizona. He stopped several times throughout the night to relieve himself of the gallon or so of coffee he had drank as he drove. As daylight came he turned onto US 63, still headed north. It was 11:30 am when he pulled into his mothers' driveway. He had promised to see her before heading back to Arizona. Two days was normally long enough before they started getting on each other's nerves. He spent those two days taking his mom out to eat, visiting his sister and catching up on his rest. The third morning, they said their goodbyes and Stony turned north on I-44 toward St. Louis, where he was to depart for Phoenix on an afternoon flight.

After arriving in St. Louis, Stony checked in his rental car and grabbed a bite to eat before finding the terminal where he was to catch his plane. He hated this part of traveling. An airport terminal filled with nothing but strangers, all hurrying, but trying to make polite conversation as they passed. Usually he slipped away to the lounge to sip a tall scotch and water to sit in a dark corner to watch. The hardest to watch was people who had someone they truly cared for, walking through the concourse arm in arm. You could tell from the little pats on the hand or the squeeze around the waist that says 'It is okay, I am right here'. The looks and glances that spoke volumes to those who cared enough to observe. Every time that Stony saw the couples with that special look, the lump would come up in his throat, and he would long for just one more moment with Marilyn.

2

Elaine has just hung up the phone after having a lengthy conservation with her sister. Carol Lee had lived in California since 1969, loved it there, and had begged for the last two hours for Elaine to come. At least, for a visit, and if she liked it like Carol Lee, why not make her home there? Elaine has promised she would come as soon as she wrapped up a few loose ends here at home. She poured a cup of coffee and relaxed at the kitchen table, thinking a change of scenery might just be just what the doctor ordered.

She looked at her reflection in the kitchen window, looking back at her was a nice looking woman. Maybe not beautiful, but very acceptable, she thought. Her hair, once brown, was now a champagne blonde. She had done it on a whim, way back when she thought there was still hope for the marriage. 'Eyes of blue, 5'2"…Blondes have more fun, all that sort of thing. But she found she liked the look, it softened her appearance, so she kept it blonde.

She stood and turned away from the reflection. She had long

passed the phase of really caring that she always looked her very best. What was in the reflection of a mirror was now secondary to how she felt about herself as a person. What was she going to do with the rest of her life?

She strolled throughout the house and tried remembering all the good times. The excitement she had felt when she and Darrell had first been married and began setting up housekeeping as Mr. and Mrs. Darrell Davis. The first year and a half had been good, very good.

Nevertheless, slowly but surely they had grown apart. She had married while still wet behind the ears. Soon their son, Evan, was born. Elaine worked five days a week at her job as a cosmetologist and Darrell worked at so many jobs that she no longer could tell how many he had actually held. It had not taken much of an excuse for him to quit one and start looking for another. Their lives together had been up and then down, starting from scratch and stopping again, just to move and begin all over again.

Elaine had finally pretty much figured out that there was no such thing as true love. She had been so sure that what they had was true love, and that it would last forever. Then love became that unattainable state of mind that she was sure could be there if she would become the 'right' kind of wife. To work standing on your feet all day making enough money to sustain the household, never being sure that your husband would still have a job at the end of the day. She would come home and prepare an evening meal, which might or might not be eaten. How many times she had placed meals on the table that had grown cold before he would come in the house, because there was always something he had to do that was more important.

Washing clothes, cleaning their home, and all the while taking care of the needs of Evan, because daddy cannot be disturbed while working on some project in the garage, tending the yard or mowing the grass, or even just watching something on television. Daddy's time was important to daddy.

To begin there was too much fairy tale, and then later, too much reality to continue. The longer they stayed together, the less time they actually spent together. Both of them had begun to live their individual lives, instead of one life as husband and wife. So inevitably, they separated, divorced, and continued to live their lives, individually. Then, there was no pretense of even caring what each other was doing and she could live her life now with no concern about what someone would or could find fault with in her actions.

Her son, Evan was now serving in the US Navy. She and Darrell had divorced when he had been five years old. She had tried to instill the importance of being a responsible person, as well as a loving, caring individual, and she was now proud of the man that he had become and the path he was now taking with his life. However, she faced the task of now doing for herself instead of him and she felt lost.

After the divorce, she tried the dating scene, the nightclubs, the parties, but found herself not liking all the games. Playing games with peoples' hearts was not to her a 'game' at all. If that was what love was all about, then she wanted no part of it. She would rather just live her life and maybe one of these days she would find a like-minded companion. She wasn't sure exactly what that meant, but later on in life she would like to travel and it sure would be better to be with 'someone she enjoyed being with', than to go alone.

She had gone through so many changes in her life that it just seemed second nature now to have a plan B. The difference between her and many other divorced, single mothers was the fact that she now almost embraced change because to start over was the chance to get it right.. She tried to make every decision count for something good, and she never wanted to look back and say I took the easy way simply because it was easier.

Elaine was now a very self-reliant person, because she had depended on herself so many times, there was no doubt that she could do whatever was necessary to survive any situation in life. Some circumstances had been so hard she never thought she would survive to another day. Nevertheless, she now knew, looking back at what she had been through that by simply putting one foot in front of the other and not thinking about the miles ahead of you, a person could survive.

The day her son had left on that military transport bus, she realized that she was alone. Maybe she should think about a change in her life. Maybe California was not such a bad idea after all. She could always get a job and she no longer had a reason to stay in Missouri. Therefore, after taking three days to arrange for the disconnection of utilities, phone, cable TV, and giving a forwarding address for any correspondence that she might receive, she locked the front door and left.

3

She approached the ticket counter in the St. Louis airport. California, here I come," she said. "I actually am getting excited about what my new life will involve."

As she took her seat in the waiting area, she knew it would be fun to see Carol Lee again. It had been so long since they had spent time together. Who knows, I might even find romance, again. Ha, ha, she smiled to herself, I will probably end up an old spinster, but maybe I will have lots of money, then I will not mind it so much. Elaine glanced up as she was smiling and noticed a man looking directly at her. Oh no, he is going to think I'm … no, she took second glance, he had already looked away.

Good, that is the last thing I need right now. This trip is for me and I do not want to spend the time on the plane politely making conversation. As he walked by her, she managed to make the mental assessment that he actually looked like a person with whom she might have an interesting conversation. The way he carried himself looked like the kind of confidence that self-reliance can give to a person. She had heard that about herself many times. Most people found her intimidating, because she gave the impression that she really did not need anyone to help her through life. That is what he reminded her of, someone who really was not interested in what other people thought or if they cared. He looked like he could take care of himself.

The announcement to board the plane brought her attention back to getting her luggage, her book, and ticket in hand so she would have everything ready when she got to the ticket counter. The flight would take about 4 hours and even though the weatherman had predicted a slight delay over Arizona because of the seasonal windstorms, there should not be any trouble with the connecting flight to California.

As Stony was settling into his assigned seat, he looked up to see the young woman that had caught his attention in the waiting area. He had been looking at her on purpose. She had caught his attention because he liked her bearing. The way she carried herself had made him stop and look at her. Then she had glanced up and looked directly at him. Breaking eye contact with her was the best way he knew to discourage conversation. He wanted to get some rest on the plane and the last thing he wanted was acting interested in someone's inane conversation. Watching her walk down the aisle, looking for her seat he had to admit maybe her conversation might have been worth listening too. She was attractive, carried herself with poise, and look, she could read. I would sure like to see the title of that book, he thought, just to see what things interested her. Do not even go there he said to himself, what on earth are you thinking? She is very not interested in a crusty old military man like me. Besides that, she is so far out of your league; you could not begin to get a second glance, let alone conversation from her.

When the engines started, Stony strapped on his seatbelt, and the plane slowly taxied out to the active runway. He could hear the sounds of the hydraulics and occasionally the sound of steering cables as the pilots went through the checklist. He could hardly wait for the take-off so he could lay back the seat and get some shuteye. Having flown in the Navy some 10,000 hours, he found that being airborne was the greatest place in the world to sleep. He loved it! The plane rumbled down the runway heading for Phoenix, where he would get off and drive the next 55 miles to his home in the mobile home park in Coolidge.

Stony had bought an older mobile home about six years back, and had spent a lot of time fixing it exactly as he wanted. There were orange, lemon, and grapefruit trees surrounding his lot, cactus and rose bushes were next to the house as a buffer to the windstorms they received every year. He had been gone much of the monsoon season this year and was anxious to get back to survey any damage he would have to repair.

He loved spending time outdoors, and he had thoroughly enjoyed his time in the desert. The Indian reservations were becoming familiar stomping grounds to him as he had made many a friend with the local Indian tribes. Stony had hiked and hunted a few times and in places where most white man never went. Some white men never learned that a little respect for your fellowman could make your way a little easier to travel. He had fished Lake Roosevelt, Lake Apache, and Canyon Lake with some success. The fish here were not the size that Florida lakes held, but they were very respectable in their own right, and he had enjoyed catching every one of them. Keeping busy was his way of helping his mind stay away from memories. Sometimes, it worked and sometimes it did not. He had even tried dating occasionally, but found that for the most part it was more hurtful than helpful. Most females had a real hard time understanding his conversation and he sure did not have a clue where they were coming from. Maybe that author was right, they did come from another planet, but more likely, it was just him. His thought process just was not like anyone else. He was pretty much a loner and he rather liked it that way.

By the time the plane reached altitude, Stony was fast asleep and oblivious to anything around him. This was one place he was comfortable and he planned to take advantage of the sleep he had lost on his trip.

4

JERRY BRADFORD HAD been a pilot for some fifteen years, ever since he graduated from the Naval Academy. He had flown the P-3 Orion in Anti-Submarine Warfare during his tour of enlistment in military service. Jerry had decided that the airlines offered more opportunity and would be considerably more lucrative than staying in the service. Once hired by the airlines, he had started flying as a flight engineer, then third pilot, and finally after three years, promotion to co-pilot. First on cross country's and overnighters and in less than two years he had become Pilot.

Flying stretch tens on regular coast-to-coast flights, he usually averaged about 6 to 8 flights per month. Jerry was married with two children, two young girls, each beautiful in their own way. However, their youngest daughter had major health issues. There had been more than one major surgery on her brain. Just when the doctors thought they had removed all of the tumor, this time she would recover and all would be well. Luckily, the tumor was not cancerous and surgery had kept her free from the most serious side effects. However, each time it would reappear and surgery would be on the schedule once again. Each surgery had put quite a strain on their finances. They had managed to amass what seemed an insurmountable medical debt, and with no end in sight because she had to undergo yet more surgery before she reached the age of ten, if she lived that long. The cost would be somewhere around three hundred thousand, if everything went well and there were no complications. And, there were never any guarantees.

Jerry's assignment for the afternoon was this hop from St. Louis to Los Angeles via Phoenix and then round robin back the following day. He was up early spending some quality time with the girls. Then helped his wife, Jillian, prepare breakfast.

Then as Jillian cleaned up the dishes, Jerry wandered to his desk and began scanning through some personal papers. These papers included his will, insurance policies, just making sure everything was in order. All the while, he monitored the weather channel watching for anything that might cause concern for his flight course.

He placed every important paper back in the little safe, properly indexed and easy to locate. This routine he had preformed before every flight he had taken; he did not want Jillian to have any trouble finding what she needed in case of an emergency. He had seen other wives trying to deal with the grief and he knew that this was just one last thing he could help her with, if there was a need.

Jerry turned his attention to a cup of coffee and the uneasy feeling that had wakened him at 4:30 this morning. He was unable to put a finger on this feeling, but found himself wanting to look over the $750,000 life insurance policy he had recently taken out. He had not told Jillian about the new policy, but she did know about the airlines insurance policy for $250,000. He knew she would find the new policy if there was an accident, but as long as she did not know about it; she would not worry more than she already did.

Reassured that all was in order Jerry kissed his two daughters and

Jillian, and he hoped the extra long hug and kiss he had given her was not an omen of things to come. He could rest a little easier knowing that if something did happen, Jillian and the girls would have enough money to pay the bills and be able to live until the ever-efficient Jillian would figure out what course to take with their lives.

As he went to work, he knew that he must not dwell on his families' problems, because it would impair his ability to fly, and therefore, put his passengers at risk. He got his mind back on his business when he heard the forecaster predict the wind conditions out west. Crap, he thought, there was going to be a little bounce over northern New Mexico and Arizona. There was a front located right over the mountain range and he knew that these systems usually bred monsoonal rains and winds so strong they pushed a wall of sand as they moved across the desert.

He was a little concerned about landing at Sky Harbor Airport in Phoenix, thinking about how strong some of those wind shears could be, not to mention the wall of sand they might encounter. Oh well, that is why they pay me the big bucks, Jerry quipped to himself.

He thought about that good bye kiss and given the time he might have taken Jillian back upstairs to the bedroom for a proper farewell, but at least he had that to anticipate until he got home tomorrow night.

Jerry picked up his flight bag and headed to the field to file his flight plan with the tower. As he did his preflight inspection, soon all thoughts of anything but the trip were gone from his mind. After climbing the stairs, he entered the cockpit to finish the take-off checklist.

He taxied the airplane out to the end of the runway, turned the plane and waited for clearance for takeoff. The tower finally radioed their clearance and Jerry began to power the plane until it started climbing and they ascended past the outer marker right on time. After setting the course and selecting the autopilot, Jerry informed the passengers they could unfasten their seatbelts and move about the aircraft.

The co-pilot assumed command of the aircraft as Jerry slid his seat back to make a stroll through the aisle of the plane. It was something that he had done on most flights since becoming a pilot and the passengers seemed to relax a little when they saw the pilot out talking to them and walking through the aircraft. After finishing his rounds, he returned to the cockpit with a cup of coffee and soon busied himself looking over the charts for the airport at Phoenix.

Jerry laughed as he was telling the cockpit crew about the fellow already sound asleep back in the tail section seats. He must be quite used to flying to be able to go off to slumber land that quick after takeoff.

Elaine had stood it about as long as she could, deciding it was safe to go she left her seat to find the restroom. As she stepped into the aisle, she noticed the fellow from the boarding area was seated two rows behind her. On his face was a soft smile, his eyes were closed and she heard snoring as she passed his seat.

How could anyone go to sleep that fast and that soundly, in a noisy aircraft, with people talking all around, and ice cubes clinking?

After returning to her seat, she opened her book and began to read, hoping it would pass the time more quickly. The flight was uneventful, and she noticed she had been reading for almost 3 hours when she saw the fasten seatbelt sign begin to flash. The crackle of the speaker reminded everyone to fasten their seatbelts, and then the pilots' voice was telling the passengers that there were some strong upper level winds and things might get a little bouncy before they would be landing in Phoenix. He reassured the passengers that we would be on time as we are now beginning our descent to Sky Harbor Airport. Depending how much weather we had to navigate around, we would be landing in approximately 30 minutes.

5

STONY WAS AWAKE instantly when he heard the metallic thud below his seat. He had heard similar sounds when he flew with the aircrew in the Navy. Back then, he would have been up looking for the problem. He knew that thuds were usually an indication that something had failed to function properly, but being unfamiliar with this particular aircraft maybe, it was perfectly normal. They were definitely experiencing turbulent weather, but he could not help but think that the noise sounded like a high-pressure hydraulic line had blown loose. However, the crew did not seem overly concerned as they went about making the passengers comfortable, doing their best to stay on their feet as the big plane bounced around in the darkened sky.

The intercom crackled again telling us that there would be a short delay for clearance to land, due to the Ground Control Approach or GCA being down. That cannot be good Stony thought, that is what tells all the pilots when and where they were in relation to the airfield. In addition, which runway they would be using when they approached to land. The pilot again reassured them that it would be temporary, and that we would be in holding pattern until the tower gave us clearance to approach and land.

Stony looked out his window and noticed the heavy blue-gray clouds that hung around the plane. They appeared to have a kind of orange colored hue to them and he recognized them immediately as an Arizona dust storm. He knew that the sand that gave them that orange color was not a good thing for the jet engines.

In the cockpit, Jerry's co-pilot had been on the radio with the tower and had learned that the monsoon storm was directly over the field. Haboobs, as the locals called these storms, contained the most concentrated sand and dirt mixture that any wind could carry; it was like a black wall moving across the desert floor. Many interstate highways would close completely down as the storm approached. Yet, there were always traffic fatalities due to drivers thinking they could just drive straight through.

The winds started quick and strong and picked up just about any loose material that was lying on the ground. They were gusting shears with thunder, lightning, and straight-line winds that could do as much damage as a Midwestern tornado. Jerry's uneasiness now had a name. Winds were bouncing them all over the sky, the thunder and lightning was enough by itself to frighten the passengers. The plane buffeted back and forth, which to Jerry seemed hours, but was in actuality only minutes. He decided that maybe if he dropped in altitude they might be beneath the worst of the turbulence. I am sure we would all feel more comfortable in calmer air, he thought. After trying to get clearance, for the third time, the tower informed him they were not sure of his location.

"Hell's bells," Jerry shouted to the cockpit crew, "the damned tower doesn't even know where we are. They have been experiencing rolling power outages, the GCA is still not working, and the airport is socked in at present." Jerry made the decision to just maintain his holding pattern, stay where he was and start their landing checklist so they would be ready when they did get clearance to land.

Suddenly the flight engineer noticed a fluctuation in the pressure on the hydraulic system. When they had lowered their flaps to 10%, the pressure dropped drastically low. The engineer tapped the gauge, but the needle stayed in the low zone, it did not kick back up as expected.

"I think we have more problems than just the weather," the engineer told the Captain.

"Yes," said Jerry, "I've noticed the plane seems to be getting sluggish." They definitely needed to land and soon, if they were losing hydraulic pressure, it would affect other important things, like the landing gear. They could not wait until it was all gone, before attempting a landing. Jerry declared an emergency landing to the tower. There was no response. He yelled into the microphone again declaring the need for an emergency landing, still no response. Jerry told the co-pilot to recycle the radio frequencies, hoping the tower could pick up their communication.

"Mayday!" "Mayday!" "Mayday!"

They could only hope that the tower might still be receiving their calls, but just could not transmit an answer back. The situation was deteriorating rapidly, it was becoming increasingly harder to turn the aircraft, and in trying to communicate with the tower, they had lost their orientation to the field. Jerry was sure they had been blown off course, but which direction, and how far?

Things were steadily getting worse. The controls were responding erratically and the circuit breakers began popping on the electrical panel. Suddenly the control of the aircraft was priority one, it was all Jerry could do to hold on to the steering mechanism. If we do not get down soon, we may not be able to land at all, he thought as he struggled constantly with the controls.

The speaker crackled once again as Jerry informed the passengers of their predicament. "We are going to have to attempt an emergency landing on the desert floor." He said, "The stewardess will help you with the procedures for a crash landing. Please pray, and may God help us all."

So this is the way it will end, Stony thought. He rather chuckled to himself. Oh, well at least it will be quick. After all, death was far from being unfamiliar to him. He had considered suicide on several occasions over the years, but each time thought about his children dealing with the self-inflicted death of their father. This would be much more along the lines of an acceptable death, and an accident on top of that, the insurance money would double. He would leave the kids a little nest egg, a cushion against the financial war of everyday existence. Not a bad deal, he thought, maybe this way I can contribute something by dying that I never could by living.

Stony had faced death many times, and always managed to survive. Hell, he thought, I am ready. I kept the promise to my wife and if we meet on the other side, I can look her square in the eye and say, 'I did what you asked'. Thoughts of his life with Marilyn filled his mind as he leaned over in his seat and covered his head with his hands. The classic 'crash' position was something he could do without a conscious effort.

Elaine had cinched her seat belt down, bent over her knees, and prayed. A prayer that God would take care of her son should she not survive. She was not afraid. She had depended on her faith for every situation in life. Today was no different, even with the other passengers crying and screaming that this could not be true. Elaine was at peace. She had been a Christian long enough to know that adversity in life, was always rewarded with strength, faith, and wisdom. Evan would need all three, when he received the news that his mother had died in the crash. She held a picture of her son in her hands as she recited the Lord's Prayer, waiting for what she was sure would be her first glimpse of heaven.

Jerry had his hands full trying to get the aircraft down to earth without losing total control. The co-pilot was busy trying to get anybody on the radio, while the flight engineer was locking in the emergency beacons and SAR signals. If both worked, the rescuers would have no trouble finding them.

Suddenly at about 1200 ft altitude, the starboard engine shut down and the aircraft began to roll right. Using all the strength he could muster to hold the plane level, Jerry had both feet on the glare shield and instrument panel. The next thirty seconds were unbelievable. The plane stalled, then pitched nose upward as it slammed into the earth. The tail section sheared completely off the aircraft; a small portion of the fuselage was broken off as well. The plane continued sliding across the desert sand as the left wing ripped off and slammed into the body of the aircraft after striking a rock formation. The fuel exploded literally destroying everything that was aft of the cockpit door. Except the nose itself, this rotated and slammed into the rocky side of a mountain, the opposite side of an arroyo. The nose section began slowly sliding downward into the small canyon, finally stopping when it reached the dry streambed at the bottom. Then what was left of the fuselage exploded filling the sky with debris. The dust and smoke enveloped the entire impact area for approximately 4 minutes. When the dust finally cleared, there was ash, cotton stuffing, clothing, and tiny particles of metal still falling like a light rainstorm. The smoke was trailing upward from several different locations, but no sound could be heard. Total silence... No cactus wrens chirping, no ground squirrels chipping, no wind blowing... nothing but absolute silence.

After what seemed an eternity, the wind slowly began whistling through the charred and twisted shards of metal that now seemed to be growing out of the scorched and blackened sand. Monoliths silently reaching toward the wide expanse and brightness of the sky. Nothing moved, and the only recognizable piece left, was now lying upside down on the horizon. The tail section seemed to rise out of the desert floor like a sail in the sea of destruction that was a mile long and about 300 yards wide. The cactus and creosote bushes were now part of the smoke signals streaming upward to the Sky God in the middle of the Arizona Southwest.

6

Stony awoke with sweat streaming into his eyes, and one barnburner of a headache. He was confused, trying to remember where he had been drinking the night before. Realizing his head throbbing seemed different somehow, he felt his body being pulled upward. As his mind cleared a little, not up, he thought, down. I am hanging upside down. He began feeling for his seat belt and finally the release that would free him.

He fell about three feet face down in a heap on the floor, or rather the ceiling of the aircraft. Laying there for a while because his feet and legs refused to work, his senses began to return and he heard the moaning, groaning, and the crying of the others. Realizing that even as he became aware of the sounds of pain, they began to cease. He managed to roll over on his back and finally was able to focus on the twisted metal of the aircraft that had pushed up around his seat, kind of like a small cocoon.

The smell of burning flesh filled his nostrils and he looked around for other passengers, which might be needing help. The man that sat next to him was hanging limply above him now with a small shard of thin metal protruding from his chest. Without moving, he could see no more passengers, so slowly he began to inch his way from under the wreckage. He tried to stand. He made it to his knees. He began to take inventory of his body parts, everything he touched seemed to be hurting. Slowly gaining a foothold, everything seemed to be where it was supposed to be, just a few cuts and scrapes and an extra knot on his head. Turning slowly to take in his surroundings, all he could see was total and complete carnage. He had not witnessed destruction this bad since Viet Nam, where he had asked God that he never see it again.

Stony took a couple of steps then turned to survey the scene behind him. Pure and absolute devastation. Clothing scattered and body parts strewn in all directions. The site was too much too quick, he wretched violently for several minutes. The heat was stifling, his stomach churned and he was sweating profusely.

"Get control." Aloud he said. "Come on man, get a grip" as he staggered a few more steps. Cursing under his breath he wondered, "How many people were on this plane?" Not knowing which direction to head first, he stepped a few more feet, and then stopped, thinking he had heard a sound. "Was that a voice?" "Is there anyone out there?" He yelled. "Can you hear me?"

There it was again, a muffled cry, "Help me, please." He turned trying to locate where the sound had come from. He turned his head from side to side, listening. Nothing…

"Are you there?" He yelled, again. "This is stupid." He muttered, "There isn't a complete body in sight."

Then he heard it again, "Help me."

Stony called out, "Just keep talking so I can find you."

"Help me. Here, I am over here." Sounds like a child, he thought as he stepped over the pieces of debris, trying to find the exact location of the voice. "Hurry," the voice was getting weaker, said, "I can't move." Stepping to a pile of twisted seats, covered with the overhead compartments that had broken in pieces; he began to pull each loose segment that would come free. Finally, freeing a large piece revealed a big enough space that he thought he could at least see what the situation was underneath and the best way to free the person caught there. Crawling under the edge of the torn metal, he then saw the small body of a young woman lying in the sand with at least two dead bodies that had dropped across her. Both men were large enough on their own to be impossible for her to remove by herself, let alone the two together.

"Hold on, I'll have to get these bodies off you, then, we'll see what's left to get you out of here." Stony told her. "Just lay still, relax, and let me do the work." As he carefully surveyed the scene, he tried to decide which was actually lying on the top of the pile. All the entangled bodies making it hard to determine whose arms and legs belonged to which body. Finally just grabbing an arm, he began getting the bodies clear of the girl, he grabbed her closest arm and tried to pull her body out, but she would not budge. Her body was being held somewhere, but he could not tell what was holding her.

She cried out in pain. "No stop, my left arm is pinned under something."

Stony was trying to pull her legs to straighten out her body, "Sorry," he said, 'I'll try to free it, just hold on a little longer." He backed out of the hole and moved around to the other side of the pile, hoping that he could reach her from that angle. As he got to the other side of the jumbled pile, he knelt down and began scooping at the sand and pulling pieces of seats and small chunks of wood out of the way. Soon he could see her hand, and then her arm. He kept digging and then he could see what was holding it in place.

The armrest of a seat jammed into the ground was pushing her arm just below the elbow, deep into the sand. The seat was holding her arm and making it impossible for her to get any control at all. He grabbed a piece of metal and making a scoop out of it, he slowly pulled the sand from around her arm. He pulled sand from under the seat until he could get his hands underneath it and knew she could be freed from the other side. Then again, he returned to the original space, climbed in once more to get a hold on her body and began helping her pull herself from under the seat that had held her captive. Once he had her clear of the wreckage, he lifted her up and carried her to a rock formation close by, hoping to get her out of the sun and the searing heat.

Noticing that she was now unconscious, Stony gently laid her down and then went to find something for a backrest. Returning with a portion of a seat cushion, he propped her head up. He began to examine her for other injuries, and discovered that the pinned arm was indeed broken. It appeared to be a clean break and since she was out cold, he put his feet on either side of her shoulder and began pulling on her arm. After aligning the two broken ends, he fashioned a temporary splint out of two plastic armrest covers. He picked up a tattered shirt from the ground and tore it into strips to use for tying the makeshift splint in place. Not pretty, he thought, but it would be better than nothing.

With the two pieces of bone back together, she could move her fingers and arm, even though it would be painful. Luckily, she had passed out shortly after he freed her arm. When the circulation resumed, it would bring the pain. At least she had slept through the ordeal and she might as well rest, she is going to need what strength she can muster to survive the next few hours. He knew it would not be long before the rescue squads would be coming to check the crash site for survivors.

As she slept, Stony set off back to the wreckage looking for and listening for anything that would indicate someone else had also survived the crash. He came across what had been the kitchen area of the plane. Looking for the in-flight containers, normally made with stainless steel, he knew they would probably survive the impact. Soon he was lost in the task of scavenging the crash site for anything that might be of use. When his arms were full and he could carry no more, he started back to where he had placed the young woman in the shade. He realized he should be conserving his own strength. They both would be needing water and he sure could use the shade, it must be 100 degrees out there between the cactus and sand. Thus, he sat and rested for a while.

Elaine come to just as Stony had gone out of sight, and was immediately confused as to how she had gotten out from under the pile that had held her down. She started to put her arms down to her side to push herself up, but the pain of the broken arm was so sudden that she once again lapsed back into unconsciousness.

Stony found one of the water containers still intact and a drawer full of in-flight packets with coffee, sugar, salt, pepper, along with packets of plastic forks, spoons, and knives, and paper napkins. The fact he had some instant coffee somehow calmed his nerves, but drinking a cup would have to wait. He was still looking for any live persons among the wreckage. It was slow going, as he picked his way through the devastation. He found a backpack that must have been stored in the overhead compartments. He unzipped the case and found clean clothes and an empty canteen with two telescoping cups attached. As he turned to head back to where he had left the young woman, something that looked like the edge of a shaving kit caught his eye. Burnt clothes and something unrecognizable covered the leather case partially. If it was what he thought, it was very unrecognizable. Trying not to look directly at what was on top. He grabbed the edge of the bag and pulled it out. He found it full of stuff that might make their stay a little more comfortable. Inside was soap in a plastic container, toothpaste, toothbrushes, a razor, some aftershave, and a nearly full bottle of aspirin.

Elaine was looking at Stony as he approached her sanctuary with his arms loaded down with the salvaged items. He took out the canteen from the flight bag along with the two cups and handed one to her. She took it with the good arm and looked at him gratefully as he poured them both a drink of water. He then opened the bottle of aspirin and as he handed her a couple of tablets, he said, "You are going to need these, if you take them now it might keep the edge off the pain that is going to come with that broken arm." "Drink the water slowly; we may have to make it last a while."

"Oh," Elaine said, "That has got to be the best water I have ever tasted. Are you a Doctor?" She asked. "And do I need to call you in the morning, if we're still here?"

Stony answered rather gruffly, "You don't have to call me anything. They were just in some of the stuff I found. I figured you could make good use of them, but far be it from me to tell another person what they ought to do. They're here if you need them."

Surprised by his sharpness, Elaine sat quietly, and then when he did not look back to her, she softly said, "Let me apologize. I hope you did not think I was making light of our situation. I do certainly thank you for your thoughtfulness. I'm sure later I will appreciate even more having something that will help with the pain." Then both sat quietly for a long time, each lost in their own thoughts, as they viewed the field of devastation that lay before them.

"Stony," he finally said, "That's my name. I assume that somebody may have tacked a name on you at one time or another?" His voice rather trailed off and Elaine got the distinct impression that he really did not want to know anything about her. He had just felt compelled to soften the earlier outburst. No sense in having dissension among the survivors, after all we were going to have to get along for a little while, until someone comes for us.

"My name is Elaine." She replied. "Is anyone else alive?" "Is there anyone beside us?"

He was still staring out at the blackened remains, "Not that I could find. However, I did not come across the cockpit, yet, so maybe there will be someone. How is your arm feeling?"

"It will be fine, thank you for putting the splint on it." As she answered she was getting up, slowly and a little shaky, she asked, "I will go with you, we should check to see if anyone needs our help."

Stony nodded, and then together they started looking for other survivors. After about 15 minutes of searching for any movement and listening for any sound of life, Stony noticed that Elaine had stopped off to one side, bent over, and began to retch. He suddenly felt very sorry for this young woman, knowing that she was seeing things that would forever be in her memory. The sad part was that she had not seen the worst of it yet. Hoping that Elaine had not noticed that he had seen her, Stony moved on. He happened onto the first aid kit still attached to the wall in the kitchen area of the plane. Burnt, but still intact, definitely something they could use. A few minutes later, he found the other fresh water container. "Come here," he called to Elaine. "This will help us to stay hydrated." Elaine drank the water and then he noticed that her eyes were full of tears.

She began to sob as she confided to him, "I've never seen anything like this. So many body parts, I do not believe there is one person still whole. How could we have survived this?" The look on her face spoke volumes. Stony had seen that same look on the faces of young men after their first encounter with the enemy in Viet Nam. A bewildered, disbelieving look that comes from uncertainty, fear, and anxiety, wondering how they will ever get out of this situation.

"Elaine," Stony said, "Why don't you take the water and first aid kit back to our rock pile, and see if you can round up something that will make bedding for us. We should spend the night here at the crash site in case there is someone searching for us. I know it is going to be uncomfortable for you, but the best chance of rescue is by staying close to the plane for now. I am going to see if I can find the cockpit, because that is where the black box will be and I want to make sure it is not too far away. I promise I'll be back as quickly as I can." She took the water and first aid kit, glad to have a task to get her mind temporarily off the situation.

"Yes, I'm sure you know best. I assume that since this scene appears not to bother you as much as me that you have been through something like this before. Am I right?"

Stony looked in her eyes and wondered that she could be so observant at a time like this, but said, "I'll be back soon." As she turned toward the rock pile, he turned his attention to finding the rest of the wreckage, hoping it would lead him to the cockpit, and possibly other survivors. After about an hour, he had covered about one half mile, and still no sign of life. He looked up the side of the mountain and noticed what appeared to be fresh scraping. Knowing of nothing else that would make scars like that on rock, he knew the cockpit must be close.

A few more minutes of walking, and he stood on the edge of a small arroyo looking down at what was left of the aircraft's cockpit. Searching for a few seconds for any movement and noticing none, he began to work his way down the side of the rock face in the desert channel. Arriving at the cockpit, he immediately tried to open the door, hoping the impact had loosened it. However, it was locked tight. Looking through the broken window of the door, he noticed that still strapped down and hanging next to the door, was what aviators called the crash axe. Being pointed on one side and having a sharp axe on the other, it was made for moments such as this. Stony worked for several minutes trying to free the axe from its holder. Finally getting a firm hold, he jerked it through the window and began to chop at the door of the cockpit. When there was an opening large enough for him to squeeze through, he found three bodies still strapped in their seats. Checking for life on each one, the flight engineer and the co-pilot were dead, but the pilot was still breathing.

Apparently, the pilot had been unconscious the whole time because there appeared to be no indication that he had tried to undo his seat belt. Stony carefully cut him loose and wrestled him outside onto the desert floor. He could hear the shallow breathing and knew that the pilot was not in good shape. He had suffered some major injuries. Stony knew that his chest and been crushed and his lungs were filling with blood. He was slowly bleeding to death internally. As Stony looked around in the cockpit for anything that would be useful, he found a butane lighter, the flight book, a box of matches, a roll of lifesaver candies, "Well, those didn't work so well." He muttered to himself, and finally a roll of pencils and a ballpoint pen.

Looking for some way to haul the pilot back to the camp area, his eyes fell on the cockpit door. It took most of his strength to hack at the door until finally it fell from its hinges. He then fashioned a travois of sorts making use of the belts that had held the crew. Stony strapped the pilot to the door and then using his own belt as a handle, he began the climb. He managed to get to the rim of the arroyo before falling exhausted to the ground. He rested a minute as he checked the pilots' condition before starting out for the crash site. As he set out across the desert floor, he was strangely comforted by the thought that someone, would be there waiting.

Elaine had watched as Stony had disappeared into the desert, watching until she could no longer make out his image. She was thinking of her first impression of that graying gentleman. Moreover, how something about him had caught her attention when they had passed each other at the airport in St. Louis. His quiet certainty had shown his confidence and for some reason she had the thought that he did not need others to validate his existence. Now that she had the time to remember what had actually went though her mind she wondered why such a thought had occurred to her. His rough exterior and gruff manner must keep most people at a distance of this she was sure. It was exactly what he intended, but by the way he had tended her arm and made sure she had medicine for the pain, she knew he considered others and could even be gentle when it was necessary.

After he was out of sight, she began gathering the material things they would need for a decent night of rest. While making the campsite she was hoping the whole time that they would not need it, because the rescuers would surely be on their way by now.

She located some seat cushions and clothing which she tied together to construct some sort of tent or lean-to under which they could find shelter from the heat of day and the chill of the night. In her scavenging, she happened upon a metal case that contained a signal pistol and six cartridges, plus a piece of plastic about 3 ft. square. Considering she had one working arm, and using only the fingers of her broken arm, Elaine had prepared quite a campsite. Still searching for anything that could be used, she found what appeared to be the in-flight service cart and sliding open the drawer she discovered several packs of smoked almonds and some extra coffee packets. Well, she thought, if we can get a fire started I will use one of these drawers to heat water and make us a hot cup of coffee.

Darkness was fast approaching when Stony arrived back to the crash site. He noticed immediately Elaine's handiwork, making a lean-to with clothing tied together gave the appearance of Grandma's crazy quilt. It actually looked inviting, and he could see her now out gathering firewood for the night.

He dragged the pilot into the campsite and then dropped to his knees into the sand, exhausted and thirsty as hell. Elaine had seen him drop to the ground and run over to him and asked, "Are you okay? Can I get you some of the water?"

"Yes that would be great." he replied. She handed him one of the expandable cups filled with water. Elaine checked the pilot, saw he was still breathing and at once tried to make him more comfortable.

"He was very pleasant to the passengers, when he came out and talked with them. I think you were asleep when he did that." Stony joined with her in rearranging the belt straps that had held him down. Their hands touched when they both reached for the blanket at the same time, as their hands met, so did their eyes. Then just as quickly as the moment came, it was gone.

Stony dropped his grip on the blanket and immediately turned to build a survival fire at the front of the lean-to. Elaine lowered herself to her knees and sat back on her heels. She watched intently as Stony dug with his pocketknife a hole about eight inches around and about ten inches deep. Then he dug another hole next to the first one about eight inches deep and poked a hole at the bottom joining the two holes together. Glancing up at her and noticing that she was watching, he explained that it would provide a draft for the fire. He then broke up a couple of the sticks she had found and dropped them into the hole. Within minutes, they had an extremely hot fire and the smell of coffee filled the air from the brew in the cart drawer.

Elaine had marveled at the performance she had just witnessed. A pocketknife, a few sticks and two holes in the ground and she could boil water in a matter of minutes. She was laughing to herself, 'Must have been a boy scout'. When she noticed he was digging another hole with his pocketknife just big enough to place the other drawer in the center of the shallow hole. "If you don't mind my asking, what are you doing now?" She asked.

"It's going to make water." He replied. He then stretched the plastic sheeting that she had found over the drawer, and then placed rocks on each corner. He finished with one smaller stone on center top of the sheet, making a shallow upside down pyramid. "The moisture will gather on the underneath side of the plastic. It will trickle down to where the small stone is resting and then drip into the drawer. There should be enough for us to gather it in the morning. Who knows, we may need all the water we can get before this ordeal is over."

"That is simply amazing, I would never have thought of that. Where did you learn such a thing? Were you a boy scout?" She asked.

Stony chuckled to himself thinking, 'Little miss, you'd be surprised how much I know about surviving.' Nevertheless, aloud he replied, "This is why I drew my pay in the military. If you survive, you get your paycheck." He sat down where he could see the pilot and close enough to hear any change in his breathing or if he might try to say something. However, he doubted very much if the latter would occur at all. Stony had seen injuries like this before and he figured the pilot would not make it through the night.

They sat on the seat cushions, drinking coffee, eating smoked almonds, and then finished the short meal with a lifesaver apiece.

They had not said anything for the longest while, both seemed to be reliving the day's experiences. Both Stony and Elaine were simply looking up into the clear night sky lost in their own thoughts. Suddenly the silence was broken by the pilot's choking. Stony jumped up and was instantly kneeling beside the man's body. He noticed blood trickling down from corner of his mouth.

This is not a good sign Stony thought as he yelled to Elaine "Quick, come help me turn him on his side." They rolled the pilot up on his side and Elaine placed a cushion behind his back. She heard the deep rattle as he was trying to breathe and glanced up at Stony.

"He's not going to make it 'till rescue, is he?" She asked softly.

Stony quietly shook his head no then said, "We need to get some rest or our chances won't be much better than his." As they turned to walk back to their lean-to, Stony went on to say, "Elaine, why don't you get some sleep and I'll stay up for awhile watching our patient and keeping the fire going."

"What are you going to do for rest, Doctor Stony?"

He smiled for the first time and replied, "Hell, I never sleep much at night, anyway. I am plenty used to it. You go on and try to get some shut eye while you can." Elaine was surprised by his answer and even more, by his smiling. How easily he seems to handle such an impossible situation.

7

THE NIGHT DESERT sounds mixed peacefully with the dancing of the fire light on the underside of the lean-to. Silently Elaine slipped into an exhausted sleep. Stony sipped the last of the coffee and watched the desert sky. He was alert to any sign that an aerial search had begun. He could see nothing but blackness. The stars so bright and the air so clear that people seeing it for the first time feel that they can reach out and touch the sky.

It was one of the reasons he loved Arizona.

Breaking the silence of the night, the pilot's raspy breathing was starting to sound shallow and quick. How long, Stony wondered, would this broken shell of a man push back at the inevitable approach of death? Where did he find the strength? I do not even have morphine or anything else to relieve his pain. He sure was a tough cookie, there must be something driving him to keep up the fight. Just as Stony was thinking these thoughts, the pilot's eyes suddenly opened and he began choking once again. Stony grabbed the water and poured a small amount of water on his lips and tongue while trying to hold his head up to prevent him from strangling himself on his own blood.

The pilot began trying to speak, the sound of his voice coming out more as a rasping noise. Stony leaned closer to hear what the pilot was saying.

Elaine awoke sensing the change in the atmosphere of the camp, opening her eyes she immediately saw Stony leaning over the Captain, trying to make out his words. Elaine heard Stony tell the pilot, "Listen pal, I don't know how you'll take this. If I were in your shoes, I would want to know. You are hurt real bad, busted up inside, you are hemorrhaging from your lungs." Stony said. "Did you let anyone know where we were before the crash?"

Jerry, the Captain, whispered, "No, we couldn't reach anyone. Either the receiver in the plane was out, or their radar was not working. We never got a confirmation that they even knew we were going down." As his voice faded, the pilot reached up and grabbed the front of Stony's shirt, pulling him close, he pleaded, "Please, take my wallet to my wife. It's important," he paused, trying to take in air, "tell my wife that I really love her and the girls. All I have ever wanted was to take care of them. Please, promise me you will do this. Promise me..." his voice vanishing as he fell silently into the arms of death.

"Damn it. Damn it." Stony cursed, "Another promise, I don't want to make another promise. I have lived my whole life trying to keep a promise. Damn it all to hell, anyway." Stony turned to walk away and Elaine heard him mumble as he left, "How in the world am I supposed to keep this one?"

Hearing most of the exchange, Elaine wondered, what could be so complicated about giving this guy's wife his wallet? Lying quietly, listening to the night sounds, she finally noticed that the rough breathing of the pilot was no longer part of the darkness. She had been listening to the grumbling sounds of Stony complaining, and was now sad that a life had passed and neither one of them had been aware of it. She sat up and Stony turned toward her, then he quickly turned his face away from her, she could swear there had been a tear running down his cheek. She started to say something to him about the death of the pilot, but he was already stepping away from the fire and into the shadows of the desert night. As she covered the body of the pilot as best as she could with a large shirt she had found earlier, she closed her eyes and she whispered a short prayer for the soul of a fellow human being. After a quiet moment, she knelt closer to turn the body and retrieve the wallet from the back pocket of his uniform.

Suddenly, Stony grabbed her hand, "I made the promise. I'll deliver on it." His voice was as cold as ice, his grip as strong as a vice, and she knew that his gentle demeanor had to be the self-discipline of a very strong willed man. She was awed by the inner strength of this stranger, and instantly curious about the other aspects of this man's character.

The chill of his actions demanded she immediately comply. She let go of the pilot's body and said. "Sorry, I was just trying to help."

"No, I'm sorry." Stony replied, returning to the soft, quiet voice of before. "It has been a long day." He knelt to pick up the lifeless body of the pilot, "By the way, I hope I didn't hurt you. I didn't mean to." He carried the body about twenty feet away just in the edge of the shadows, laid the body to one side and silently began digging a shallow grave. Elaine stayed where she was, not sure whether to offer her help or not, finally deciding if he needed help he would surely ask.

After roughing out a hole deep enough to cover the man's body, Stony opened the wallet, finding out the pilot's name seemed important now as he was about to lay him into the grave. "Jerry Bradford, St. Louis, Mo." He read aloud. He covered the body as best as he could with sand, then began piling rocks on top. After twenty minutes, and many trips into the desert for more rocks, he seemed satisfied that scavengers could not get to the body. He came back to the fire.

Returning to the lean-to, Stony poured a cup of water, drank about half and then handed the cup to Elaine. She took the water and thought, 'peace offering' I guess. No words were spoken as they both lay down for the night collapsing into hours of fitful dreams. They would both need what little sleep and rest they could get from what was left of the night.

Morning came and with it, the flying insects and scavengers attracted by the stench of decaying flesh.

Elaine smelled the odor before she opened her eyes, then immediately felt the smothering heat. The temperature must be ninety degrees already, she thought as she rolled out of bed with a taste of bile in her throat, and before she could reach the outer edge of camp, she was violently vomiting. Her stomach finally settled as her nose became adapted to the smell of death. Looking around to see if he had witnessed the pathetic display, she became aware that she could not see Stony anywhere.

Stony had just reached the summit of the mountain he had been climbing for the last two hours. He had started well before dawn while the air was still and the smell had been mild to what he knew was coming. What he discovered here did not improve his day. He leaned dizzily against a rock and looked in all directions. All he saw was desert on three sides and on the fourth side to the northeast were only more mountains. He recognized only the few dust devils that were whirling on the desert floor. There was nothing even resembling a search party, and even as he thought it, he knew that the search parties would first be sent to the plane's last known position. He was sure that the plane had not gone down anywhere close to where their flight plan was supposed to be. Remembering the pilot's last words, he was well aware that it would be days before anyone would be looking for survivors where they were because nobody knew where they were. Not their control tower, not rescuers, not even the captain had known, and certainly not Stony or Elaine. Hell, Stony thought, we will be lucky to live long enough to be rescued. Staring across the terrain and figuring they must be somewhere southwest of Phoenix, maybe even in Mexico. He knew their only chance of survival was to the northeast through the mountains, as rough as that would be he knew it was still better than traveling the scorching desert floor. Walking back to the crash site, Stony envisioned all the things that were probable if they were to be stranded in this desert. From snakebites to wandering dehydrated and disorientated until death would become welcome.

The crash site was almost a pleasure to see as he topped the last rise by late morning. He noticed that Elaine had redesigned her attire to compensate for the heat, and as tired as he felt, he could not help noticing that she brought relief to his dry and strained eyes. She was now wearing a white blouse with the sleeves torn off. A ball cap that she had found was on her head with her long blonde hair pulled into a ponytail through the hole in back. A pair of pants with the legs torn to the length of walking shorts, drew his attention to her legs. The dress suit she had worn was now gone and so were the heels and hose. She had located a pair of sneakers that some passenger had no doubt packed for walking the beach. Overall she was quite fetching in her make shift wardrobe. Stony thought she looked like a tomboy character out of a Huck Finn scene getting ready to play baseball with the neighborhood children.

Suddenly he became aware of the smell, God Almighty, he thought, the stench became almost unbearable, as he closed the distance between them. Walking up to where Elaine sat, he asked, "Are you ready to travel? We need to get out of here as soon as we get everything we can together."

She had not taken her eyes off him since he had walked into sight. "No one is coming to rescue us, are they?" Knowing the answer before she asked, she turned and began gathering what she thought they might need to survive.

As she was stuffing what bags they had scavenged, he replied, "No I'm afraid not, I really don't think anyone even knows where we are."

"What did you see out there? How far did you go?" She asked.

"Nothing but more desert and desert we do not want to cross." He answered. Stony took a stick and drew a rough map in the sand where he thought they were. When he looked up at her, he thought she would be on the verge of tears.

Instead, she answered, "Well, we better get started then, hadn't we?" Sounding almost nonchalant, "We really don't have much time to waste if we are to get to a place where they can find us. Surely, we will have a better chance if we can get higher up on the mountainside. Don't you think?" Elaine had wrapped up everything she could carry, folded it the best she could into a man's shirt that she had fashioned into a sort of backpack. Tying it around her waist, she turned to him expectantly.

He took the water jug and went to the shallow hole he had placed the plastic sheet over and there he retrieved what little water that had accumulated. Peering into the jug he said "Looks to be about a half pint." He then folded up the plastic sheet and put it in his pocket, took the stick and wrote a message in the sand. Last, he drew an arrow to the northeast, then turning to Elaine signaled for her to follow him.

They were heading to the mountain range that Stony had spotted this morning that looked to be approximately five miles across the desert floor. By noon, he figured that they had covered maybe a mile and a half. It seemed they were traveling at a snails pace. As Elaine trudged along in the sandy soil, she tried not to think about how hot it was or how far they had to walk. She felt like they were walking in circles because every step she took, the desert floor and everything on it looked the same as those they had just passed, rocks, sand, sagebrush, creosote bushes, and cactus. She had not known there were that many varieties of cactus. Just as she was about to ask for a short rest, she glanced up and realized they had reached the foot of the mountain range. Stony spotted what looked like a shady overhang on the far hillside, pointing it out to Elaine told her they could rest there. She simply nodded her head in reply and concentrated on putting one foot in front of the other. After glancing at her watch, she realized it was only a few minutes after 2 p.m., not bad, she thought. I figured it would take all day to get to the other side of the desert. Reaching the shady alcove, they both sank to the cool rocky ground. They lay there for the better part of an hour trying to catch their breath and cooling their overheated bodies.

The sun had been relentless for the past four hours, but they knew dehydration was their worst enemy right now; it was the better choice to go while they were relatively fresh. Elaine was not sure how much farther she could have gone. Her arm had swollen and was pretty tight in the splint now; she was considering the possibility of circulation being shut off to her lower arm. Stony also noticed how swollen her arm had become and flinched, knowing how painful it must be. He realized that she had not complained once during the arduous journey they had taken. Tough little gal, he thought, as he motioned her to move closer.

"Here, let me help." As he retied the splint, he could read the pain in her eyes, and instantly he grabbed the first-aid kit and handed her a couple more aspirin. She gratefully accepted the pills and drank the half cup of water he offered. "Well, I'm not sure, but I believe this tastes even better than it did this morning." she smiled in gratitude.

Stony picked up a couple stones about the size of pennies and then handed them to Elaine. "Here, put these in your mouth, they will keep your mouth moist."

"Are you kidding me?" She asked.

"No, I'm not kidding. I'm quite serious." He replied.

She could tell by the look on his face that he was indeed serious, so she popped the pebbles into her mouth and in a few seconds realized it worked! Just like he said it would. "Shouldn't you be drinking water also?" She asked. "I don't need you to drop out because I'm getting all the water."

Stony managed a small smile and replied, "Hon, we've been dehydrated for the past eight hours, a few more hours won't hurt."

"Well then Doctor, why am I drinking and your not?" She asked.

He thought a moment, "Pain does funny things to dehydrated people and, what I don't need is a raving lunatic on my hands. Hell, it's dangerous enough out here without that."

Finally, after resting for about 2 hours in the cool shade of the overhang, they started for their next stop. Neither one sure exactly where the spot would be. They stopped when Stony told her that he was beginning to get dizzy. They shared water this time and one lifesaver apiece, rested several minutes, and then continued. They passed through a small canyon. Stony hoping that it would not be a box canyon. They really could not afford to spend the time or energy trying to climb up the steep walls that would surround them at the end. Two hours later the canyon became just a dry wash that passed directly under a sheer rock face. It was at least shady here and a few degrees cooler. Staying with the dry wash, they covered about a quarter mile in distance. Stony knew they would need more rest soon and definitely something to eat. The dizziness was becoming bothersome and Elaine had fallen twice in the last hour. He figured that they had covered somewhere between six and eight miles since this morning. He began scanning the rock face looking for a place to stop for the night. Elaine saw a dark indention in the rock about 30 feet above the floor of the wash and about 100 yards ahead. She pointed it out to Stony and he started in that direction.

What they found looked like the start of a mineshaft. One started somewhere in the distant past, but never finished. The opening was about three feet wide and five feet tall and went back for about eight to ten feet into the rock face. Perfect! Stony thought, a great place to bunk up for the night. It was weatherproof and from the looks of the sky, bad weather was on the way.

They both began to clean the sanctuary out as best they could and then built a fire by the entrance. Stony pulled out a piece of seat material he had brought along and handed it to Elaine.

"How about pulling the threads from this seat cover and braid them together to make a little rope? Maybe we could use it to build a snare." Elaine took on the task without question and Stony looked around outside for anything to eat. To Stony's amazement, he found a small rattler under a rock ledge about twelve feet from the tunnel entrance. Carefully he prodded the snake out into the open. As soon as the head cleared the rock, Stony took his head off with the crash axe. He peeled the snake out of his skin and cut it open to remove the guts. He then took a small stick, used it to skewer the rattlesnake, and placed it over the open fire. They would eat tonight. Stony thought, we will have roasted snake, with a lifesaver for desert, followed by a cup of coffee. That is not bad for a survival dinner. He hoped that Elaine would not be squeamish about eating snake. Any meat will be very nourishing and they both needed to stay as strong as they could. However, he need not have worried. She did not have any problem picking the meat out of the snake's ribcage just like an expert. Between them both, they had picked every edible piece of meat from the carcass.

Finally, Elaine spoke, "That wasn't half bad and just think the meal comes with its own toothpicks."

"Hell," Stony smiled, "You would pay big bucks for a meal like that in a fine restaurant. Of course, the packets of salt and pepper helped."

Having satisfied their hunger, Stony and Elaine leaned back against the mine wall and began watching the small fire. Soon they were relaxed and lightly dozing from the results of the filling meal and the warmth of the fire.

The loud clap of thunder replaced the crackle of the fire, they both jumped awake and then heard the wind begin to pick up speed as it passed the entrance of the tunnel.

Stony could see the dark clouds in the night sky and asked Elaine to get the plastic sheet. Handing the plastic to him, she watched as he made a rain catch close to the outside edge of the tunnel. The wind was blowing the plastic edges, making it hard for Stony to place it where he needed to catch the rain. She then handed him the braid she had made earlier from the seat material. She grabbed a corner of the plastic and held it in place so he could tie down the opposite corner. Looking at the braid, he remarked, "The braid works perfectly, I'm beginning to think that maybe I'm not the only one who has some hidden talents."

"No, I was not a girl scout." But she smiled at the compliment. After the plastic sheet was finally in place, they both returned to the warmth of the fire, waiting for the coming rain that would at least give them some drinking water.

The lightning lit up the sky bringing the rolling thunder, but only a light rain was falling. Fifteen minutes later the plastic sheet held enough water to fill their water jug. They refolded the plastic and put it away for the next time. The temporary bed pulled close to the fire was inviting them to take advantage of the shelter and get some rest. Sometime during the night, the fire had faded and both Stony and Elaine had moved closer to the warmth of each other's body. As the tunnel got colder, Elaine had snuggled up under Stony's arm. It did not take Stony very long to become aware that her warmness was more that just normal body heat. Damn, he thought, I was afraid this might happen. Elaine's head was lying on his chest and he realized she had developed a fever. This was the last thing either of them needed. Her chance of survival was slim enough with the broken arm, but adding an infection was really going to cut into her percentage rate. In addition, he would have to stay a little closer to camp to keep and eye on her. He needed to be free to go hunting for food and search for anything that would help their chances of being located.

He got up carefully and stoked the fire, then grabbed the first aid kit. He got three more aspirin from the bag and poured a cup of water for Elaine. Knowing she was sleeping deep because of the fever he cautiously woke Elaine by putting his hand on her ankle and patting softly. She indeed startled awake, then after she saw him handing her the aspirin she remembered where they were and realized that he was just trying to help. Stony noticed that she was shivering as she took the pills, so he picked out a shirt from the clothes bag, and wrapped it around her. "I imagine that the crash, your injury, and our trek across the desert finally caught up with you, Elaine." Stony said. He put a few more logs on the fire then set down next to her, putting his arm around her body and pulled her close. As she relaxed against him he knew that she had fallen back to sleep. Rest was what she needed most so he would let her sleep until she awoke. There was no hurry right now because no one was looking for them. Heck, he thought, they might not even know there had been a crash.

Stony took advantage of Elaine's sleeping to inspect the area around the entrance of the little tunnel. He was looking for anything that would indicate that wild game might also take shelter in this small area. He found sign of rock squirrels under several of the creosote bushes. Picking the bushes that showed the most recent activity, Stony chose the hole that looked most used. He carefully tied a slipknot, opened the circle just wide enough to cover the animals' head as it entered. He laid the snare around the entrance of the animal hole. Taking sand in his hands, he sprinkled it over the small braid rope to conceal it from the animal. He backed off into the rocks to watch for any animal that might pass this way. Glancing at the sky, he realized that he had been unconsciously listening for any aircraft that might pass over their location. He brought his eyes back to the snare, they would need to eat and he knew that it was never too soon to start gathering what they could to build their strength. They would not be staying at this site long. They needed to keep moving in order to get as high an altitude as they could. Both to be seen and to see what was around them.

The sun was already beating down on the desert and Stony noticed that there were no damp spots on the ground. You would never know that it rained last night. Hearing a small noise he turned toward the snare, he had caught a squirrel in the trap. Wow, it had not taken as long as he thought it would, the squirrel was flopping wildly under the bushes with the snare tightening around his neck. Stony ran over and with his fire axe quickly separated the head from the body.

"Well, let's get you cleaned." Stony said as he began to field dress the squirrel out of his skin, preparing the body for the spit he had built over the fire. He started back toward the tunnel, admiring his catch. He had taken only a couple of steps when his shoe caught on something sticking out of the ground and he nearly tripped and fell. Looking back to see what it was he noticed what appeared to be the shaft of a spear. He pulled the old broken spear out of the sand and saw immediately the obsidian point was intact. Now he thought he knew what had likely happened to the miner that had started the old tunnel. If it could only talk, what stories that old spear could tell. He chuckled to himself on the way back thinking about the ways this new weapon would be useful. Crude, but very deadly, I am sure it will come in handy.

Elaine had awakened just before noon, the fever had broken and she was soaked with perspiration. As she sat up, she became aware that her head was throbbing with one hell of a headache. Slowly wobbling outside toward the thickest bush she could find making sure that Stony could not see her, she promptly squatted and relieved herself. She slowly stood up and instantly caught the scent of meat cooking, and she started back toward the campfire Stony had made to cook the squirrel.

"Well, good afternoon, sunshine, I thought maybe you were going to sleep all day." he said.

"I might have returned to my bed, but I smelled something delicious. What have you found to eat this time?" She asked. After she picked up the water jug and quenched a little of her thirst, she took two more aspirin and sat down next to Stony at the campfire. He handed her a chunk of squirrel on a stick and she ate it never questioning the prey or the flavor of it. A good sign, he thought, she knew there was no choice, so she ate. 'The Great White Hunter' had provided once again. For some reason he felt proud of being able to supply what little food he had.

He showed her the old spear he had picked up out in the dry wash and told her what he thought had happened to the prospector that had started the mine tunnel.

"I think that you've done a great job with just the fire axe, do you really feel you need another weapon?" Elaine asked.

After a short pause he said, "Never can tell what may happen out here. We are one hell of a long way from anywhere."

She sensed that she had hurt his feelings. He had been so excited about the spear and the imagined tale of the miner and the Indian. He thinks I am making light of his eagerness. I swear, she thought, it must be that Mars and Venus thing.

I will talk to him later about it, maybe after he chills out for a while. I guess I will back out of this conversation, I am rather tired and on edge anyway, we both need a little space. She went back to her makeshift bed and by the time her head was on the pillow, she was fast asleep. She never knew that Stony had set out on yet another scouting expedition.

Stony carried with him the crash axe, the four-foot rope that Elaine had made and his newly acquired spear. He watched the wash for tracks and looked ahead as if he were stalking a deer, slow and methodical. He had worked his way up the canyon about a mile when he spotted hoof prints in the sandy floor of the dry wash. They appeared to be deer tracks but they were smaller and a little more rounded on the toe end. Peccary, he thought, for animals that big to be out here, there must be a source of water somewhere close. He decided to follow the tracks that led him for about another half mile, and then turned abruptly up a hill to his left. Stony searched the hillside for any sign of life. Nothing! He took about ten more steps and looked again up the hillside. He noticed an area that had thick, lush, green vegetation. It appeared to be approximately a hundred feet from the top of the hill. Hell's bells, that is about a two-hour climb, but it is in the direction we need to go. Stony marked the trail and headed back toward their temporary shelter cave. Maybe there is an old ranch or a squatter living up there. Either way maybe we can find out tomorrow if Elaine is feeling strong enough to walk that far.

Stony arrived back at the camp to find Elaine sleeping, restlessly she tossed and turned, her clothes wet again from the perspiration. Her fever must have kicked up again. As he got closer, he could hear her trying to talk, but only mumbling a word now and then. If the fever goes too high, she might become delirious. He was afraid that her arm might be filling with infection. He was not a medical doctor, but he would do the best he could to keep her fever down. For the next four or five hours he used his handkerchief to wet her lips and apply water to her forehead and neck. Finally, she started relaxing more and more and became less restless. The sweating had stopped and her breathing was deeper and soon she was sleeping peacefully.

Well, I have to find fresh water and food or this little gal is going to be in real trouble. He took quick inventory of their meager supplies. He filled his canteen and left the rest of the water next for Elaine. He built up a fire in the doorway of the entrance, and then headed off toward the mountain in hope of finding somebody or something that would help their situation. About an hour into the climb up the side of the mountain that held the green patch of vegetation, Stony was becoming very uncomfortable in the heat. He found some large bushes and sat down in the shade. He drank a small amount of water, even though he knew he was dehydrated. He understood about the possibility of disorientation and likelihood of hallucinating. He had seen it dozens of times on the local news. This scorching desert could become a killer if you did not keep track of what you are doing. He was finding it hard to focus on anything very long and his hope was that there would be water where he saw the green patch on the mountain.

As his breathing returned to normal and the dizziness cleared from his head, he proceeded upward again toward the top of the mountain. He kept thinking about the situation he was in and why after all these years of wishing he was dead and gone, here he was taking care of somebody else. This train of thought only served to make him angry so he turned his mind to the task of climbing. His head began pounding. His heart was beating so hard he could feel it through his throbbing ears. Okay, stupid, you are moving way to fast for these conditions. You have to slow down and pace yourself. He reached up to wipe the sweat from his face and in that split second, his foot caught the edge of a rock and immediately he felt himself bouncing back down the hill. He was aware of his body hitting bushes, rocks and even a cactus now and then. Trying to concentrate on what was passing by. He hoped he could catch hold of something strong enough to stop his fall. When he finally did stop rolling down the desert slope, he was unconscious. He was not aware of the boulder his head had struck on the way down.

8

He lay there for approximately 20 minutes before he realized he could feel coolness on his back and neck. He tried to clear the cobwebs from his mind, and blinking his eyes to see through the blurry fog that now surrounded him. After a few minutes, he reached back to feel what the coolness was on his neck and shoulders. Turning over he found he was lying in water. Wow, good thing I did not fall face down he thought. Reaching out his arm, he filled his hand with enough for a small drink, and then planting his hands on either side of his body, he lowered his face into the water to drink his fill. Finally, feeling some relief from the thirst and thinking a little more clearly he sat up to survey his surroundings. The beautiful crystal clear little pool was the only thing he could see for a few minutes because it seemed so totally out of place here on a mountain in the desert. Maybe I am hallucinating, he thought. No, I can feel this.

The pool looked to be about six feet long and maybe three feet deep. He washed his face and noticed there was a small crack in the base of the largest stone at the end of the pool. It was not just a rain catch. It was fresh constant flowing water. He washed his face again, soaked his head, and filled his canteen with the life-saving water.

He slowly made the trek up the side of the mountain, collecting his weaponry as he found it scattered across the sand. He noticed he was only about seventy-five feet from the top of the hill and as he looked around, he realized this little oasis was the one he had been looking for. The little spring was almost hidden from the world. If he had not tripped and fallen he probably would have passed right by without seeing it. The only thing giving it away was the bright green of the nearby brush that grew at the edge. The pool, protected on two sides by boulders and the shear rock face where the spring originated, the water flow was just enough to allow a small trickle to run out and over the side for about twenty-five feet. At the bottom, there was a small muddy area, and within fifteen feet, it just disappeared into the rocky, sandy desert floor. Good thing I was stopped where I did, that extra twenty-five feet might have done the job that the airplane crash had not.

It truly was an oasis. Elaine can have all the water she needs now, no more skimping with a drink here and there. Well, all I want now is more food. This water is bound to attract animals in the area. This is an excellent place to get our next meal. He began thinking about getting Elaine and all their stuff up here, because this was the perfect place to maintain their strength. It has water, access to food, and we could build a small lean-to that would give us protection from the heat and rain. Stony turned his attention back to the top of the mountain, maybe if he climbed all the way to the peak he could see if there was an easier way from the other side of the mountain. Well, it was worth a try, weaving his way around boulders and rocks and brush until he was there.

He stopped and stood staring across the desert and then around toward the crash site, which he could not see. He looked back down the mountain toward the mineshaft, which he could see. The severity of their situation smacked him squarely in the face. He slowly turned in all directions, looking as far as he could see. Nothing but miles and miles of dry desert floor. There were no signs of civilization, no farms, no houses, no highways, no dirt roads, not even a path. By all appearances, it looked to be untouched by humankind.

No sign of rescuers, he looked to the skies in hopes of spotting any type of aircraft, nothing there, either.

"Well, I guess we … are the only hope we have."

Immediately his mind began to race, damn, we are in serious trouble here, he thought. He figured he could see about 30-40 miles, could we walk it? Sitting down on a large rock, he contemplated his next move. Chances of them walking out were perilous even if their bodies were in perfect shape, which they were not. I am not as young as I once was. Civilian life has made me soft. She has a broken arm for sure and we might not be aware of any internal injuries. Either one of us could have problems that we just do not now about yet. Hell, it looked like the devil's oven out there. The shimmering waves of heat that went on forever, it conceivably could be hell. Maybe, he thought if we walked at night, but he already knew the answer to that was possibly one percent higher than walking in daylight. This is not the time to play macho man and try to prove I can do it.

The only realistic answer was too tough it out right here, until somebody found them. The FAA would be searching for the aircraft eventually. Here with a shelter, the water, and the opportunity for food, their chances for survival were the best. The FAA is surely aware that the aircraft did not land when and where it was supposed to, so, they will hunt, and eventually find the aircraft. With the signs we left behind they will know there are survivors somewhere.

"Okay, it's settled, we'll stay here and take our chances at the mountain oasis." Stony said it aloud. It seemed to make the decision more definite. He then set about making what comfort he could formulate by clearing a level spot for the future lean-to site.

"We will need some firewood for camp and some bigger logs for a signal fire that we will put on the top of the hill, where it can be seen from all directions." In about thirty minutes, he had gathered a pile of wood he thought was large enough. He then picked his way back down to the oasis and searched for any small recess in the side of the rock face but fairly close to the pool. Finally finding an alcove, the place he thought would work, he gathered small firewood for the camp and placed it in front of the alcove. Cutting two limbs with a forked end and then a piece for a cross bar to lie on top of both forks. He gathered and piled rocks around the poles to keep them in place. Then he began placing longer logs on the crossbar running toward the back of the alcove until there was a solid roof. He picked up rocks and laid them down both sides from the front forked posts that would be the entrance, to the rock wall. Stony hauled mud from the water hole and packed onto the roof of logs until it looked like an amateur version of an adobe roof. Tired, but pleased with the shelter he had built, he started back down the mountain toward the tunnel entrance. He carried the full canteen of water so Elaine could drink her fill.

It was good dark when he arrived and found her sitting up and looking a little pale, but otherwise she was in good spirits.

Elaine saw Stony approaching and said, "Good grief, what in the world has happened to you? You look awful." She stood weakly and instructed him, "Come here and sit down, I need to check your head. Is that blood I see?"

Being way too tired to argue, he sit down and let her probe and mash every bone in his head. "I'm okay," he said, "I got side tracked, and happened to trip and fall, and as usual I landed on my head. Nothing new, I've been doing it since I was a kid."

"Well, other than a knot or two, it seems to be intact." She said.

"Actually I think we have more important things to discuss right now than my hard head. This is something that will affect our immediate future." Stony looked intently into Elaine eyes, making sure he had her full attention. "I found water and close to it I made a shelter for us. So, if you are able in the morning, we will have about a two-hour climb. I figure this will be our last move for awhile." He waited for her reaction.

"Why are we going to stay there, if we're supposed to be going for help?" She asked.

"I am going to be honest with you. You are as much a part of this predicament as I am, so I will give you my opinion and then I will gladly listen to you. We are both adults and we both need to know what might be ahead for us. The decisions we make from here on need to be mutual. Okay?" Stony began to explain about the miles of desert in every direction around them. "If we try to walk, we will eventually run out of water. That is the bottom line. I feel that our best chance of survival is to stay where at the least we have water, shelter, and a good chance of getting all the wild game we need to eat. We can, I believe, stay alive until help comes."

He told her about building a base for a signal fire on top of the mountain for the time when the search teams expanded their search beyond the original flight path. He finally revealed the information about the pilot not being able to contact anyone before the crash. "From my experience I figure sometime in the next thirty-six to forty-eight hours they will find the crash site and us."

"But you're not sure though are you?" Elaine asked. The look on her face was something he could not ignore. "I…No." he replied. "But it is just a matter of time before they make it this far. The question is will we still be alive when they get here?"

"I do appreciate you being straight with me." Elaine said softly, "I knew or felt that we would probably be on our own for a while. I'm not a quitter, and I have the feeling that even though you are aware of the worst that can happen to us, you are not going to give up any time soon. If I have to be in this situation, I am glad it is with someone like you. Surely between us there is enough fight to last as long as we might need."

Stony smiled then said, "Well then, the general consensus is that our job while we're here, is to stay alive long enough for the rescuers to rescue us. Is that the way you see it?"

"Yes, it is." Elaine nodded as she handed him a couple of lifesavers and a cup of water. "Now let's get some rest so we'll be able to climb a mountain tomorrow."

Very soon, after he lay down on his bed, all that could be heard was Stony's exhausted snore. Elaine drank all the water she could hold and watched Stony as he slept, with a little more than confused interest. He seemed to be capable of doing most anything, she thought, I just hope he is right about this mess. She lay back and thought about the last three days and how suddenly she found herself depending on a perfect stranger. She smiled as she drifted off to sleep, I can't let him know that I think he has done everything perfectly. And he does not feel like such a stranger any more.

9

WHEN DAWN CAME Stony was just stirring. "Boy, something sure smells good." His voice was dry sounding and gravely as he was trying to come awake.

"Coffee?" Elaine asked

Stony sat upright and looked around, "Absolutely, you bet I'll take a cup." As he staggered to his feet, he could not help but notice the stiffness and the sore joints as he stretched. However, the smell of hot coffee helped wiped out the discomfort he felt from the previous day's activities.

Elaine had awoke early and slipped out to use the 'little girls room' while Stony was still asleep. She used the last of the water to make coffee hoping that it and the couple of packets of sugar they used to sweeten it would give them some energy. She knew that she was weak, but she felt much better today. The swelling in her arm was actually going down. She was more concerned about the knot and cuts on Stony's head.

"How are you feeling this morning?" she asked.

He was sipping his coffee and seemed to be savoring every drop.

"I heard you mumbling in you sleep last night. Did you get some rest?" Elaine asked hoping he did not have more injuries than he admitted.

"I did rest very well, thank you. In addition, I do talk in my sleep now and then. It is just the after effects of combat in war. Don't think anything about it, really, I feel much better today than I did yesterday. I was very tired last night, I'm sure that some of the fatigue is from the crash, just catching up with us." Stony took the last drink from his cup and began packing up their meager belongings.

Elaine repacked the makeshift backpack, trying to get everything that they might need. She knew they would probably not be coming back to the crash site or this little camp. She finished packing and with one more look, she scanned the area looking for something they might have forgotten.

"Have you gotten everything?" Stony asked.

"I'm as ready as I'll ever be." Elaine answered.

They set out heading for the mountain to Stony's oasis. The climb was uneventful and because of their early start, it was cool enough that they did not have to stop for rest or water.

Elaine had been thinking most of the way and had not realized that they had worked their way up the mountain so quickly, until Stony stopped on the edge of the small arroyo where they could look down, "There's our little slice of heaven." He pointed to the oasis as Elaine come to stand beside him. She could not believe this place existed in this God forsaken country. It was actually very beautiful she thought and amazingly much cooler as they approached the water. She just stood and stared for several minutes, taking it all in.

Her thoughts went back to what she had been thinking about on the trek here, on the man that she had seen at the airport, then on the plane itself, and now thrown together for survival. Some people might consider this fate or destiny, or karma, what ever it was it seemed they were supposed to meet. The last thing she thought she needed was another man. Nevertheless, she felt safe with this Stony. The man had many talents, one minute hard and stubborn, the next gentle and kind. He seemed capable of handling any situation that might be thrust upon him. Mostly quiet and determinedly sure of himself and the decisions that he could make in an instant. She had never met anyone that she felt trust in so quickly, as if it was the most natural thing in the world. Her emotions were taking her to places she had not planned on going. Oh, what was she thinking? I have heard stories about people thrown together in stressful situations that would form an attachment to each other. Desperation could make a person do some strange things, but, I am not going to think about this now, neither one of us need added problems to contend with. All we are supposed to do is survive and if we do, there will be plenty of time to think and talk and come to a decision.

"Are you feeling alright?" Stony asked. "Do you not like it? You sure got very quiet. Do you need anything?"

"I'm fine," she said, "really, just fine. Yes, I like this place. I think it is beautiful. And since we'll be staying, I guess we need to get unpacked."

They both unpacked their make shift knapsacks and placed the items where they both could find them. A plan of action began to immerge as they discussed their situation. If an airplane did fly close, he showed her where he had piled the bonfire woodpile that was on top of the mountain. He instructed her on how to load and fire the flare gun. The first flare into the pile of sticks and brush in the middle of the stack of wood. "This will get the fire started," he said, "Next, you will reload and fire the second flare straight up. Between the smoke of the signal fire and the glow of the flare, surely someone will notice." Elaine slowly looked around while on the summit taking in the beautiful view. Then suddenly she was flooded with the feeling of total isolation. She was overwhelmed with the realization of what had actually happened to them. These last three days and the very serious situation they were in, she began to sob. Facing death, destruction and hopelessness was almost more than she could bear, weeping uncontrollably, wishing that all she had been through was just a dream. However, knowing in fact that it was reality.

Stony heard her gasp and turned to see her breakdown, her body shaking with deep racking sobs. He approached and gently took Elaine in his arms and held her tightly until the tears slowly subsided. Finally, after a few minutes, she was trying to dry her tears and wiping to clear her face of the emotional outburst she stepped away from him.

"I am so sorry;" she said softly, "I don't normally break down. The possibility of not getting out of here just suddenly came over me. Being busy with all the actions of making shelter, salvaging materials, and trying to gather and prepare our meager supply of food has pretty much kept my thoughts from getting to the morbid consciousness that death could still claim the remaining passengers of the plane crash."

"I know, I've been wondering how long it would be before your shock and adrenaline would finally hit rock bottom. In addition, you are right we could die here. Right here on this mountaintop. However, you know you cannot dwell on this train of thought. Between us both, we have provided for ourselves as best as anyone possibly could. Considering what we had to choose from, I think our likelihood of survival is very good. We have shelter, water, and there will be food, because its here for us to find and harvest. Furthermore, we are on top of a mountain, from this altitude our chances of being seen are the best they could be. Now, come here." He held out his arms, she leaned toward him, and they were holding each other. He smiled down at her and said, "You know, it's really kind of pretty up here, it's like you're on top of the world." He squeezed her and then whispered, "You are not alone out here. I have survived three plane crashes, SERE training in the military, fifteen years of being on my own, and five children growing to adulthood. There is not much I have not tried or seen at one time or another. If you had to be stranded with anyone, your best bet is me. Therefore, we are not going to dwell on what could be, but think only about what will be. I am not afraid, I can take care of the things that you cannot. There's only positive thinking from here on, which is until we get rescued, and after that you can take all the time you want to feel sorry for yourself." He hugged her reassuringly, and then said, "Maybe it's time we try to find some food. How about you? Are you hungry? My stomach is letting me know that my mouth needs to chew on something."

"I'll be okay, thanks for the pep talk. I am not really feeling sorry for myself. That is not my style. I think I was just afraid. I've never faced anything like this before and it's hard to be optimistic when you don't know how to help yourself." I have always counted on myself to do what needs done, and I just got off the path and was a little lost. But now that I know I have Daniel Boone with me," Elaine smiled, "I'll count on you for guidance and maybe I'll even give you total control on those things I haven't learned yet about survival. But I must tell you I am a quick learner, so total control may not last long."

She was laughing now, the fear forgotten, as she headed down to 'Camp Oasis'. "I think I will clean up the camp site and maybe look for some firewood, that I know how to do. Thanks again, I really do feel much better now."

Stony smiled watching her practically skip down to camp, feeling a little better himself. He turned and walked down the hill looking for the two boulders he had spotted earlier today. Between the two boulders, there was a game trail. Animals had worn a path, while going to drink from the pool. He quietly worked his way around to the upper side of one boulder and figured a way to climb on top of it. He found he could lie prone on top of the rock and with the spear in his hand, it hung directly over the narrow trail, about 2 ft above the path. He squirmed around to get to the best position. He knew he might be here awhile so he worked on balancing himself atop the rock well enough to make a jabbing movement without falling off.

Then he lay very still, waiting for whatever game would eventually walk by on the trail. The sun was relentless and the stone was getting extremely hot on his skin. The buttons on his thin cotton shirt were biting into his chest. The sweat was rolling down his face into his eyes and yet he remained motionless, waiting patiently.

Finally, after what seemed hours, a movement caught his eye, a sow and three piglets were making their way up the path, and heading straight at him. "God, please help me kill this peccary for we certainly need the food." As the sow slowly made her way toward him, he concentrated on his grip of the spear. He did not want to lose the pig and the spear if she took off running. At the precise moment, the sow came under the spear, Stony jabbed straight down as hard as he could. He felt the shudder under his hands and then it launched forward nearly jerking Stony from his precarious perch. He still had the spear in his hand, getting his balance back he then stood where he could see below. Somehow, he had missed the sow, instead getting one of her piglets. It laid kicking and bleeding about ten foot up the trail. The piglet became still and Stony could no longer see any movement from the animal.

Sliding off the rock, he walked slowly toward the piglet keeping an eye out for the mother. She could come back when she discovers one of her babies is missing. Stony hoped that she was too busy with the two she had left and that all would be heading down the hill for a safe place to hide.

Picking up the piglet, he figured it weighed approximately fifteen pounds. Perfect, he thought, young and tender, it was going to taste delicious. He began to skin out the carcass, saving everything that was edible. They could eat the meat, and also the heart, liver, and even the brains. He was pleased that he had provided the promised meal with such tasty meat. Carrying the carcass into camp, he smiled at Elaine, lifting the prize for her to see. He skewered the meat with a small branch that would act as a spit over the fire. They both enjoyed the smell of the meat as it cooked. Making sure it was well done so there would be no parasites or bacteria to harm their bodies, Stony began to cut chunks of meat off, handing Elaine the first bite, he took the next piece until they could not hold another morsel.

"Well, now that my mind is not on my hunger pangs, I realize just how gritty and dirty my body feels." Elaine was looking at the dirt and sand that was sticking to her clothing and skin. With my stomach satisfied, I would like to be clean."

As Stony thought about the meal she had just eaten, she was probably feeling much stronger. He noticed a little color had returned to her face.

"This must have been what the cavemen felt like most of the time." She commented, as she stood and started toward the supplies that were in the hut.

"Yeah, but they were used to it." Sensing that it might be a good time to let her have a little time alone, he said, "Oh, by the way, I'm going up the hill to see if I can spot any search planes and that pool is looking like it would make a mighty big bathtub. So, feel free to freshen up, I'm sure you will sleep a whole lot better tonight if you do."

He grabbed the signal pistol kit and started up the hill for the summit.

As he left the camp, Elaine realized that he was being the perfect gentleman. He was letting her clean up and giving her privacy while she did. She found the soap in the shaving kit and headed for the pool. Taking a bath seemed suddenly to be very enticing. She walked down to the pool and shed her clothes, and slipped slowly into the water. "Oh, this is heavenly." She whispered. Feeling the water as it enveloped her body, she was amazed at how alive she felt at this very moment. The cold water covered her body as she moved farther out so that her whole body became immersed as she found a small rocky ledge at the edge of the pool. Actually, laughing aloud with the pleasure she was experiencing, she did not care whom or what heard her.

Stony sat and watched out across the desert for the better part of an hour, belly full and lost in thought as the darkness covered the mountain. He heard Elaine laughing and his mind drifted back to the warmth of her body pressed against his when she was crying earlier. He actually entertained a moment of sympathy for how frightened she must have felt. What really bothered him was the fact he felt the beginnings of sexual arousal. Hell, he thought, I have not felt that in months, maybe even years. Damn boy, what is wrong with you? He had not let anyone get that close to him for a long time, he had been through enough with women to know that he did not want tied down again, ever.

Satisfied that there were no search planes anywhere near, he started back to camp. The glow of the fire was flashing across the little oasis and as he came into the edge of the clearing. Immediately he noticed the back of Elaine's head, she was still in the pool. He turned and stepped back into the darkness. He had no plan to look in her direction, but he heard water splashing and he glanced toward the pool. Elaine had stood up with her back to him as she rinsed the soap from her body. Oh, my God! He thought, she was drop-dead beautiful with the water running down her back in the dimness of the firelight. He turned away immediately. You are out here stranded in the desert, trying your best to survive. Do not even go there! He was trying to make the picture in his mind go away. Do not do something stupid! This is not the place or the time to entertain such notions. He eased back up the side of the hill, back up to the summit, to sit in the darkness. Needless to say, this time he was not thinking about rescue. He felt guilty and yet was not sorry for witnessing such a beautiful sight. At this moment, he felt like he had seen something that few men had ever experienced.

Elaine had rinsed out her clothes and hung them to dry on some bushes at the edge of camp. Surely, she would hear Stony coming down the hill in plenty of time to slip them on. It felt so good to air-dry her body after washing all the grit and grime of these last few days. Checking the clothes in a few minutes, she felt they were dry enough, so she quickly slipped back into them. Making her way back to the campfire, she sat fluffing her hair dry with her fingers when she heard Stony approaching.

"Well, how was the bath?" He asked. Stepping closer to the fire, glancing in her direction, remembering exactly what she looked like naked. He was trying his best to appear nonchalant and indifferent.

"It was wonderful." She answered. "It felt great, almost sinfully good, I certainly feel like a new person."

"I want to know one thing." Stony asked. "Did you leave me any hot water?"

They laughed, both feeling relaxed and truly comfortable now in each other's company.

"If you want me to I will change that splint on your arm. It looks like it is about to fall off anyway, did you get it wet?" He asked. "Better let me re-do it."

She gratefully handed him the first-aid kit, and he set about taking the remaining bandage off and rewrapping her arm carefully, trying not to hurt her. How gentle this man could be she thought, she actually thought his touch was almost a caress. You had better be careful, she told herself, do not be reading more into this than there is, he is just helping me. What was it he had said? Something about doing for me the things, I cannot. Well, wrapping my own arm was surely one of those things. "Thank you, very much, for everything that you have done for me. You can be so gentle and caring." She looked at him and smiled.

"We are not out of this yet, I'm sure you will see a different side to me before this situation is over. Most people find me hard to live with under the best of circumstances. My children would probably be the first to tell you that my soft side has rarely seen the light of day. I find it is easier to show the hard side first, and then most people leave me alone. In addition, there is no question about where I stand on getting involved with other people's lives.

"So, you have children?" She asked.

'Yes, one son and four daughters." Stony replied. "I think I was too hard on them. Men are not supposed to be moms, and after their mother died, I did not know anything but control or discipline. As a result, they did not really get the caring and tenderness that only a mother can give. They're grown now and have families of their own. I am pretty sure, if they had their choice, it would have been me that died, not their mother. She had that knack for nurturing. She left a big hole in all our lives."

Elaine sat listening as Stony opened up and talked about his family. She sensed that he had needed to talk to someone for a very long time. She learned that his wife had died when the children were quite young. The boy was the oldest and he had been only nine when he lost his mother. The youngest girl was two days from being a year old. Elaine understood perfectly how a callous outlook on life could come from such devastation. He had been so out of his element as a parent that all he succeeded in doing was alienating first his children, then his family and then everyone he met, keeping everyone at arms length.

She learned about the promise that Stony had made to his wife before she died. That he would stay in the service until retirement and keep the kids together until they could make it on their own. It was a promise he had kept even at the expense of making them all miserable. This person had given up his life for over fifteen years just to keep a promise. The only way he knew how. She learned that he and his wife had been high school sweethearts and were inseparable until the war. He had gone to Viet Nam a young daddy and lover full of life, only to come home a bitter and hostile man who had seen way too much and had grown old long before his time. Then have his life companion taken away by death shortly after his return to the states. He had never had a period of adjustment back to a normal relationship, let alone a situation where he would deprive himself of anyone that could get close enough to help him talk about some of the stuff that was bothering him.

Stony grew silent. He stood up and said, "Sorry, I've talked too much." He walked toward the little pool. He sat mulling over his sudden compulsion to talk. Why in hell did I spill my guts to this lady? My emotions were just too close to the surface, after seeing her in the pool. She sure did not need that piled on her too! He bent to wash his face, then slowly walked back into camp and the little adobe topped hut. Elaine was in bed and was fast asleep when he came back. He stood in the doorway watching her as she slept. She really was a beautiful woman, he thought. He noticed her full breasts rising and falling with her breathing. Damn, she really was a knock out. He was surprised that he was just now seeing his companion for the first time after three days and nights.

He returned to the fire and threw on another log, then retreated to his bed. The bed that Elaine had made for him with articles of clothing that covered a thick carpet of weeds and grasses. He last thought was that it felt like a bed fit for a king, and then he was asleep.

"Are you okay?" She asked. As he opened his eyes, he was looking directly into the beautiful blue of hers.

"Yes, I'm fine. What's wrong? Has something happened?" He asked.

"No, nothing has happened and nothing is wrong, I was just a little worried about you sleeping so long. You know with that knot on you head." She answered.

He sat up and realized that was probably the best night's sleep that he had had for a long time. The sun was high in the sky and he had not felt this rested in years. He had become accustomed to short periods of sleep and even shorter periods of rest. That was the norm since he had come back from Viet Nam. He looked at his watch and was still surprised to see that is was close to 9:30. "Good night alive," he said, "I cannot remember the last time I have slept past 5:00 a.m. I guess I was more tired than I knew."

Elaine handed him a cup of coffee and said, "It's well done, and has been for a couple of hours. I hope it's not too strong."

Stony took the cup and thoroughly enjoyed the overcooked bite of the coffee. "That was perfect," he replied. "It's nectar from the Gods, and way better than some fancy coffee shops I've tried. That's just the way I like it."

"And you are a big fat fibber." She shot back. "Here," she handed him the oddest contraption that he had ever seen, "you look like you've been in bed for a week. Your hair is an absolute mess. Maybe this will help you." She began explaining the ugly devise that he held in his hand. "It's a piece of cactus with four forks imbedded in it. I know its crude, but it does work." She said. "I used your big spear to shave off the thorns, then slit four openings to hold the forks, and by golly, it worked!"

He noticed her hair was neatly combed. She was very fresh looking. Yes, I can see it does, and I'll try it out as soon as I finish my coffee." Smiling as he took his time draining his cup and even asking for another. "Okay," he said, "I'm going, I'm going." Off he went towards the pool. Leaning over the edge of the water, he washed his face, wet his hair and then began slowly combing it with the makeshift comb. To his surprise, it worked quite well, a little awkward but it did get the job done. By God, she ain't half bad to be stuck with either, a man would never have thought about making a comb, but using it he somehow felt more civilized. She is really something, beauty and brains too! He remained by the pool, hoping that he had not talked too much last night. He had never talked to anyone like that before, but it had felt so natural with Elaine, the words had just tumbled out.

He tried to recall some of the good times that he and his wife had together. He tried to remember her body and how she had looked naked. He did not try to call to mind his wife very often, but now for the first time ever he was having a hard time with the details he had been sure he would never forget. Fifteen years, and now all he could see in his minds eye was the backside of one appealing woman rising up from a pool in the middle of the desert. Damn, boy, get your mind right. She is too young and beautiful to want a tired old man like you. Your mind should be on the business at hand, like survival. Quit being stupid! Stony apologized to Marilyn as he walked back to camp. I am sorry that I can't remember like I used to. I am sure it is just from being in this hot desert and the stress of the situation. Do not worry, Hon, I will be fine after we get back home, and everything gets back to normal.

'Well, you look almost human with your hair combed. What's on the agenda for the day?" Elaine asked.

"I think that since we have this shelter to live in, there are probably a lot of things that we can make use of from the crash site. If we are going to be here a while we can just make it more livable. I'd like for you to stay here and keep the home fire burning, and on the lookout for planes. Someone needs to be close to set off the flare and bonfire." He looked at her for her response and was not surprised by what she said.

"I question that decision. What if something were to happen to one of us, especially you?" She said. "I'm not sure I want to be by myself all day long. It will take you at least eight hours to go there and then come back."

"Listen to me, you are much stronger now, your fever is all but gone, there's still meat to eat, and water, you will get along fine. What if there is something there we might have overlooked? Something important?" Stony asked. "I'm stronger now too, so I will probably make it faster alone. I just feel it needs to be done. Now, please, stay in camp and take care of yourself for the day. The rest will be good for you. You can gather your thoughts, and maybe you can come up with something that will help our situation."

Elaine finally gave in and agreed that it might be the most important thing they could do for now. "I'll keep the fire burning until you come back. It will most likely be after dark and you might need a beacon. And I'll keep my ears open for the sound of planes." She promised. "I'll take care of everything here, so don't worry about me. You just take care of yourself, I've kind of got used to seeing your face around here and I don't know that I'm through trying to figure you out, Mr. Stony. So, come back."

He filled the canteen and picked up the crash axe, "I'll leave you the signal pistol, the spear, and the left-over food." He leaned down and kissed her on the cheek, "That's for good luck. I promise I'll be back before you know it. I'll be fine, so don't worry about me either."

Stony started with a rather brisk pace, but since childhood, he knew he could sustain that pace with a stable and steady tempo. He learned from his paternal grandmother who happened to be one-half Cherokee Indian. By maintaining this rhythm, he could cover a lot of ground and not tire easily.

10

The local search and rescue squads had searched for three days and nights. There were air searches that covered the White Mountain range from east to west, and north to south. There was nothing indicating a plane crash. There were squads left to a ground search in the Superstition Mountains. As the air patrol expanded their search from central and northern areas of the state, their next target was to cover the Mogollon Rim area. One squad was even searching in northern and western areas of New Mexico. No one had found anything yet. It was unusual that there was nothing found. Mr. Robert Farley, representative of FAA, was pacing the floor trying to comprehend the meaning of these dead ends. "For crying out loud! It has been three days and nights. Where could they be? The Governor of Arizona will be calling back in about an hour for a progress report. What in the world, am I going to tell him? We have thousands of man hours from the National Guard, rescue personnel, and hundreds of volunteers, but, sorry Governor, we can't find a crashed airliner anywhere."

Bob was a large man, not fat, just big. His thick black hair had a tendency to drop a curl or two on his forehead. Especially when he was pacing the floor and he was pacing now. His co-workers often referred to him as the 'pit bull'. Mostly behind his back, but he had heard it before. He was always ready to take on any hunt. When he got his teeth into it, he would not let go. He had taken years on investigations. He had to be satisfied that he had all the information he could before his final report went to the powers to be in Washington, D.C.

Bob had been on vacation in the West Indies when he received a call to head up the search effort. His reputation was known from coast to coast, if it could be found, Bob Farley would find it. He was best in the business. The Governor had contacted Bob, telling him that the Air National Guard was ready and waiting for an assignment. "Bob, all you have to do is tell them where to go."

"Yes Governor," Bob told him, "But at this time, we don't know where to go. Trust me. You will be the first to learn of the location as soon as we find it."

The control tower personnel had listened to every communication tape from that night. The past three days filled with trying to find anything that might lead them to the crash area, hopefully with some survivors. However, that chance was getting smaller every day that they did not find the plane. Arriving in Phoenix two days ago, Bob immediately assumed control of command central and established a session, which brought the search team leaders into a brainstorming conference every three hours. It bothered Bob that the aircraft had been inbound to Sky Harbor, circling from the west coming east toward the airfield. Then ground control had suddenly lost power and did not regain command for approximately twelve minutes. A monsoonal black out! While not uncommon in this area, they had never lost power for more than a couple of minutes. When the power came back online, that flight was no longer on the radar screen. The control tower had depended on the radar to pinpoint the plane so it could continue its landing. While there was nothing on radar, they tried immediately contacting the plane on the radio. There was no answer, no SOS, and no airplane. Seemingly, it had just vanished.

How could an airliner just disappear?

Bob had isolated the exact spot where the plane had been when the communications were disrupted. He could not believe that the crash had happened somewhere beyond their search areas. Bob stood looking over incoming information and the search chart. He slammed his fist down on the table.

"I know we have information missing here or we're just not seeing it, by God, we've got to find that plane soon or it'll be too late." He reached for a cup of coffee then returned to settle in at the table that held the search chart. It had been placed in the center of the room which had been designated the War Room. He studied the first search areas and noted all of the sites they had explored were along the originally filed flight plan route. That was the most logical thing to do he thought, but it had not worked. There was simply nothing in any of those areas. Hell, there should be wreckage, some wreckage, somewhere along that route. "Someone get me a damned phone, and have the General of the Air National Guard on it." Bob snapped. One of Bob's aides handed him the phone, "General, Bob Farley here. We have entered our third day of this search effort. It is on the edge of turning into a recovery, not a rescue mission. I intend to find something soon. Do you understand me? I want you to dispatch every damned Apache helicopter you have. Search every canyon, river, arroyo and hog wallow from the Grand Canyon to the Phoenix city limits. Find me something!"

Bob knew that every minute could mean death for a survivor and he took it personal, as if he was responsible for the crash. The people that worked with Bob knew that because he took it personal, he searched for these people as if they were members of his own family. It was no wonder that his success rate was the highest in the business.

He just simply would not give up. They also knew that the longer the search went, the more demanding his orders would become.

"We are going to have to expand this search," Bob barked. "Expand it to at least 100 miles west from the Arizona/New Mexico state line. Okay people, get on it, NOW!"

The thing that troubled Bob was that no one had been able to pick up the Emergency Beacon Signal from the plane. Normally it only takes a few minutes to find a downed aircraft, had the plane crashed so violently that is destroyed the EBS? If so, he thought, there would not be any survivors. He needed answers, but more than anything, he wanted to know where that damned airplane was. And the 120 souls on board. He needed to think of them alive, not dead.

"What am I missing?" He asked.

11

STONY HAD MADE good time crossing the desert floor. Heat from the sun did not really get hot until about an hour ago. It is not even noon yet, so he still had about 2 hours before he would have to get out of the heat and rest for the return trip to the oasis.

He had tried to think about the kinds of things that he and Elaine might need until the rescuers came. He figured that suitcases were the best source of essentials, medicines, and clothing. When he finally reached the crash site and started combing through the wreckage, there were not as many suitcases as he thought there would be. Nevertheless, he started to notice the carry-on bags strewn around the body of the plane. Well that makes more sense he thought, the carry-on bags had been with the passengers. The suitcases were in the baggage compartment in the belly of the aircraft, most of which was now buried in the desert sand and would be impossible to get to without some major machinery. Carry-on bags would probably be holding the kind of stuff he was looking for anyway. So, not wanting to waste the time he had he began grabbing as many bags as he could carry at one time and then headed for the biggest spot of shade he could find. Putting the things he thought they could use in a pile to one side. He threw the bags in the other direction and out of his way. After several such trips his keep pile was about as much as he would be able to carry back to the oasis camp. He had retained a large size canvas bag that he began putting the supplies in. There was an assortment of medicines, even a couple of antibiotics, and a thermometer. One small case had contained a travel mirror, hairbrush, toothpaste and even a couple of travel size bars of soap. He had come across two small battery powered radios, but they were not working. Either they were out of range or the batteries were dead. Stony had come to the wreckage from the galley area and had found more of the coffee, sugar, and some powered creamer packets. There were actual coffee cups and some small plates. He stuffed them into the canvas bag. As he walked toward the tail section where he had been seated, he found another small radio that seemed to have power but was not receiving any signal. He put it in the bag thinking he might be able to tweak it a little or maybe just getting it back to the mountain would open up a signal path.

About 100 yards beyond the tail of the plane, there was a pile of debris that looked like it might be a piece of the cargo section. By making contact first on the desert floor, the bottom of the tail section had been dragged completely off the aircraft. Stony noticed a couple of crates that were semi-buried in the sand. He walked to the crates trying to read the shipping labels and then suddenly busted out laughing. The crates had been broken apart in the crash, along with the contents. That is all except one beautiful bottle of Rose Mateus wine. It was standing upright in a small patch of sand between the two crates. "What are the chances of a glass bottle making it through a plane crash? Maybe this is what some people would call divine intervention." He could not help smiling to himself. It was a little out of the ordinary that this one bottle was surrounded with chunks of debris and yet stood there like it had been placed by someone waiting for him to find it. He laughed for some time at the strange little scene. Finally, he picked up the bottle and placed it gently in the canvas bag.

He continued looking and did find some articles of clothing that they could use. There was a cargo strap, a piece of the aircraft skin about a foot and a half almost exactly square. The canvas bag was finally full enough that he began entertaining thoughts about getting back to the oasis camp and Elaine. This trip had not been in vain. He felt that with what they had gathered the first time and now that he had focused on the specific items could be put to good use, he knew that their chance of survival had definitely increased. Scanning back over the crash site, he thought, I hope I do not have to come back again.

He lifted his face to the sky. He knew he would need to rest for a little while before starting back. If he timed it right he could be there before it got black dark.

As Stony got closer to the mountain, he spotted the small fire that was burning for him. "Well, how about that. She did keep the fire alive." He muttered, and kept walking toward the burning light. As he got closer, he got a whiff of meat cooking. He stopped for a minute just to take in the site. "It's been a long time since I've come home to a meal already fixed and lights on to welcome me." He had not noticed how dark the desert had become until he saw the small fire. Now he quickened his pace to get there. Struck with a feeling of being alone, he had not felt this want to be with someone for a long, long time. He became aware of his heart beating faster, and his breath getting short, and he realized that he had been afraid. Afraid that something might happen to her and that she would not be here when he returned. "Okay, calm down, slow down, she's there! The fire is going and she preparing a meal for you to eat. You will scare her to death if you go running in there like a crazy man. Just take it slow and easy. Think about something else, she has learned to read your face pretty good for a rookie." He smiled at that thought and as he walked into camp, she glanced up and smiled back. Maybe she missed me too!

"Ah, the smell of food," Stony raised his nose in the air and closed his eyes, "I didn't know I was hungry until I smelled that. Whatever it is, I'm sure it's going to taste delicious."

Elaine had killed another rattlesnake. She had skinned it, threaded it onto the stick that was their spit. It was cooking slowly over the small fire that she had kept going until he returned.

"I see you have been busy since I was left." Stony said with a wide smile, "I'm surprised to see the meat of choice is snake tonight. Have you acquired a new taste?"

"This one tried to crawl into our camping area and I had to defend our territory," she replied, "so he sacrificed his life for our survival. It really is amazing how just a little salt and pepper can enhance the flavor of food. I think you will be quite satisfied with the meal I've prepared."

"When you are as hungry as I am, I think I could have eaten it raw, but I'm glad that you didn't have any trouble finding food. You probably could take care of yourself if you had to. I will not worry about that as much now that I know you are capable of providing for us if the need should arrive. Have you ever done anything like this before?

"Only an occasional camping trip now and then." She replied.

He asked, "You told me you were a quick learner, and now I know there is some truth to that. Is it ready to eat? I'm starved."

They ate the snake and as Stony was going through the items he had brought back, it dawned on him that Elaine had been talking non-stop since supper. She told him about killing the rattler. She told what she had done with the time while he was gone. She finished her narrative with, "I'm sure glad you're back, I was getting a little worried about you." The comment caught Stony a little off guard because up 'til now she had seemed to be confident. "Thank you." Stony said, "It's kind of nice to be needed." Even in the darkness, he thought he could feel a slight blush had come to her cheeks. He picked up the bag and handed Elaine the clothes including underwear that looked like it might be close to her size. He then handed her the box of travel soap and said, "Thought you might like this for your next bath."

She jumped up and gave him a quick hug, "Oh, Thank you." With soap in hand, she immediately headed for the water hole.

"Wait, I'm not through yet." He called after her, but she was already gone out of sight. "I didn't get a chance to tell her about the mirror, or the hair brush, or the toothpaste. She'll really like that, I'm sure."

The water was so cool and the night was like a curtain around her. She was lost in the luxury of the bath, so much so that she had no thought about the man sitting at the campfire. When the thought did come to her mind, she thought that right at this moment she did not even care if he was to look. What the heck, she found that thought a little exciting. She had not been close to a man for quite a while, physically or emotionally. A person could not help but be drawn to another person in a situation as they were in. For some strange reason she felt happy tonight. I do not mind at all if he wants to look in this direction.

Stony sat there for some time before allowing himself the pleasure of glancing in her direction. He was not disturbed that she might see him looking. As far as he was concerned, she was a knock out and he did not want to miss a chance to view the beauty of her.

The fire cast enough light that he could see her as she soaped her body with the tiny treasure he had given her. She was totally oblivious to anything outside the edges of the small pool. He could not remember the last time any woman had intrigued him so completely. She was bringing out feelings that he had long ago hidden from everyone, even himself. Since his beloved wife had died so many years ago, he had not wanted to feel anything like that for another woman. He had totally blocked any action that might lead a woman to think he would be interested. Feelings that he had forgotten you could feel, thoughts that raced in his mind, he could not control them this time. The yearnings that were coming over him, he thought were long passed.

"I'm going up the hill to look for search parties." He yelled to Elaine as he found himself walking away from the campsite, trying to get away, far away from her and the turmoil going on in his body and mind. Damn, he thought, I cannot even remember the last time I have wanted to make a woman mine. "I'll be back shortly." He headed for the top of the hill trying not to think about the touch of heaven that was in the pool below. When Stony reached the top, he turned on the little radio he had brought back with him. "Now we'll see if the battery works." He mumbled to himself. As soon as he flipped the on/off switch, the radio chattered to life. He searched for any news that would let him know that someone was indeed searching for the crashed plane. There was an announcement about a search, but the best he could tell they were looking on the eastern side of the state. Surely, they are not looking for us way over there. Stony sit down on a large rock and began looking to the empty sky.

Elaine finished her bath and knowing that Stony was up the hill, she walked totally naked across the campsite to the clothes that he had brought back. She dressed and began to search for her homemade comb. She walked into the hut and immediately noticed a hairbrush lying in the middle of the floor. There was a mirror lying to the side of the brush and around the two objects, Stony had drawn a circle in the sand. He had left them where she would have no trouble finding them. Then she noticed the toothpaste and travel toothbrush, "Oh, my gosh!" she started to laugh as she bent to pick up all that he had put out for her. She went straight to the pool and brushed her teeth, astonished that her mouth could feel this clean. She returned to the hut and sitting down, began to brush her hair free of the tangles. She felt like a new person. A clean body, clean teeth and she could actually run her fingers through her hair. This has been a wonderful night, she thought.

She returned to the fire to wait for Stony to come back, she lay down by the warmth thinking about the man on top of the mountain. How safe he had made her feel. Attempting to understand what his life must have been like since he wife had died years earlier. She wondered about the women in his life, had he found any sort of happiness? How many had there been? Had he tried to make a life? Or had he just lived a life, waiting for what was so inevitable to come? If he tried to make a life with someone, what kind of woman had she been? However, if he had just existed, then the women were likely to have been prostitutes. How do I feel about that? He definitely had an attraction about him, he could be charming, tender and gentle, and he had a confidence that she found extremely appealing. He was surprisingly thoughtful when he wanted to be, but there was another side to Stony. He had a core that seemed to be strong as steel. It apparently had been forged by adversity, danger, and responsibility. He could be stone cold and immovable when he felt the need. Hmmm, maybe that is how he got his nickname, or that could be his real name? She would find out eventually, because if she had anything to say about it they would be spending some time together. "This is stupid." Elaine was thinking aloud, "He probably has no desire for any kind of relationship, especially with the situation they are in, he has enough to think about right now, and his mind is on keeping us alive until help arrives."

After about 45 minutes, Stony returned to camp and showed Elaine the little radio he had found at the crash site. He said, "The best I can tell, we are somewhere between Yuma and Phoenix. That was the two channels that I could pick up with the strongest signal." He then noticed that she had in fact found some clothes that fit good. "Oh, by the way, you look very nice." He said. "You clean up pretty good for a girl, especially one that is camping out."

"I can't say the same about you," she said, eyeing the clothes he had worn for the last four days. "The soap works, the bar is smaller now, but I saved it for you. I figured that you probably feel as gritty as I did."

"I get the hint." Stony answered, "I can smell myself. Let me pick out something I can wear. Then stand back because you are going to see a new me." She watched him as he made his way to the pool. As he began stripping off his torn and dirty clothes, then she turned and walked into the hut to give him some privacy.

Just as he stepped into the pool, he turned to see if she was still watching, but she was nowhere in site. "Oh," as he sank in the water, "This can't help but make a difference in the way I feel." He spent the next twenty minutes washing and rewashing his body trying to erase the smell of death. The smell felt like it still clung to his skin. After the grime and sand were finally gone, and his body felt almost new, his thoughts drifted to Elaine and how she had looked in the light of the fire.

She had held up pretty good for a female, he thought, but if I did not know better I would think she missed me a little. This had been a long day for him as well, and he smiled broadly, lay back in the cool water with his hands behind his head as he leaned against the warm rocks at the edge of the pool. "Yeah, I think the little lady missed me while I was gone." He closed his eyes and just relaxed while his mind enjoyed the thought of Elaine.

When he returned to camp, he noticed the fire was just about out. He glanced into the hut and saw that Elaine was sound asleep. He tended the fire until it was going once again, then he also lay down on his makeshift bed and tried to put together some plans for tomorrow. The radio had said the search was on, but if they were searching the other side of the state, and if they were in fact looking for our plane, then it would be several days before they started to expand the search area. So… There were things that needed to be done before we even hope that the searchers would be over their area. Things like food, firewood, and a female standing in a pool of water. Stony drifted off to sleep with the picture of her in his mind. He saw the light from the fire reflected on her wet body. "Ice cream for my eyes." he whispered, smiling to himself.

12

Morning brought with it, a sudden rainstorm. Elaine awoke to the sound of rain beating on the tarp spread from the front of the hut. The wind was trying its best to whip the fastenings of the tarp loose. She jumped up and checked to see that the clothes and firewood was still dry. She and Stony had put them in a secure place, just in case this happened, and when she inspected them, they were still dry and in their protected place. Thinking of Stony, she looked to his bed and was surprised to find him gone already this morning. He had built up the fire and had coffee brewing in the metal drawer that was their coffee pot. I wonder where in hell he is off to now, Elaine thought as she poured a steaming cup of coffee. She sat down close to the fire to offset the chill of the rain.

Stony had walked back down toward the game trail that he had used before to catch the piglet. He had started digging a small pit across the trail. The cavity would be about 13-14 inches deep and approximately that wide. He had centered it as best as he could in the middle of the trail. Picking up the piece of aircraft skin he had brought back from the crash site, he punched a hole in one corner of the metal with the back of the fire axe. He then took the cargo strap, tied it in the hole, and finished by cutting an X in the center of the square shaped metal. The blade side of the fire axe was sharp and heavy enough that he simply let it fall into the flat metal. Each leg of the X was about five inches long. Stony held up the semi-square hunk of metal, smiled and said, "That ought to do fine." He laid the metal across the hole he had just dug and covered it with a light coat of sand. After standing up, he stepped back to see how good his camouflage looked from a distance. It blended in with the rest of the trail. "That is going to work very well," he muttered to himself. He then proceeded to pull the cargo strap around a large rock and tied it firm. He did not need it to pull loose easily. Now the trap was complete. When an animal came down the trail, he would step on the X in the middle of the plate. Its leg would slip into the X and the stiffness of the metal would prevent it from pulling its foot out. As it struggled to walk and pull out of the trap, the metal would cut into the leg and cut tendons, muscle, and possibly the bone. If the strap did not hold, the animal would try to run and the opposite leg would be cut as well. There would be a blood trail if in fact the strap did slip off the rock.

It had begun to rain as Stony was tying the strap to the large rock. He had kept working because he knew once the trap was set; he did not have to be here to see that it worked. He knew it would work. By the time he finished, the rain was pouring and the wind was picking up and the air was chilly blowing on his wet clothes. He needed to get back to the hut, put some dry clothes on, and warm up. The wind was making it cold and he did not need to be sick with pneumonia.

Elaine saw him coming up the hill and poured him a hot cup of coffee. "First things first," she quipped, "Here's some dry clothes, you need to change before you get any colder. You look like a drowned rat, where have you been?" As Stony began undressing by the fire, Elaine turned her back and waited for him to get the dry ones on. "I did feel like a drowned rat." He replied as he fastened his pants. Elaine thinking he was fully clothed turned just as he was turning around toward the fire. He had just finished snapping and zipping his slacks, and as he reached for the shirt, she noticed the scars on his back and shoulder. However, even the bullet wounds could not detract from fact that he was actually quite muscular in build. There was red hair on his chest that she imagined was soft as velvet. His stomach was flat and no flab that she could see. Not bad, she thought, especially for an 'old man', his words, not mine. She could think of at least a dozen men that were twenty years his junior that did not look as fit as he did. Stony finished buttoning his shirt and set down to drink his coffee while it was still hot and let his body absorb the warmth of the fire.

"What were you doing out there to get so wet?" she asked.

"I was making a leg snare on the trail." He answered. "One we don't have to stay and watch, I don't think it will take long before we'll have some more food to eat."

The rain was letting up, the wind was dying down, and they could tell the area was going to be humid today because the heat was already feeling considerably warmer as they finished their coffee. Elaine set about hanging his wet clothes on nearby bushes to dry. Stony was sharpening the fire axe with a piece of sandstone he had picked up near the camp.

All of a sudden, the air filled with a violent, shrieking noise. It overflowed into the little oasis. Elaine jumped about a foot in the air, whirled around, and yelled. "What in the world is that?"

Stony said, "Don't worry," as he laid down his sharpening rock and picked up the spear and the fire axe, "I told you it wouldn't take long, I'd say from the sound it's another peccary. It will probably be dead before we get to it, do you want to help me?"

"Sure, I don't mind." She was thinking that his voice sounded different.

"Thanks," he said, "I might need a little help with this one."

She followed him down the trail to a spot where there was blood everywhere she looked. The animal had stopped its terrible squealing. When she looked up Stony was signaling her to stay put and be quiet. She watched as he followed the cargo strap off the side of the trail into some rocks and low bushes. Suddenly the strap pulled violently to the right and with its teeth clicking together the peccary charged full bore right at him. Elaine happened to glance at Stony's face; the look was not one of fear, which you could expect, but rather a look of determination. Maybe a little like a gunfighter just before he draws his weapon. Stony's eyes were concentrating on the pig, his jaw was clamped so tightly together that muscle in his jaw looked like it was ready to pop right through his cheek. His legs, planted wide apart, fully braced for the confrontation. When the pig was within maybe three feet of him, Stony thrust the old spear dead center in the peccary's chest. Stony managed to hold on to the spear until the pig quit moving. The incident had not taken more than 45 seconds and Stony appeared to be in total control. On the other hand, Elaine was shaking like a leaf. She felt so weak that she sank to the ground just to have something to hold on to because she was absolutely exhausted. She could not help but notice the slight smile on his lips and yet his eyes appeared vacant, the reaction seemed like the look of victory, he had won, that is all. Stony's knuckles were white as he stood solidly holding the old spear as though he was expecting the peccary to get up and make another lunge for him.

Elaine spoke softly, "I believe its dead now." He was so focused she had not wanted to distract him. A person could get injured from a "dead' peccary, she knew that he was making sure that it was in fact dead and not just waiting for a second chance to fight for its life. "Really, I think he's dead." She repeated as she watched him, wondering what was going on in his mind at this moment. If she had had any doubt about his capabilities before, she was beginning to understand. It was quite possible he could handle any circumstance in which he found himself. She found herself with no doubt that Stony would protect her from harm. Trust was something that she had not let herself feel for a long time, maybe even never.

"I believe you're right." He straightened up and began to pull the spear out of the animal's chest.

She wiped sweat from her face suddenly feeling the heat of the day beating down on them. "You didn't even break a sweat." She said, "How do you do that? Oh, never mind," she said, "I'm not sure I even want to know. Okay, now that we've got it, what do we do next?" She asked as she stepped closer to him to stare at the dead pig. Stony turned toward her and she saw a kind, gentle, and caring man. He had very soft thoughtful eyes. It was totally opposite of what she had seen just moments before.

"You don't need to do anything, you just head back to camp and I'll get this thing skinned out and sister, we will eat well tonight!"

"I don't mind staying to help. Maybe I need to learn how to skin out an animal, just in case you're not around." She looked up at him and smiled, "But, then if I learn how to do everything, then I won't need you. I'll make sure the fire is ready and I'll see you back at camp."

As she walked up the trail, Stony called after her, "Oh, by the way I have a surprise for you, but you'll have to wait until the meat is cooked."

"I'll be looking forward to it." she replied as she turned and walked up the trail, leaving him to finish the job. When she got as far as the spring, she sank down to her knees and bent to splash the cool water on her head and face. At last, the nausea was about gone. She was sure that seeing the killing of the animal plus the extreme heat had been what had caused her to feel slightly sick. I will be fine when I cool down back at the camp. He can change his demeanor so fast, she thought. She almost could not keep up, but somehow through all the transformations she managed to feel safe. She had no doubt that he was doing everything he knew to help them survive however long it took to be rescued. Thinking back over the last few days, she had to admit it had been a hell of a trip so far.

13

Back in Phoenix Bob Farley had just received the morning brief from all units involved in the search. It was day five and Bob's hackles were up. "Damn it, why in hell have we not found those poor souls? How damned hard can it be to find an aircraft that was supposed to be on final approach. Just minutes from landing and it disappeared from the whole damn world." He summoned the heads of the search teams together. He wanted to give them his directive. They had all seen how Bob's attitude changed as each day came and went. He became more frustrated every day that a plane crash was not found. He was definitely in a sour mood. Bob walked to the middle of the airport war room, looking about the room as the search team leaders gathered.

Facing the leaders he said, "There are people out there somewhere." His dark eyes were literally snapping from face to face. "We can only speculate as to what condition they are in, but I am sure they are expecting us to find them. It has been five days. I do not care what it costs, or how many agencies have to be involved. Hell, I do not care if we have to call in the whole damn states of Arizona, New Mexico, or California. I want that plane found and damned soon! If there had been survivors after the crash, they probably have starved to death or died from thirst by now. Has anyone come up with any ideas about where this plane could have gone down?"

No one in the crowd offered any suggestions. "Okay, this is what we're going to do. Get all the tower tapes and the tracking information and we are going to stay here and plot the entire flight path from St. Louis to Phoenix." The crowd then started to protest because this had been completed days ago. Besides, they did not think there was anything that they could possibly have missed. "I know we've done this already, but I'm telling you people, we have missed something. We are also going to expand the search pattern again. Let's look from Flagstaff to Lake Havasu and the entire northwest corner of Arizona. Go all the way down to Needles, Ca. and then back to Phoenix! Remember! No comment to the News media, we will tell them something when we find something concrete. We do not need speculation. Day five, people! Please bring me something." Picking a couple of Rescue Team Leaders, Bob started for the tower to listen to the tapes again. "Three heads are better than one and if we don't find something we will volunteer three more heads to come and listen."

14

STONY SAT QUIETLY eating the last piece of pork tenderloin. The fire was crackling and he was lost in thought staring into the flames. Savoring the taste of the meal, listening to the night sounds, this was the perfect ending for their day. As Elaine returned from fetching water at the pool, the stillness drifted away and his attention turned to her. There was no need for constant communication. They had become comfortable in each other's company. She sat down by the fire, stared into the flames for a minute, and then asked, "Where did you learn all these things you've been doing?"

"Like what?' Stony responded.

"Well, like making water, catching animals with a piece of metal, building a fire down in a hole in the ground, finding and making shelters or setting bones or eating rattlesnakes, things like that, just to name a few." She replied.

"Oh, I imagine most of it was learned during survival school. That was way back in 1968, just before I was deployed to Viet Nam."

The question came at the perfect time, because for the next two hours Stony spilled his guts about a part of his life he had never discussed with anyone before. He told about his experiences at S.E.R.E. School. Survival, Evasion, Resistance, and Escape. That is what the letters signify. All members from every crew that would be spending time in country, or over southwest Asia, had to take and pass the course.

He told her about the tours he had spent in Viet Nam, things he had never talked about and yet it came so easy from him to Elaine. It suddenly dawned on him that he had talked too long, and was somewhat embarrassed by that. "I've had the floor long enough," he said and walked over to the canvas bag and pulled out the bottle of Rose Mateus. "This is your surprise." He said as he leaned toward her to pass her the bottle.

"A good meal deserves a great glass of wine." He said. They both laughed, and as her hand reached out for the bottle, their fingers touched. She looked up to see him staring deeply into her eyes. Neither moved from the touch, nor did they say anything to spoil the moment, a moment that felt like electricity moving from his hand to her hand. Their eyes seemed to search each other's souls. For that moment in time, there were no barriers, no differences, and no boundaries. Just an openness that neither had ever felt before. From their eyes to their very hearts, they felt for an instant the 'extraordinary' emotions. This was a moment to savor and be remembered for a lifetime.

The fire cracked and the spell was broken. Stony released the bottle and Elaine got up to look for the plastic cups to fill with wine. Elaine stood in the cover of darkness, quivering inside. Never had she experienced such an overwhelming stir of emotions and the suddenness of desire that had just passed through her body. She had read about the uncontrollable passions of lovers, but she had always regarded these stories as make believe. All of her life she had been pretty much in control of her emotions and yet not more than 30 seconds ago, she found herself wanting to be held, engulfed in his arms, bodies touching, doing whatever it took to keep feeling that electric current that had passed between them. Passages of romantic novels spun through her mind, women who could not resist the touch of a certain man, falling in love, and with no encouragement, they turned their whole lives over to him, totally controlled by the emotions of desire that raged in their bodies. "I thought that all those stories, all those women, were just the imaginings of an authors' mind." She whispered to herself. 'Nonetheless, I feel I have known him all my life.' She knew the gravity of their situation and that rescue could still be a long way off. Her survival would probably depend on the abilities of this man who guarded their lives with such determination and self-control. She was not afraid, maybe a little confused, but she had opened her heart to this man who was still very much an unknown individual. However briefly, the feelings were still very comforting.

Stony finally dug the cork from the bottle and poured it into the plastic cups. Elaine sat back down as he handed her the cup. "Now let's toast the dead souls of the aircraft." They drank. "A salute, to the pilot whose final thoughts were of his family." They drank again. "A salute to nature for providing us food and water." They drank again. "As well as a salute to the rescue crews who will be finding us before long." They finally ran out of toasts about the same time they ran out of wine. Heading off to the adobe hut and settling into their separate beds, lost in their separate thoughts, both soon were sound asleep.

Dawn found them huddled up closely together with Elaine's head on Stony's extended arm and his nose buried in Elaine's hair. She had her splinted arm across his chest and as he began to awaken, he smelled the aroma of her as she lay sleeping. He realized it did not feel unnatural at all, in fact, it felt good to have her so close.

The pounding of his head soon put an end to the moment. He slid silently out of the makeshift bed, and made his way to the pool. Stripping out of his clothes, he then eased into the cool water all the way over his head. The pounding had now taken 2nd place to the memories. The dreams had returned last night. The ones that kept him awake most nights since 1969. He should have known they would be there after last night. Stony remembered that he had talked about the war to Elaine. The flight surgeon had said that time would erase the ugly memories of that stinking war, but that had been a lie. He could still smell the disgusting odor of burning flesh, and the feel of the babies he had held until they drew their last breath.

His crew had taken medical provisions and food into a village in Viet Nam, but had run out before all the villagers could be inoculated and fed. They would have to return the following morning with more supplies. However, the next morning when they walked into the village, a pile of arms and legs greeted them. It seems the Viet Cong had entered the village after he and his crew had pulled out. They had made an example of the entire village by promptly amputating either the arm or leg that had been vaccinated. They had stolen the food that had been left and there was a message in blood on the side of one of the huts. "you no come back".

That was probably the most horrible sight that Stony had ever witnessed in his entire life. It had never lessened in details and it had replayed in his mind thousands of times. Stony then realized that even with the plane crash and the mangled bodies, he had not had a nightmare about the crash. However, every time that he talked about his war experiences, the traumatic dreams came back.

The mutilation of the people in the village had been so disturbing, there had been no erasure or lessening of the memories as Doc had promised there would be. That was one reason he did not talk about that time in his life. In addition, of course, their welcome back to America had not been so good either. People were yelling at us, cursing us, and even throwing bags of human waste at us as we entered or left the sanctity of our military bases. These people might have lived down the street or even next-door. Ordinary people! We were not welcome at our own children's school functions, block parties, or any civilian get-togethers. Even neighbors would look away when they confronted you on the sidewalk.

Veterans did not dare apply for a job. If you filled in the section about military service with any dates that were in the Viet Nam era, you were immediately rejected. We were all trying to adjust back to civilian life. His wife died leaving him with the children, the youngest two still in diapers. From that point on, any pleasure that life had held for him was now gone. Disappeared in an instant.

His American dream did not exist. He had succeeded in becoming an invisible man. Just existing day to day in a world he did not recognize. After a while, he did not want to recognize, did not want to care about anything. Had it not been for a pilot's dying request and now a beautiful woman, this would have been a perfect opportunity to vanish from the face of the earth. His children could have collected his insurance and might have even found kind words to say about a dad that was never around when he should have been. He had instead served his country for bureaucrats who turned out not to really give a damn about the expendables.

Stony just could not leave people helpless and in need. He did not want to but he could not stop himself. He offered to help wherever he could but angry with himself later because he was obligated once again. It always ended with just more trouble for him and no or little appreciation from the rescued. He had concluded that it just was not worth it. All that being said, it would forever be his Achilles heel. The one flaw in the armor he used to protect himself from disappointment. He dipped once more before getting out of the pool, hoping to leave all bad memories behind in the cool water.

Elaine awoke to find Stony heating water for coffee. She had spent the night listening to bits and pieces of what must have been a nightmare. She heard him mumbling about children and those low-life bastards. He tossed and turned until she tried to comfort him by moving closer and holding him. She even wiped the tears from his face as he moaned and whimpered like a child. Elaine found it difficult to believe this self-sufficient, strong independent man crying over anything. All the same, she wanted to find out. Whatever was troubling Stony had to have been quite shocking.

"Good morning." She said softly as she stirred from the bed.

"Hello," Stony replied, "Did you sleep well?"

"Yes," Elaine answered, "a very restful night for one of us."

Stony stiffened, he knew what was coming. "I'm sorry if I woke you. I know I can be a little restless sometimes." He was trying his best to head off any questions.

Elaine stood and slowly walked straight toward Stony, looking directly into his eyes, all the way to his soul he felt. She stopped and knelt down in front of him, never taking her eyes off his. "Look, Stony, I wouldn't have made it this far had it not been for you. You made this happen." She spoke softly, "You have been the protector, the provider, and Lord knows, our only hope of ever leaving this desert alive. I have two perfectly good ears and if I understand or not, I can listen. As strong and willful as you are, it will help if you talk about what makes you tick. So maybe, if you talk about just your life in general, your loves, your likes and/or dislikes, your children, your wife or your war." Elaine went on, "I'm no psychologist, but I know that no man can be an island forever. My office hours are open to you, sir, 24-7. But only for you." After having said this, she patted him on the leg, knowing by the look on his face that she had gotten her point across without pushing too hard. She had learned there were some people you just could not push. In time, she felt he would come around. Time, she thought, apparently they had plenty of time.

Stony had never known but one person in his life that could get inside his shell, his late wife. This woman kneeling in front of him some how had that ability. She said the right things with that all knowing look in her eyes. She made him uncomfortable as hell at times. However, she seemed to be truly genuine and actually interested in his well-being. However, he had to change the subject.

Stony stood up and said, "You'd better start following me around. That way you will learn how to catch things to eat. Just in case."

"In case of what?" She asked.

"Well," Stony answered her, "Just in case something was to happen to me. At least, you might have something other than snake to eat. We'll take it easy today, but first thing in the morning, I'll start teaching you some of the things I know."

Elaine went back to the little hut, thinking about what he had said. What is he up to now? He is probably going to leave me here and try to walk out of this desert to find help.

Both of them did a lot of thinking that afternoon. Stony was considering trying to walk out for help, but he just wasn't sure that Elaine could handle it alone, especially if he did not make it. A few days and she would probably make it fine, but he did not think she had the strength to do all the things that would keep her alive long enough to be rescued.

Neither one of them sleep well that night. The situation was getting worse and both of them knew it. Time was not on their side, but neither one wanted to admit even to themselves that they might not be leaving this desert. All it would take is one misstep, one accidental fall, one mistake and their lives could be forfeited. They knew that to sit and do nothing, would gain them nothing. They both wanted to work at doing what they could to help their chances of surviving just long enough. Just long enough for someone to figure out where they were.

Daylight finally came and after they had finished their coffee, they set off down the trail below the water hole. It did not take long for them to realize they were getting weaker with each passing day. The heat was affecting them quicker. They were sweating more and their strength drained with the simplest of tasks. However, they could not quit, keeping busy would keep their minds off it and they were getting better equipped to help their situation.

Stony told Elaine how to clean out the hole in the trail and reset the metal lid with the X in it. All the time explaining how the leg snare worked. "Now that's one more thing you know how to do." He said. "Are there any questions?"

"No, I think I've got it. I am ready to go back to camp and get some of that pig you caught in your little trap. Pig on a stick sounds pretty good right now."

They made their way back to camp and after a brief rest after lunch, Stony told her he would go back and check everything over one more time. He asked her to go over what she was to do if she heard an aircraft fly overhead. "I want you to know what to do if you get woke up in the middle of the night, and you're still half asleep." He said.

"I promise I'll repeat it to myself until I can do it in my sleep." She smiled in reply.

He had been uneasy since last night. He worked his way toward the mountaintop to check the signal fire pile one more time. It had to be ready to go in an instant. It would only take a few seconds for the plane to be past them and gone. He always listened to his gut feeling. There were even times it had saved his life, so he knew he needed to be cautious and aware of his surroundings. The desert was not a forgiving place. When he arrived at the top, he scanned the sky for any activity. Nothing appeared to be moving but the waves of heat that were endless across the desert floor. You could see them for miles and miles across the sand. He started repacking the brush pile and tightening up the sticks. Just one shot from the signal flare gun would be sufficient to start a fire. He piled dry brush in and around the stack of wood. Finally, he had stuffed enough in the pile, he was sure it was ready to go. He was getting tired and a little dizzy from the effort and the heat. He had to sit and rest awhile.

He stared out over the floor and mountains across the horizon as he sat, hoping against hope that he would catch the sight of billowing clouds of dust behind a vehicle. He strained to hear the hum of an airplane. He saw nothing but emptiness. If you looked at the picture as a whole, it was a strangely beautiful place. He laughed to himself as the thought occurred to him about how many times he heard people talk about this land and always the phrase 'the wide open spaces' would be found somewhere in the conversation. Their predicament gave new meaning to those words, so casually spoken. There was really no way of determining how wide these spaces really were.

Out of the corner of his eye, he thought there was a flash. He turned immediately and sat staring into the northern sky. After staring for several minutes, he figured it must have been wishful thinking. He stood and glanced around one more time before starting back down to the little oasis below.

Elaine had gotten dirty and hot while working on the leg trap. The arm that was broken could be used, but very slowly and awkwardly. She checked the flare pistol to make sure of its location and that it would be working when they needed it to work.

The pain in her arm was beginning to rise especially after all the work she had done today. It had hurt all morning, but she thought she had hidden the fact pretty well from Stony. Even when she was resetting the leg snare, she managed to keep her pain from him. The last thing he needed was to think she would not be able to do what was necessary in camp. She knew that she had overdone it a little, her fingertips throbbed as bad as her shoulder and the pain now spread into her neck. The coolness of the pool might relieve it for a while. She had to have some relief from the pain and pressure of the splint. So, now that he was gone, I will practice a little physical therapy.

After being in the pool for while, she thought this might be a good time to wash some of their clothes. She managed pretty well until the wringing part, and then her arm began to scream with sharp stabbing pains. So deciding to leave the clothes wet. She got out of the pool and loosely hung the clothes around the campsite on the small bushes to dry. Knowing the pain would not completely go away unless she quit all activity, Elaine returned to the hut and lay down to rest her arm.

When Stony returned to camp, the area looked like a Chinese laundry. He turned toward the hut, saw the top of Elaine's blonde head, and started to kid her about all the clothes, when he heard her sniffle. Was she crying? He stepped closer, "Are you alright?" He asked.

In a shaky little voice, she replied, "No, I'm not. I am feeling a little sick and my arm is killing me. I know, I will live through it, but right now, it is hurting like hell. I just overdid this morning. If you will turn around, I will slip my clothes on."

"Okay sure," He replied. As he turned his back to the hut he thought, she must really be hurting to have said anything. He knew she was not a whiner, she had not complained about a thing, so far. He had to admire her will, he had not really thought about it much, but his wife had been the same way. Even before she died, she rarely let you know she was in pain.

"I'm covered now," she called, "You can come in. I need your help, please." Stony turned and made his way to the hut, and as he entered, he saw that she had wrapped a man shirt around her like a bath towel. He could not help but notice how damned sexy that was. Hell, she even looks good when she sick.

"We've got to do something with this splint." She said. "It's beginning to hurt quite a bit." She knelt down and stuck her arm out toward him. He went down to his knees and started removing the splint slowly as not to hurt her any further. As he undid the gauze wrapping and the circulation began to flow into her hand, she gasped and jerked her arm back a little. The shirt she had on slipped open. Grabbing with her good arm, but before she could get a hold on the fabric, Stony had seen the smooth skin of her breast. She quickly glanced up at him, but his expression was strictly business and his eyes concentrated on the splint. He removed the splint and began to massage the arm gently up to her shoulder. It would loosen the muscle tissue around the break. In a few minutes, Elaine told him that her arm was feeling much better. After he was sure the circulation was reaching all the way to her fingertips, he worked on refashioning the splint on her arm and then wrapped it a little looser this time. He had shifted the splint a little to the front part of her arm.

"How's that feel?" He asked.

Elaine smiled and said, "Much better, Doc. Thank you very much." She began flexing her fingers and slowly rotating her shoulders to stretch the muscles in her neck and upper back. "Oh, it feels so much better."

Stony finished up, turned, and moved outside the shelter heading for the pool, mainly just to put distance between him and her. He had definitely seen more of her than his eyes had indicated to her. He wanted his back to her for now because the swelling in his pants made for problems. He was not ready for this. He had not experienced this yearning for years. He felt like a teenager trying to hide something that was as natural as breathing. I know, thought Stony that she had to know that she had given him at least a glimpse of what was under her shirt. Had it been an accident? Maybe she was just testing the waters to see if he was interested. On the other hand, maybe she was just in so much pain, that she had been unaware of the exposure until she felt her shirt slip open. Always the questions…. did they want you or did they just slip-up?

Stony busied himself collecting firewood for the coming night, trying very hard to push the memory of that lovely flesh pressed against her shirt. And those legs… they are absolutely prefect. When he first saw her legs, his first thought was of that picture of the actress as she stood over the metal grate on the sidewalk. Elaine's legs looked forever more like a movie star's. Every red blooded American boy's dream. "God, I sure hope they find us soon." Stony mumbled to himself and as he returned with the wood, he found Elaine fully dressed. She had brushed her hair, but she was still the cutest tomboy alive. She had rolled her jeans up to her calves, and the man's shirt tied in a knot under her breasts. It did not seem to matter what she put on, it seemed to define her excellent figure.

"Do you like it?" Elaine asked, taking on her best impression of a southern belle. "I checked my closet and I swear I just couldn't find a thing to wear. So, this is a little something I picked up at the local Macy's."

They both laughed, and seemed to be trying their best to act as if nothing had happened. Yet it was paramount in both their minds, neither one wanting to read more into it than it just being an accident.

'Here, let me help with the wood." She jumped up and started toward him. "The least I can do since you gathered it, is to stack it by the fire."

After the fire was fed and finally big enough, they re-roasted the cooked pig, one more time. As they were sharing their nightly cup of coffee, Elaine said, "You know, blacked pig on a stick might just catch on. Maybe I'll open a restaurant when I get back." It had been a comment to try to lighten the mood around the fire. They had barely spoken through the whole meal.

"I wouldn't be making fun if I were you." He snapped. "Just eat. If it weren't for 'blackening' of the meat, there's no telling what kind of bacteria we would have already eaten. We could have been dead or at least sick as hell. The cooking kills any bacteria that might be on or in a wild animal. This is just one more thing I've done to keep us alive until someone comes to our rescue."

The smile on her face was immediately gone.

"I've tried my best to do just that. Do you really comprehend how bad this situation is? We are not on a camping trip here."

The tone of his voice was enough to make anyone afraid. Her expression now replaced with hurt by the anger he had just directed toward her. He was instantly sorry. He hadn't meant to sound so abrupt with her and now was sorry he'd said anything. His thoughts had been of her, back in the hut with her legs (and more) exposed. After all, he was just a human, and did not need that kind of distraction, not now.

"Are you mad about something?" Elaine asked. She had thought they had come to an understanding, maybe not spoken, but there had been equal respect of ideas and actions. "I thought we had been working together pretty well. I now know that you think you are doing all this by yourself. Well, if I am no help to you then I guess I'll just do my best to stay out of your way. I'll try not to make unnecessary remarks. If you want, I don't have to speak at all." She stood up and started toward the hut. "And, yes" She spit the words in his direction,

"I do know how bad our situation is. I just don't dwell on the bad aspects all the time, like some people I know." She stopped, turned to him and said, "If you don't need anything more, I'm going to bed." She turned and started away from him.

"Wait, I'm not mad at you." Stony said, "I'm just tired. I didn't mean to direct that at you. I knew you were joking, so, just ignore me. I am out of the practice trying to use tact when I speak. Please do not go just yet." He held up his hand, indicating for her to stop.

She stopped when he asked, but took her time turning to face him.

"Please, let me apologize. I am truly sorry for snapping at you. I had a few things on my mind today and I have been preoccupied with my own thoughts. Are we okay?" He asked her, once again very aware of her beautiful face. This was going to be harder than he thought. "It's just been too long since I've been in the company of someone as direct and truthful as you. Most of the people I talk to are hard and crusty ex-military men. I need to work on my exchange of conversation."

Elaine stood for a minute then said. "Alright," Elaine said "but, if I do something wrong you promise you will tell me. I know you have your hands full baby sitting me and taking care of everything else too. I am trying to learn as quickly as I can those things that I can do to help."

"Would you sit back down?" He asked. "Please?" She complied but did not say another word. The silence became deafening. The crackle of the fire was the only sound he could hear in the dark night air. Then he began to speak slowly and deliberately choosing his words. "Look, I think maybe I have to apologize to you for not being the gentleman that you think I am. It has been a very long time since I was even remotely close to any woman. Especially one that looks as good as you do. I have watched you at the pool a couple of times. Yes, I have desired you many times over the past few days and nights. You reminded me of a relationship which I treasured very much. You present the same characteristics that I have missed so much these last 18 years. You have looked into my soul the same way my late wife did when we were together. I feel vulnerable when you look at me that way.

I find you extremely attractive. Don't worry, I know you do not understand my ups and downs, nor have you figured out what kind of man I really am. I do think that you truly care for me and that is enough for me right now. I am still sorting out whether I am just lonely for my wife, or if I might have found another woman I could fall in love with, I'm sure when we get rescued that you'll go on to your sister's and start that new life you were talking about. Thank you, for our time together and for making me face the fact that I have missed one hell of a lot of living. You are a very special woman and I consider you a friend, and I've had very few of both in my life."

Elaine was sorry for her hurtful outburst and almost embarrassed by his confession. She found herself thrilled by his genuine honesty. That is not something you find much anymore, she thought. How hard it must have been for him to confess his feelings to me. She thought she had pegged him as one who would not give quarter to any emotions. Especially to someone he had only known for six days. Elaine's impulse was to reach out her hand and touch him, so she did just that. She reached for his hand, patted it, and still holding it said, "Thank you for being honest with me." Tears now filled her eyes as she told him, "I honestly don't know what I am feeling right now. I have been struggling with some emotions myself. But do not sell yourself short. I think you are the only real man I have ever had the pleasure of knowing. You are right. I do care about you, a lot." She looked into his eyes and softly muttered, "A whole lot!"

The crackling fire caught their attention. The night was growing late but neither of them wanted to move away. Making small talk for a while, Stony began telling her his story. He tried to put into words the things he had faced in his life. He hoped this might help her to understand him a little better.

Elaine stretched out by the fire, listening to this man pour out his soul for her to see.

Yes, she found herself very attracted to this man with his strong hands and a heart as big as all outdoors. She learned that he had a never quit attitude, even when the odds were against him. Stony was definitely one of a kind man, and she knew for sure that he would live to deliver the pilots wallet along with the message he had left for his wife and children. Elaine found comfort in her thoughts. Here was a man of his word. She could depend on him.

They eventually had made their way to the hut. Soon they were both sound asleep.

15

The morning sun came up on the seventh day. He could feel the difference inside himself. He talked last night to Elaine as if he had known her all his life. She seemed genuinely interested in his stories. Some of them he had not told to anyone before, but it seemed the most natural thing in the world to do. She had a way of making him feel at ease. I have tried not even thinking about some of the stuff I told her last night.

He awoke this morning feeling 20 years younger and light as a feather. That must be what they mean 'to bare your soul'. More than one counselor had told him he would feel better and be able to deal with bad memories and nightmares. If I could just get some of it out of my mind by talking about it. Well, I cannot deny I do feel better this morning, better than I have for a long time. Since I feel so energetic, I will go down the hill beyond the pool and check our trap.

Stony had not heard anything during the night, but he felt he should check it anyway. As he slid down the bank below the pool, his eyes focused on the leg trap site trying to catch a glimpse of any animal that might be caught. When he reached the bottom, the sound of the small stones rolling down the hill finally quieted. The sound he heard now was very familiar to him. He stood perfectly still. He had heard it many times on the field trips he had made into the desert. There was no mistaking what it was, but he could not see it. As he slowly turned his head trying to pinpoint the rattler, there was a blur of action from directly behind him. He tried to step out of range, but too late, the snake sank its fangs deep into the calf of his leg. Immediately he felt the fire as it began to spread slowly around the bite. He tried to kick it off, but the fangs were caught in his pant leg. Stony reached down and grabbed it behind the head. Turning to a huge flat rock, he threw the snake down and smashed it with his boot. He stood for a second thinking about what had just happened, and then he sat down and rolled up his pants to a point above the bite marks on his leg. Pulling his penknife out of his pocket, he sliced open the two puncture marks. If he could make his leg bleed, some of the poison would be forced out with the blood. He squeezed, massaged and pushed at the skin around the bite to get the maximum amount of blood out of his leg.

He then cut a strip off the tail of his shirt, rolled it into a tourniquet, and placed it just above the bite to suppress the flow of blood to the rest of his body. Stony began making his way down to the trap and found a desert jackrabbit caught and now dead. He reset the trap, picked up the rabbit and the snake, taking the time to clean both animals before beginning the trek back up to the oasis above. As he made his way into camp, Elaine saw the blood on his leg. "What happened?" She exclaimed as she started toward him.

"Well, I had a little run in with this little fellow here." He handed her the skinned out snake. I also got a jackrabbit so we won't have to worry about eating for a little while." Stony replied. "That will be a good thing because for the next few days I will be too sick to even get out of bed." Elaine was instantly concerned about what needed to be done to help him. She wasn't too frightened because his attitude seemed relaxed and in no hurry to do anything.

"I'll need to get this wound scrubbed out, so if you will get the soap and a rag of some sort to clean out the blood and dirt. We will be doing all we can do right now." Stony was talking as he headed for the pool. Elaine grabbed the first aid kit just in case there was something inside they could use. She helped him scrub out the cuts he had made on top of the bite marks. Finding an alcohol rub in the first aid kit she saturated the area that was already beginning to swell. She then tore a strip of cloth from a blouse that she had washed out earlier, as she began to wrap his leg she insisted that he lay down and elevate his feet. When she finished the bandage, she helped him to stand and they started for the hut where he would be out of the heat.

Stony was trying to tell her something, but he was already slurring his words and she could not make out his exact words.

"Listen," she said, "Don't try to talk, you just lay down here and get as comfortable as you can." She started untying his shoes and pulled them and his socks off his feet. She looked at his face and thankfully, he had passed out as soon as he was down. The toes on the bitten leg were already turning black. He was getting hot to touch. "Oh, please help me, God. I don't know any more to do for him. I do not know a thing about snakebites. Please, guide me in taking care of this good-hearted man. Do not let me lose him, not now. Not when I've just begun to have hope again."

Elaine started by unbuttoning his shirt and pants, rolling him from side to side to remove them from under him. I will need to get something that will hold some water and some more rags. At least I will keep him cooled down. She loosened the tourniquet because the swelling was becoming evident, keeping the blood flow regulated could help prevent permanent damage to his leg. She swabbed his upper body with the dripping wet rags, hoping that the moisture left on his body would prolong the coolness for him. Finding a chance to step away from him she located the canvas bag that held the medicines

Stony had brought back from the crash site. The tetracycline tablets were lying on top when she jerked the bag open. "I'm taking this as a sign. Thank you, Lord." She looked at the dosage on the bottle and pulled out two of the tablets. Putting her good arm under his neck, she raised his head high enough that he could swallow the pills. "Hope you aren't allergic to these," she said as she placed him back down on the bed. For hours, she never left his side except when she had to go to the bathroom bush. She wiped his face, his body and his legs, she could tell the fever was going up not down. Taking a pan, she went to retrieve more water from the pool. When she returned she found that Stony had thrown up while she was gone, and his whole body was shaking violently. She cleaned his face and body one more time, and then scooped the sand covered with his vomit and carried it outside to dump it a little ways from the camp. She covered his body with all the clothes they had, trying to warm him up. The fever was worse and he was chilling horribly. As she sat watching over him, fear began to crawl into her heart. She tried to fight the tears and the fears from coming, but she was fighting a losing battle. "God, please, give me strength to help this man. He is a good man and I know that you know that. But, you have to have more for him in life than he's had in the past. Please, God, help me."

She continued to bath his face as his fever worsened and she held him close when he chilled. Hours passed, she had no idea how long she had been by his side.

Day 7 had not been a good day, she thought. Slowly the realization came to her of how alone she would be without Stony. She learned something new everyday that she was with him. She was scared, very scared. "I don't want to be alone here. I don't want to be without you." Elaine whispered to Stony as he slept.

Morning came and Elaine had not slept at all through the night, but she knew she could not quit. She tried every way in the world to make him more comfortable. First the water to keep his fever down, then pills for the pain and poison, then either less cover or more cover. Then she would start over again, water, pills, and cover, water, pills, and cover. "Damn it, where are the rescue crew? It has been eight days for crying out loud." She was getting exasperated. "You'd think someone would have figured out by now where we are." Elaine was exhausted, she knew if she did not get a little rest she could be down herself. Stony seemed to sleeping a little more peacefully, she lay next to him to keep him warm and close so she would be alerted if something changed in his condition. She remembered putting her good arm over him and snuggling closer, and then she was fast asleep.

When Stony started thrashing about she was instantly awake. "What is it? She asked. "Are you okay? What can I do to help you?" He was still asleep, he seemed to be trying to yell, but she could not understand any of the words. He was dreaming, reliving something from that terrible war that would never make sense. As he quieted down, she began to make out the words and what she heard made her sob. "My God!" She whispered, "No wonder he didn't get rattled by a simple plane crash." If all she heard was true, she now understood why he did not sleep well. When you are awake you keep all those memories hidden, when you are asleep they come unbidden and unwelcome.

Watching his chest, she noticed that his breathing was becoming more erratic. She lay back down next to him, and cradled his head with her arms, squeezing him tight to her breast. She began talking to him. "Damn you, Stony, don't you do this to me. You are the one that started me wondering if maybe we could have a life together. Then you go and do this, what were you thinking about? You are a naturally cautious man, why didn't you see that snake? What ever it was I hope it was worth this. If you die on me, you will never know that I think I am falling in love with you. No one has ever made me feel so protected, and so special. You have to hang on. Do not let go of the life that you and I can eventually share. If you think that I am going to let you get out of this world without a fight, you are sadly mistaken. When we first started out on this journey, we made a pact that we would put all our energies together to survive. That is our #1 priority. I am not saying 'your' priority; I am saying 'ours'." The tears were running down her cheeks and dripping on Stony's face. She bent over him to kiss his forehead, then his eyelids, then finally his lips. She moved her mouth until her lips pressed against his ear. "Don't you dare give up on me. You have to fight this thing. Fight as you have never fought before. You're fighting for both our sakes." Elaine held him like this for hours. Cheek to cheek with this man she wanted to spend the rest of her life with, she just hoped it was not too late.

16

Bob Farley was sleeping fitfully in his motel room. The clock had just ticked to 3 a.m. when he suddenly sat straight up in bed. "That's it! That's got to be it!" He was almost shouting as he jumped out of bed and into the shower, trying to clear his head. Today would be the ninth day since the plane had disappeared. Why had he not thought of it sooner?

The key was the weather; it had to be the weather. "I can't believe that I never thought of this before. The monsoons could play tricks with the wind in the southwest deserts. He was immediately thinking of all the possibilities, he needed to check the conditions at the airport around the time of the disappearance.

He got dressed and drove his rental car to the terminal, onto the tarmac behind the tower at Sky Harbor Airport. Bob bounded up the steps three at a time, bursting into the control room. Even at this hour the air traffic control personnel was hard at work.

"I need the recorded weather reports from nine and ten days ago, now!" Bob's voice boomed even over the din of activity. The Senior Controller glanced at Bob and made the mistake of asking, "What do you need those for? And why the rush?" Bob was face to face with the captain in two steps. "I'll tell you why." Bob bent closer so the Captain would not miss a word. After approximately two minutes of discussion, with the captain nodding his head yes and the only words out of his mouth were, "Yes, Sir!" The Senior Controller turned away to retrieve the needed tapes, he saluted Bob and said, "Yes, Sir. Right away, Sir." There was no doubt to those within earshot that Bob must be next to God himself in authority, they had never seen the Watch Captain jump to do anything for anyone, until this morning. Those watching saw the Senior Controller survey the room looking at anyone watching, as if to say, I'd better not hear one word of this incident from anybody outside this room.

"Could I have some coffee over here?" Bob bellowed out.

A nearby controller pointed to the far corner behind some file cabinets. "The coffee brewer should be finishing a fresh pot right about now."

Bob filled a cup and stood in the dull red glow of the tower confines. Watching landing planes as they punctured the sky over the ground lights of the airfield. He listened to the controllers giving instructions over the radio. God, how I love airports, he thought. Bob was all business when it came to work and right now, he was in his element.

The door flew open and there stood the Senior Controller with a box of tapes in his arms. "Where do you want these?" He asked.

"I'll take them back to my office. In addition, while you are at it, call the meteorologist who was on duty nine days ago. Tell him I need him in my office ASAP!" Bob was already walking away toward his office, the last few words thrown over his shoulder.

Bob called in his team while waiting for the weatherman. He had laid out fresh maps of the area, and shoved back all the chairs that had been around the table and pushed them back against the walls. He wanted everyone on their feet and thinking. The weatherman arrived the same time the team walked into the room. When everyone had entered the room, Bob walked over to the door and flipped the lock. He then turned toward all the questioning faces in the room and said, "I want to know every weather scenario conceivable at any given time on the night in question. I want it plotted for each and every aircraft that was in the sky over this airport. After we have correlated that information to this box of tapes sitting in the middle of this table we should have what we need to find this missing plane." He turned to the weatherman and said, "You, sir, were on duty that night, so I want you to explain the winds that those planes encountered to my team. Do not leave out anything no matter how trivial you think it might be. Team!" He shouted. "I want this information NOW!" His voice came down a notch, "But not so fast as to make mistakes. It has to be correct. We are still going on the assumption that there are people out there who are still alive, and they are counting on us to find them."

The sound of breathing was all you could hear in the room.

"Okay, people, let's come up with some valid answers." Bob was looking around the table when the room came alive. Team members grabbed the tapes from that fateful night nine days ago. Checking with the weatherman, they began to put together a duplicate flight pattern of all planes and their positions in any given minute. Over the next three hours, every airplane track was plotted, but none of them went anywhere except where they were supposed to go. The weatherman was checking over his weather charts, measuring the isobar patterns, checking and re-checking wind direction and wind speed.

They played the missing aircraft's tape repeatedly until they had copied each transmission verbatim. They noted that just prior to the blackout that night. The tower had reported a monsoonal storm approaching from the northeast. That was two minutes prior to the last transmission from the lost aircraft, then the blackout. The team and weatherman concentrated on those two minutes. They brought every possibility from precise course to fifty miles off course. The weatherman plotted the winds for each hypothesis and where the track of that aircraft would be if they encountered that wind.

This continued for hours and every plot concluded that the plane would have crashed in highly populated areas, or in and around the Tonto National Forest Area and Roosevelt Lake, Canyon Lake, or maybe Apache Lake area. The search teams are called and given these corresponding coordinates. They were briefed to canvas these areas for any sign of the crash site.

The local television stations volunteered their choppers and pilots, if they could make and keep the tapes that were produced in a rescue or recovery mission. Bob agreed, with the parting words. "I hope your tapes will show us something. If anyone can find it, surely your news hounds can. My team has plotted one hundred and twelve different scenarios. I just hope you have enough tape to cover them all."

Bob turned to his team and said, "Let's take a break for dinner and some well deserved rest. We cannot do anymore right now. It will take the searchers awhile to cover that whole area. Do not come back for at least six hours. Get your minds on something else. That way when you get back to look again, your minds will be able to take a fresh look." He left for dinner himself, then come back to his office for a quick shower, a change of clothes, and then back to the charts. Bob poured himself another cup of coffee and spent the next thirty minutes on the phone to D.C. and the central office. The hopes of finding anyone live had long since disappeared, but there were people of some importance that were applying pressure on the FAA and telling whoever would listen about the incompetence to find one crashed airplane. Hell, they had searched over twenty-five thousand square miles, but to no avail. It was never enough to the higher ups.

The families wanted to know where their loved ones were.

The airplane, if it had sent a mayday or position report, it sure as hell never made it through. The rolling blackout had taken care of that. The emergency beacon signal had not functioned properly, they had not turned it on, or it was destroyed in the crash itself. The plane, the crew, and the passengers had absolutely disappeared from the face of the earth. It did not matter to Bob about what the bureaucrats thought, but he did care about the families of those that had been on board that plane. Until now, he had been hopeful of finding possible survivors.

With a bang, the outside door flew open and the weatherman walked back in with two members of Bob's team. They were bone tired but did not want to quit.

"We feel like we are so close." The weatherman said, looking straight at Bob. "What are you doing here?" He asked.

"Well, I come back to call the bureaucrats and keep them up to date on what's happening here. That's done, so we can get back to the business of finding a needle in a haystack. I appreciate your dedication, damn the bureaucrats, let's find something that will help the families find closure."

The radio crackled and the voice on the other end said, "I've got a signal flare. Fix position approximately 12 miles west of the Tonto National Monument." The pilot went on to say, "I am headed to that position now."

The small group that was standing in the war room was looking directly at Bob, with eyes as big as saucers. They all listened intently for every word. They were hoping against hope that it would be survivors of the plane crash. Bob did not share their enthusiasm. It just did not feel right. That area had been flown over several times with no sign of a crashed plane. About twenty minutes later, the report came in that an injured hiker had been found and was now on his way to an area hospital.

The sudden let down took them all by surprise. "Well, that one didn't work out like we wanted, but as professionals we can't dwell on what might have been. Let's get back to work." Bob turned his attention to the charts on the table. The hours slowly ticked by and the rest of the team eventually filtered back into the room, all going immediately to their workstations.

17

Elaine roused up to find that Stony's fever had broken during the night. She was still holding his head in her arms and her back was screaming because of the position she was in when she had fallen asleep. She slowly let go of Stony's head and began working her hands, shoulders, and legs trying to work out the kinks. As she stood, she staggered and realized she had to get something to eat and drink. She knelt by the fire and stoked it back to life. Then she began to make coffee. The snake still in place over the fire. She sit back again waiting for breakfast to come together. The food was beginning to smell good, so she downed a cup of coffee and part of the snake. Letting the sustenance seep into her body, she felt that maybe a cool dip in the pool might make her feel stronger and more revitalized. Since Stony was still peacefully asleep, she walked quietly down to the water and shed her clothes. From where she stood, she could see her reflection in the edge of the pool. Mmm, I've lost a few pounds, not bad for a middle-aged mom, she thought, as she slid down into the water.

Stony was drifting in and out of semi-consciousness. He had glanced down at his leg and could see the swelling. His leg appeared to be about half again its original size. His mind was time traveling back to happier times, the good times he and Marilyn had. They had almost 13 years of good times. Theirs had been one of those relationships where they could finish each other's sentences. A smile crossed Stony's face as he recalled how she used to surprise him by wanting to make love at the darndest times. Like pulling onto a side road while traveling as the kids slept in the back seat. They made love under the stars or out in the middle of a lake with other boats whizzing by. It was as if there wasn't anyone else in the world when they were together. God, it had been wonderful!

The smile changed to a frown as he remembered the day she died and how all their hopes and promises flew away with her soul. He recalled how he had cursed her for leaving him. Even with a houseful of children, he was lost and alone. He never was able to accept the fact that she was gone. He never quit loving her, even after all the years and tears. He had never missed a day in all those years that he didn't remember her fragrance or her smile or the feel of her skin. Even if it only lasted a fleeting moment, there had never been any room in his heart for anyone else.

Until now. He was drifting upward in a mind trip searching, listening for her voice, but seeing Elaine's beautiful face instead. Then he heard Marilyn, the smile had come back across his face at the sound of her voice, God, how he loved the sound of her. Her voice seemed to be coming out of a distant bright light, it made his head hurt from the intensity of the light. Then Marilyn spoke again saying, "It's time. It is time for you to let go and move on. Elaine is a good woman. She appreciates the man you are. Enjoy the rest of your life, turn loose of the past and live again for the future. It's time." Her voice faded and the light went dark and somehow the relief he felt was as if the weight of the world lifted from his shoulders. Relief, unbelievable relief as his body relaxed and his mind went quiet.

Elaine made her way back up to the hut feeling a little better. Choosing from the pile of clothes, she dressed for the day and began to brush her hair. As she brushed her hair, she turned and looked at Stony to see if he was fretful again or hurting. His face held a slight smile and he seemed deeply relaxed. She poured Stony some water. Kneeling down close to him, she moistened his lips by dripping water from her fingertips. When his eyes opened suddenly, he startled her but she managed to hold the cup of water so he could drink. He drank slowly and soon had his fill, he leaned back and shut his eyes again. "Stony," Elaine said, "Stony, can you wake up long enough to eat something? You really need to eat something. Come on, wake up!" The request had been pointless, for Stony had drifted back into a deep sleep. Elaine noticed that he was beginning to get some color back in his face. "That's a good sign." She said, "You can eat later, rest I guess, is what you need now."

She tried to lay back and rest herself, but with listening for any sound from the sky and checking Stony every few minutes, she didn't get much rest let alone sleep. She could tell he was in extreme pain. She hated to see him suffer through this, but she knew she had done all she could do for him. If the tables were turned, he would be on watch for planes and he would continue to take care of her. She sang songs, whistled, hummed, generally anything in her power to stay alert and maintain some sort of vigilance.

Day 10 came in with a smattering of raindrops. Even if it was temporary, it was a welcome relief from the heat. She glanced toward Stony and she met with open eyes. "Well, good morning." she said, trying to be as cheerful as was possible. Stony tried to answer, but did not have enough strength to speak. Elaine jumped up, grabbed the cup of water and knelt down beside him, holding it to his mouth so he could get a small drink of water. She whispered, "Good morning, sir, I'm glad you are awake. I sure missed your grumpy voice, first thing in the morning."

"You look nice," his voice trailed off, but he managed a small smile.

Elaine flushed, as sick as he was he could still find something to compliment. She thought, he is unbelievable, but she managed a smile herself and a small "Thank you."

Her goal for the morning was to get some food and water down him. He managed to keep a few bites down and a couple sips of water. "Do you think you could drink some coffee?" she asked. He nodded his head, "Yes, please."

By noon, he was strong enough to speak in short sentences. He was physically weak, but mentally he never felt better. The small rain spell had cleared the air of dust and the dryness smell. When they thought it was gone for good, Stony asked Elaine to go up the mountain with some dry kindling to put at the base of the signal fire pile. "Please be careful." He told her then he lay his head back on the pallet and was soon out again.

Elaine made her way up to the pile of wood, checked everything once again. It was ready to go. All they needed was a plane to fly overhead. As she walked back into camp, she noticed that Stony was moaning. Apparently, the pain in his leg was cranking up again. She knelt down to Stony's side and lifted the bandage over the bite; the smell just about knocked her over. She had never smelled anything even close to this. There were also red streaks running up his leg from the bite. It was definitely infected. As she tried to examine the wound, she touched his leg and instantly he was awake. He could tell by her face that it was not good. He told her to get his penknife from his pants and place it in the edge of the fire. The wound needed to be cut and drained. The outer surface skin was already trying to grow back together, but if she did not cut it, the infection would continue to spread inside his body.

"Tell me what to do." She said.

"You will need to boil water so you can use rags as a compress to draw out the infection." He answered then slipped back into unconsciousness.

She found the little knife and opened it up, held it in the flames at the edge of the fire. "Oh, God, I don't know how to do this, please guide my hand." Before she left the fire, she placed a container with water in it on top of the rocks to boil. She held the knife by wrapping a piece of heavy cloth around the handle. The hot knife split the outer skin as soon as it touched his leg. She pushed the little blade into the swollen area immediately above the bite marks. The bloody infection poured out freely, and Elaine wretched violently from the smell. "Take hold, girl, you have no choice here. He cannot do this, so that only leaves you." Elaine kept pressing around the leg working the infection down to the cut. She pushed from every direction around the bite making sure to get as much out as she possibly could. Glancing to his face, she pressed one more time all around the wound. She would have never been able to do this if he had been awake.

"Thank God, he is still out." She whispered. She threw the rags she had gathered into the boiling water, then grabbing the pan and rags she went back to his side. Pulling a rag out with a short stick, she applied the first compress over the bite mark. Smoothing out the edges, she realized that the heat alone would help sterilize his leg. After about five minutes, when the rag began to cool, she took it off and added the second. This continued for about fifteen minutes and she could already tell the difference in his leg. The swelling was a little smaller and the smell had diminished.

Elaine dug around in the canvas bag and found a medicine for ear infection.

"Close enough." She said as she ground up the tablets into a powder and sprinkled it on Stony's wound. Then she covered the injury with a strip of cloth she had ripped from her shirt. Having bandaged his leg, she took the dirty rags and washed them out to use again. She went back to Stony's side and lay down as close as she dared as to not disturb him as he slept. She needed to rest but she wanted to be able to hear him if he stirred. Elaine fell sound asleep and was soon dreaming about her childhood. Her family had been poor as dirt, but her desire for a better life had made her read anything and everything she could find to read. She had wanted all the things she read about concerning the 'American Dream'. That included marriage, children, and her own home. She had worked her way through Cosmetologist College. Now she would always have an occupation. Darrell had just joined the Air Force when she met him and as long as they had been in the service things worked out good. Fine at first, then his enlistment was up and even though she had wanted to stay in the military, he did not even consider that possibility. Therefore, they became civilians and their lives became nothing but struggle. Her husband seemed to find unhappiness with his job, or his boss, or he could do better, if he could just find that perfect job. Elaine finally stopped counting how many times they moved. She always made it a home, wherever they went. She had no trouble finding jobs for herself. She would make new friends, finally find her way around the neighborhood and feel like maybe this will be the place they could stay for awhile.

Then Darrell would come home and announce the news as he entered the door. "I'll be looking for a new job tomorrow." He had just quit, or been fired, and the move was on once again. Things had deteriorated until she could hardly stand to talk to her own husband. She resented him so much. He never thought about anyone but himself. He was not happy with anything or anyone. He expected a clean house, pressed clothes, and a hot meal no matter what time he decided to come home for supper. That was the woman's job, even if she worked outside the home. That was just something she had to figure out how to do. He never lifted a finger to help, but could always find things that needed to be done before bedtime, and of course there was always the 'wifely duty'. This was exactly what it was, because there was no love left anymore. Their lives had become just a routine and such a rut that neither one wanted to leave the comfort of the 'known'. After 2 years of marriage, she became pregnant. They were both excited at the prospect of parenthood. Maybe this is exactly what they both needed. A child to take care of might make both grow up and take responsibility. Raising a child might make Darrell hold onto a job. Working together, making their lives a combined effort. Not just two separate lives in one household.

It did not take long for Elaine to realize that things did not change that much for Darrell. She was still the major breadwinner, head chef, house cleaner, baby sitter, and runner of all errands. He still sat in his rocking chair watching television and he would tolerate no interruptions!

As their son grew, she was getting more dissatisfied with this 'American Dream'. This life was not what she envisioned for herself and now there was child to nurture. She might as well be on her own. She was taking care of everything, making all the decisions concerning this household. She did not want Evan growing up with this poor example of a man. Having a part-time dad was better than this one full time. Therefore, Elaine made the decision to divorce Darrell.

Her attitude had become quiet determination. She went about her life with full confidence that she could do anything she set in her mind. Many people told her that she had been called the Ice Queen, being so independent that she appeared aloof and stand offish, especially to men. However, for those that truly knew her, her goal in life was to take care of her son and herself without asking for help. She was successful in her business, because she never took anything for granted. Others wanting the control and benefit of her actions had taken so much of her early life. Now was the time for her to take the control and maneuver her work and actions to benefit her and her son. All she wanted was for her son to be independent and be his own man. She had learned the lesson of caring for oneself because nobody else would ever take care of you, like you.

After her divorce, Elaine turned all her attention to her son and his well-being. Trying to give him, what he needed and not things he just wanted. Being spoiled and indulged would bring him nothing but discontent. There was a whole world out there and she wanted Evan to have the confidence to tackle any part of it he chose. He had such determination and perseverance that she never worried that he would turn out a good man, and she told him often how proud she was of him.

Stony stirred in his sleep, and Elaine was instantly awake and checking him for temperature. However, he drifted back to sleep, and she lay awake thinking about her past.

She was not interested in starting another relationship. She had become very independent, very successful in business and for the time being her life centered on her son. Nightlife for her had been virtually non-existent. Oh, she had had a few dates and ventured out occasionally, but found most men in the singles scene were only after one thing. She really could not get into all the crazy mind games. Truthfulness or moral character was not part of the single landscape, so she just stayed home. She was quiet happy with her life and now that her son was in the Navy and on his own she took advantage of doing a few of those things she had never had time for in her schedule. She had never missed the sex or so called romance, it had never been an earth-shattering event for her. She had read magazines telling you about fantastic experiences that you could have with the man in your life. Yeah, sure, she thought. Life with her men had all ended in disenchantment. She enjoyed talking to one man in her life and that was Evan. She had decided long ago that to avoid the disappointment was to avoid the relationships.

Stony roused to turn from his back to his side, his arm fell across her breast. She did not move to push it away. Actually, it was comforting. She snuggled a little closer to him and enjoyed the warmth of him close to her back with his hand casually holding her breast. Stony was the one dreaming now, in bits and pieces. The first time he had seen her in the pool, then when her big shirt slipped to reveal what only her hairdresser knew for sure. Such a beautiful woman, he felt as if he was sixteen again, experiencing the emotional dizziness of just being in her presence. When he was there, he could forget his past for a while and get lost in her.

Elaine found she could not go back to sleep, so she shifted her position so she could look at Stony. She looked from his broad shoulders, to his chest, strong, and muscled. Light red hair scattered across the middle of his body. She resisted an urge to run her fingers through the patch of soft hair. She lay watching the rise and fall of his chest as he breathed. There was a little smile of a scar on his right ribcage. Someday she would ask him about that scar, when the time was right. She loved the darkness of his skin, tanned by the sun and the contrast to the whiteness of her skin. We look good together, she thought. Am I really falling in love? People in this situation sometimes thought they had fallen in love, only to realize later that it was just the circumstances of being thrown together because of a traumatic event. How will they know for sure? When they were rescued and got back to our own little worlds? The attraction she felt was very real, nevertheless, she still wondered.

She sat up and checked Stony's leg wound. Well, I am not a doctor but it is looking much better. Real medical attention was what he needed and soon. Elaine found a pair of trousers and split the leg so Stony would have something to wear when he woke up. She knew him to be a proud man and was certain he would not care to be rescued in his underwear.

You can call it woman's intuition, a premonition or just a feeling, she felt like day eleven would bring help. For Stony's sake, she hoped it was true.

18

THE WEATHERMAN HAD found a possibility that no one had thought of yet, maybe the plane had been several miles off course due to the prevailing winds of the monsoon. Bob called the team together and said, "If this is true, then, the monsoonal conditions of the storm may have sent them further south, maybe as much as two to three hundred miles. We have not found them north, west or east, it makes sense to head south. I have a good feeling about the weatherman's speculation. Re-plot the track using the specifications that he has come up with, a different track is entirely feasible with the wind speeds that had blown that night. The tower would have gotten them on course before landing. However, with the storm and the power outages, and if they had a problem themselves, damn, anything is possible. What do you all think?" Bob asked.

Several on the team voiced their dislike for incorporating that much variance into a possible flight path. However, after a short discussion, some agreed that if, in fact, they had been south of their flight path when they were told to enter the holding pattern, they would lose communications. "That could be why the tower did not see them on radar, they were not there. There was no telling how far they could have gone waiting for the tower to issue instructions." Bob went on, "You all know if we break off the northern search and skip over toward Yuma that we could miss them completely. This is definitely not recommended procedure."

The room was silent while the team pondered the idea. The weatherman broke the silence, "Listen, I've figured every damned wind current and squall winds and rainstorm. I am convinced you will find your airplane somewhere between Phoenix and Yuma." Bob whirled around, grabbed the phone and proceeded to move the search patterns to the south and southwest. When Bob hung up the phone, he said, "Okay, we should know something by this afternoon and I'm banking on the weatherman's prediction. I think he is right!"

When daylight is here, I want all teams to commence an integrated search pattern using the Air Force, National Guard, Civil Patrol, and news choppers. If they think they see something, I want to know ASAP." Bob left to call Washington with his morning brief. He explained that if the pilot was flying blind and failed to make wind corrections by banking on GCA to correct his flight path for approach. "Then with the power blackout and no telling what else, it was very possible to have overshot to the south. Way off their planned flight path. The possibility that they had problems with the aircraft could escalate dramatically in a storm causing confusion and total chaos inside that plane. We will probably find the wreckage on the side of a mountain." Bob thought as he sat down at the radio waiting nervously for news, any news. At least they would have died quickly.

19

Stony became restless as the morning neared and his bandage needed changing. Elaine cleaned and redressed his leg wound. Carefully she slid the trousers on Stony along with a light shirt. Elaine had washed his face and combed his hair. She just knew today would be the day! His leg was not looking good, so Elaine prayed silently that a rescue team would find them soon. She feared the eventual outcome would mean the unwelcome task of burying a man of whom she grown to like very much. The thought of Stony's infection slowly killing him was just too much to think of now. Being without him and knowing the overpowering loneliness that she would feel when he was gone brought a wave of physical nausea. He had a way about him that made you feel better about a situation no matter how bad it got. He always seemed to know the right thing to do. Smiling, she thought to herself, at least he pretended to know all the right things. She was already beginning to miss the honest but guarded conversations, the cute little grin that made his eyes squint almost closed. She loved the confidence and his unhurried drawl when he explained things. Southerners were very good at that she thought, and being southern, he was considerate of her always. I cannot even imagine how he probably spoiled his wife, of what kind of life they really had. Maybe one of these days she thought, she might even have learned what life could be with a man that had the attributes of this man. However, life does not always work out as we imagine.

Stony was getting sicker by the hour, his breathing had become shallow again and he seemed to be choking more often. Fear was gripping her like a vise, squeezing her chest, "No, God, no, don't let him slip away from me." She cried aloud. For the next few hours she watched him continuously, every time he moaned, moved, or choked her eyes were on him. She tried to keep his lips and mouth moist with a dripping cloth. She rubbed his temples lightly with the tips of her fingers, talking softly like a mother to a sick child. When his breathing became almost impossible, she picked him up and held his upper body in an upright position to make it easier for him to breath.

Soon she was rocking him like a baby, murmuring in his ear, comforting him any way she could think that might ease his suffering. He was failing faster than she imagined he would. There was no more eye flutter, no moans of pain, just nothing, nothing but the raspy gasps of breath. Elaine had decided that if Stony died, he would not be lying flat on the ground. She would be holding him and even as she thought about his death, her heart ached. Elaine began praying aloud and unashamed, "God, I've believed in you my entire life. I have trusted you with every fiber of my being, with all my heart and soul. Please, God, I am holding onto the faith you have taught me and I believe. I am accepting as truth your words when you promised that if we come to you with faith unwavering, believing in our hearts that you will answer your child's prayer. I am thanking you Lord, right now for the intervention in Stony's struggle for life. His heart is a good heart. You know that he has so much more to give to those around him. You know what kind of men are in your world. The bums that call themselves men, they are liars, thieves, and use other people for gain. Stony is not like those men."

She was sobbing so hard that just for a second she thought she was hearing Stony's breath, becoming a rhythm of gasps, whew, whew, whew. Then she realized that it was coming from a distance. "A helicopter, it's got to be a helicopter that's all it could be. Oh, God, thank you." She had not heard it at first because of her prayer, but now she could tell the whop, whop of the blades. It was coming closer. Elaine all but threw Stony's body down, and grabbed the signal gun then raced for the mountaintop and the signal fire.

The radio crackled to life in War Room Central. "We have found the crash site." The pilot of the search plane was excited and the words came in a rush.

Bob grabbed the mike and asked, "What is the fix position?"

The voice responded, "Thirty-three degrees, fifteen minutes north. One hundred thirteen degrees, thirty minutes west. Do you copy?"

"Affirmative," Bob replied, "Do you see any sign of life?" He asked. Everyone in the room held their breath, waiting, hoping the answer would be yes.

"Negative, but we are going to land for a closer look. Will reply in a few, over." The voice continued, "If anyone lived through this it would be a miracle. Hell, this thing is scattered over a mile and looks to be 500 yards wide." The silence in the War Room was almost unbearable. Some of the team whispered silent prayers, some paced back and forth, some were busy plotting the fix position of the crash site and some just sat and allowed the tears to flow down their cheeks.

No one spoke. Bob sat staring at the speaker so intently it was as though he could see through the speaker all the way to the crash site, willing the searchers to come back with some good news. Five minutes, ten minutes, then twelve minutes had passed and the speakers crackled again. "You will need to send a paramedic squad and maybe a tracking dog to the area. We have found evidence of two or three survivors, over."

"They are on their way even as we speak." Bob replied. It was not necessary for him to tell anyone anything. Within seconds, he had left the room. They had a chopper lifting off with a dog search team and paramedics, Bob would not let it leave without him. Twenty-five minutes later, he was leading the group of rescuers that were scattering across the crash site. He intended to be there when they found the survivors. That was always the best time to find out information on what had happened. Those that survived were the only ones that could fill in the blanks for the reconstruction of the crash.

Elaine had tripped running up the hill toward the signal fire. She had hit her head on a rock, knocking herself out for several moments. When she awoke to the sound of the chopper, she thought it was leaving. Crying and yelling she scrambled to her feet, found the signal pistol, she took aim at the brush pile and fired the double star flare directly into it. The burning phosphorous did its job. The smoke swirled lazily at first then picked up and moved rapidly toward the sky.

When she saw the fire was burning, she slipped back down the hill to camp when she noticed there was blood dripping from her fingertips. "Oh no." she whispered, "The fall must have re-injured my arm. My luck, I probably have two breaks now." She had not noticed the pain because the arm had swelled while she was unconscious. The homemade splint had cut off the circulation again. Her fingers had no feeling and she could not move them. By the time she reached camp, the nausea hit her hard. Every few feet she had to stop and vomit. Disoriented, and feeling faint, it would not be good if she pass out now. She made her way to the pool and soaked her head in the cold water and when her head began to clear, she slowly lowered her injured arm into the icy pool. Cupping her good hand, she drank the water, hoping to settle her stomach. When she could think clearly, she realized that she needed to reload the signal pistol in case the aircraft passed over again. With the loaded pistol in her good hand, she finally sat down next to Stony. His breathing had gotten even worse.

Her main thought as she looked at him was that she hoped it was not too late to bring him back from the dark place where he was now. She noticed the bluish discoloration of his lips and quickly rolled up some clothes, lifted his head and neck placing the pillow beneath his head. She actually placed it more under his neck than his head, but it seemed to open the airway in his throat. Immediately his breathing became deeper and a little more regular.

Just that small task of placing something under his head, had been hard with only one good arm and one hell of a headache. However, she was more concerned about his condition than her pain. Hers' would eventually go away, but there was no guarantee for him. Elaine began muttering softly, "Please hurry, please hurry and find us." She briefly considered making a trip back to the crash site, but knowing she probably would not make it, she turned all her attention back to Stony. She would not or could not take the chance of leaving him here alone.

20

THE STENCH WAS stifling. The searchers sifted through the wreckage, some were taking pictures, some taking notes, and all of them looking for any clues that might help explain the crash.

The search team had begun to cover the perimeter of the crash site with the tracker dogs, when one of them yelled out, "Here, over here!" Bob beat everyone to the location where they observed footprints heading off toward some boulders. As they reached the boulders, Bob noticed a pile of rocks that looked very much like a gravesite. Walking around the rocks Bob saw an arrow drawn in the sand, pointing toward the neat pile. The wind or rain had partially wiped some of the letters, but Bob understood as soon as he saw the letters P _ _ O T.

Another search team member found a message scratched in the desert floor, TWO SOULS with an arrow pointing off in the direction of the mountains northeast of the site. Bob yelled orders for the search dog team to hurry toward the mountains. "I can not believe it." He said. "They may still be alive." He stood surveying the scene and commented to another team member, "Whoever buried the pilot was not a wimp, Hell, some of those rocks must weigh close to a hundred pounds."

Bob pulled his radio out and proceeded to call for a military unit from Yuma to bring body bags and trucks to the crash area. They needed aid in some of the forensics, picking up all the body parts would be a nightmare in itself. He made another call for the reconstruction team from Washington D.C. They would head the all-important process of reconstructing the plane to determine the cause of the crash. He knew it would take weeks if not months to find all the bits and pieces of the aircraft. It was a tedious but necessary process to find out what had really happened here in the Tank Mountains area between Phoenix and Yuma.

The dog search team had traveled about three miles up the dry wash when one of the team noticed the plume of smoke trickling slowly skyward. It looked to be coming from a mountain top some eight to ten miles ahead. The team leader called Bob and relayed the message of their smoke sighting. He ordered the chopper fired up and the remaining rescue squad aboard. Three minutes later, they were airborne and heading straight toward the smoke signal. "Whoever that is," Bob said, "is no rookie at staying alive, probably a military man on leave or maybe a veteran of the service."

The chopper climbed to altitude and within minutes was hovering over the mountain peak. The rescue team jumped to the ground from the chopper and immediately began searching the area around the signal fire. As the helicopter began to pull up and swing toward an area they thought might be a suitable landing site, two double star phosphorus flares flew by just barely missing the aircraft. The team on the ground started shouting in the direction from where the flares had come. "Stop, don't shot! We are here and coming to you. Don't shot again." They followed the small trail toward the campsite. It did not take long to find the two survivors, one woman with a makeshift sling on one arm, awake and talking, and one man who appeared to be in very critical condition.

The leader told Bob, "You'll have to talk to them in the air and you probably will not talk to the man. His chances do not look good."

"Stony, his name is Stony." Elaine called out to the paramedic. "He is the reason we are still alive." She covered her face with her hands and began to sob uncontrollably. "Please, save him. Please." She kept repeating the phrase until the paramedic finally got her attention, "Lady, I'll try, but I need to know what happened to him?"

Elaine calmed a little and told him about the snakebite. She also repeated the instructions he had told her to follow. "I don't know what else to do." Her eyes pleaded with him, silently saying 'Tell me you know what needs to be done.'

The paramedic, thanked her, already hooking up an I.V. drip in his arm, picked up a syringe with antivenin, and injected it into his body. "Okay," He turned to her and asked, "What injuries do you know that you have?"

"Only my arm, I fell again when I ran up to the signal fire, it has swollen and I'm not feeling my fingers anymore." She replied. The paramedic gently removed the makeshift splint, examined her arm for any outward injuries. He then placed her arm palm down to her stomach and taped it close to her side. "Come on," he motioned that she needed to get to the chopper so they could help her get on board.

"No," she stepped back, "I am not going anywhere without him." She pointed straight at Stony.

"It's okay, lady," He said, "I wasn't planning on leaving anybody behind. Just cooperate a little here. We need to get started now." The team, waiting at the chopper, proceeded to load the two survivors so quickly that it took Elaine a couple of minutes to realize they were actually off the ground and on their way to the Trauma Center in Phoenix.

Bob had decided to wait and question the couple until after the medical staff had checked them. He was slowly walking around the little camp, taking pictures and making notes. He had found the canvas bag with the medicines that they had brought from the crash site. A collection that was actually impressive. He noticed the water jug and the drawer from the aircraft galley. There was the crash axe and the old spear. He picked up the signal flare gun from the pile of clothes on the floor of the little adobe hut. Noticing the path that led him to the pool and there he found the plastic soap dish. Following the path on down the slope leading from the spring fed pool, he followed the trail on to two large boulders where he almost tripped over a dead peccary lying on the edge of the path. As he examined the animal, he saw the piece of aircraft skin that was stuck tightly around its foot. Bob had seen this type of snare one time before, and he was well aware of it deadly effect. "This guy Stony must either be a Viet Nam veteran or a survivalist," He was muttering to himself, "Either way it was no surprise that these two have survived." From what he had seen, this fellow could have stayed out here one hell of a long time living off the land. He just had a little bad luck with the snakebite. Bob heard the dog team approaching down below and waited for them to arrive at his position.

After a short rest, they walked on up the hill and into the little oasis where they drank from the cool spring water. The dogs enjoyed a cool dip in the water while the team leader told Bob about his findings back at the mine entrance. Bob took notes. Bob then ordered a chopper to their position to pick up the team and himself for the trip back to Phoenix. As they climbed toward the top of the little mountain, Bob turned and looked down on the oasis camp and thought, not bad. Actually, it was quite cozy and comfortable looking. Within minutes, he was instructing the crew at the crash site about how he wanted the clean up to be handled. Taking a few moments to rest, he leaned his head back against the seat back and closed his eyes. "Thank you, God for letting us find them." Then he relaxed his body, his mind already on the details they had learned.

When he opened his eyes, he was surprised to see they were landing outside the terminal at Sky Harbor Airport in Phoenix. It did not take long for Bob to find out which hospital the crew had taken the man and woman. Hoping once in the emergency room, he would get first hand information from the two survivors. What he found was a mob of TV camera crews and reporters covering the trauma entrance. Damn, what a zoo, Bob thought. I guess I might as well face it now as he drove into the parking lot. The media surrounded Bob as he approached the entrance, he simply held up his hand for silence he spoke slowly, carefully choosing his words. "We have located two survivors. The medical personnel are examining both to determine the extent of their injuries. Now, if you will allow us the consideration of a little more time, I will tell you all that I know about the crash. Thank you." He then turned and entered the hospital.

The head nurse intercepted Bob and pointed him toward the Chief of Staff's office. "Dr. Chapman needs to brief you on Mr. Dawson and Ms. Davis' condition." After entering the office, he noticed that she turned and stepped back into the hall and pushed the door closed. Bob turned toward the desk of the Chief of Staff. "It seems," he began, "that with the exception of a few bumps, bruises, and a broken arm, Elaine Davis is remarkably well. Both dehydrated as expected. Stony Dawson on the other hand is hanging onto life by a thread. The next twenty-four hours will be critical, within that time we will know how bad the venom has taken over his system. We do know that the infection has now advanced through his entire body. He has been transferred to the third floor VIP Intensive Care Unit, and Ms. Davis is on the third floor in a private room."

"Can you tell me how long until I can question them?" Bob asked.

"Intensive Care will let you know the minute Mr. Dawson is awake and alert enough to answer any questions." Dr. Chapman replied.

Bob thanked him and then headed off for the VIP Intensive Care Unit to find Stony's room. Finally standing by his bedside, Bob thought, I am staring at the face of a man who if he survives will be a hero. The media will see to that. He actually felt sorry for this Mr. Dawson. Chances were that he would not want the scrutiny of the public or the details of his life laid out for all to see. Bob noticed a ring on his hand and took hold of Stony's rough hands. The inscription read, Navy Viet Nam 68-69.

Bob softly said, "I knew you were special, you could not have done what you plainly just did." Getting louder he said, "Damn it, Stony, you hang on. The world may have trashed you back then, but I can damn well help you now." His voice getting louder he said, "So, stay the course, sailor. That is a damned order."

The nurse heard Bob and asked, "Is there anything you need, sir?"

Bob replied as he started toward the door, "Get him well. No matter what the cost or how many Doctors it takes. You got that?"

"Yes sir," replied the nurse. "We plan on doing just that."

"That would be good. The President will be thrilled to hear it." He said when he reached the hall outside Stony's door. Bob smiled to himself because the nurse would tell the Chief of Staff and Stony would get the best of care. Sometimes being able to drop the President's name had its advantages. Hell, Bob thought, they would have every damned specialist from the west coast staring at his chart by morning. That is as it should be. He is a hero. He does deserve the best.

Elaine was about half-asleep when Bob walked into her room. Seeing her arm had been properly set. "How are you feeling, Ms Davis?" He asked.

"Have you seen Stony? Can you tell me how he is?" She struggled to sit up in bed and never took her eyes from his face.

Bob stood for a second gathering his thoughts. Knowing he would not lie to her, he wanted to soften the severity of the situation. Slowly he began telling her basically the grave condition Stony was in, but he ended by trying to reassure her that he had been in excellent health and they all had high hopes that he would be able fight his way through. "He will be having the very best care this hospital has to give." Bob waited for the information to sink in. It might take her a moment to comprehend everything he had said.

Elaine sensed this abrupt but articulate man was telling her all he knew, at the moment. She relaxed a little, feeling that she could trust him and then showed him a slight smile. Bob smiled back and instantly knew that this Ms. Davis had only one thing on her mind and that was the man laying in a room just down the hall.

"May I sit down a few minutes and visit with you?" Bob asked. Elaine nodded and Bob pulled up a chair close to her bedside. She did not know who this man was yet. Though she suspected he must be of some importance, either with the government or the airline.

"What do you want to know?" She asked him, never once taking her eyes from his.

The question caught Bob a little off guard. She was quick, Bob thought, so he figured he might just as well tell her. "My name is Bob Farley and I am with the FAA. It is my job to try to find out why this plane crashed. So, if you can recall, would you tell me about your flight after the take-off in St Louis?"

Elaine spent the better part of the next hour describing the rather uneventful flight of the plane she had boarded eleven days earlier. She told Bob that about ten minutes after they began their descent for Phoenix, the plane had started bouncing rather violently. The belt sign come on and the pilot had calmly told them to fasten their belts that the ride would be a little bumpy. She remembered that he had also told the passengers there would be a small delay as they were entering a holding pattern. "A little time later I was bending over to put my book back in my bag. That is when I heard a popping or maybe a muffled banging noise that came from under the floor. It seemed like it was directly beneath my seat. I felt like we were still quite a distance from the airport because of the short time of actual descent."

She was doing an outstanding job. Bob was impressed with her attention to detail, and the awareness she must have of her surroundings. Even now, she seemed instinctively to know when it was important to be completely thorough and detailed.

Bob asked, "What happened next? Were there any violent maneuvers or abrupt changes in altitude or course?"

"Yes," Elaine replied. "The plane made an extra hard turn to the right and the pilot came back on and told us to prepare for a crash landing. All hell broke loose then, people were screaming, crying, praying, cursing, and families kissing, saying their goodbyes. I thought of my son, but he was on a camping trip and the fact that it would take several days for him to receive the news of my death."

"Do you remember the turn itself?" Bob asked.

Elaine took a moment to think back to that night. "Yes, I think I remember the turn." She replied. "It started slowly at first, and then seemed to roll tighter and faster. I remember how the force of the turning actually began to lift me out of my seat. Even in the bent over crash position, the force tried to pull my head and upper body away from my knees." She paused, recalling the moment she had tried not to think about all those days after the crash.

"And then what happened?" He encouraged her to keep talking.

"I felt the plane kind of shudder. It sounded almost like paper tearing, but loud. Then I remember the current of air, a strong wind, blowing into the plane. That's all. I guess I blacked out then and I do not recall anymore until after the crash. I hope this helps you in your search for the cause of the crash." She finally looked away for a second and then said, "I think I can probably rest now, if you don't mind, maybe any more questions could wait until tomorrow?"

"Just a few more, please?" He asked almost warily. "I promise not to keep you much longer. Did you have the feeling of floating before you blacked out?

"Why yes, I did," she said. "I remember feeling like we were flying upside down, then nothing."

"Can you tell me where you were seated in the plane?" Bob asked absently. His mind seemed to be on something else.

"I believe it was about three rows behind the exit door." Elaine replied.

Bob took out a chart of the aircraft and asked Elaine to show him where exactly. She had no trouble pointing to her seat location. Bob took her extended hand and patiently patted the top of it. "Thank you for your time and tolerance. You have helped tremendously in my investigation." As he stood to leave, he pulled his business card out of his coat pocket, handed it to her, and asked, "Is there anyone I can call for you?" Elaine told him that she felt she could take care of that later after she rested a bit.

Bob stepped to the door and before he was out of sight, Elaine spoke earnestly, "Please, Bob, don't let him die. You and I both know he is the only reason I am alive." He turned and winked at Elaine, "Not to worry, little lady, I fully intend to see you both well taken care of and remember this, do not do anything but get well! I would appreciate it if you did not discuss the plane crash with anyone else at this time. Not everyone has your best interest in mind." He left and Elaine lay back, thought about what he had said, relaxed and soon fell into a deep dreamless sleep.

When Bob Farley arrived back at his temporary office, he immediately started gleaning over his notes, scanning the hundreds of Polaroid's of the crash site and the surrounding areas. He hoped to make some sense of the whole mess. The only discernable visible part of the aircraft left was the tail section and the cockpit. They were thousands of yards apart. He noticed that the tail section had broken off just behind the rear cabin door and appeared to be upside down. That matched Elaine's story of the final moments. It would seem the tail was first to contact the ground, shearing off from the fuselage and actually skidding some distance before coming to a halt. Apparently, the fuselage blew up on impact, and then the tail section came to rest. The cockpit even though upside down, pointed upward when the fuselage exploded. The nose section rotated as it was propelled hundreds of feet into the air. It made contact with the rock face side of the arroyo, sliding downward. It came to rest on the floor of the small canyon right side up.

Bob shivered as he started sifting through the facts, he also began visualizing the crash in his mind. He had done many reconstructions that seemed to take forever to figure out how a crash had occurred. However, this one seemed to jump out at him. He did not know the actual cause, but he knew by looking and hearing Elaine's eyewitness account that it had been horrific. How anyone managed to survive was a true miracle. He needed to interview Stony as soon as was feasible. However, he had plenty to do until then.

Uncertain as to whether that gravely ill man in intensive care would pull through, Bob's thoughts wandered to the crash site. Why had he buried just the pilot? A riddle he had to find the answer to and other details that would eventually connect all the dots that Bob and his crew needed to connect.

21

THE CLOCK IN her room showed Elaine that she had sleep until 4 a.m.. She decided that Carol Lee was probably worried sick because she had not arrived in California as scheduled. Carol Lee had no way of contacting me these past eleven days. "I'm sure she won't care about the hour, she'll want to know that I am fine." She held the phone through five rings, then a sleepy voice, "Hello?" "Hello Carol Lee, this is Elaine, your long lost sister. You know the one who was supposed to be in your house by now?"

"Oh my God! Where are you?" Carol Lee was fully awake in an instant.

"I am fine, really. There is just a little break in my left arm." Elaine reassured her. They talked for some time, Elaine filling in the details as Carol Lee asked the questions. They cried together, laughed together, and then Carol Lee told her that she would be coming to Phoenix as soon as she could get a ticket. "I'm sure I'll be seeing you later today so just rest until I get there. I love you."

While she was talking to her sister, Elaine had noticed a terry cloth robe hanging on the bathroom door. She slowly got out of bed, rolled the IV drip to the bathroom and slipped on the robe.

The IC nurse saw Elaine coming down the hall, reached into a bottom drawer of her desk and handed her a pair of hospital slippers. "Here, young lady, you might want these and they even match your lovely robe." Elaine noticed the sweet smile on the nurse's face and a nametag that read HELEN when she added, "It is a little early for visiting hours, but if you insist on traveling our halls, it would be wise to let someone know of your whereabouts."

"I just wanted to check in on Stony." She said, adding, "I couldn't go back to sleep."

The nurse, Helen, noticed the intense look on Elaine's face and told her, "Maybe I can help, just a moment." She turned to a candy-stripper and instructed her to "Push a wheelchair for Ms. Davis. See that this lady goes anywhere she wants."

Elaine was rolled into Stony's' room and as she neared his bedside she was shocked by how frail and fragile he looked. Tubes were in his nose, mouth, arms, and probable in some places she could not see. Her first thought was if he were awake, he would be raising hell about how uncomfortable he was and was this stuff really necessary. She smiled for a minute looking at the little man, remembering the rough exterior that covered what he tried so hard to hide. He had a good heart, a heart of gold if she did not miss her guess. The tears began rolling softly down her cheeks. Helen had quietly entered and stepped up beside Elaine, "He's got a chance. But, it will take a real fighter to shake off the effects of the venom. He has to want to live, so, you talk to him, honey. Give him a reason to want to live." She winked and went back to her station leaving Elaine with her thoughts.

She stood slowly and watched the monitors with all their little funny beeps, then noticed the bellows of the breathing machine. Opening, and then slamming shut tight, oh my, she thought, the machine was breathing for him. He is so weak he cannot even breathe on his own. This is not good. The tears began falling more freely, she moved closer, took his hand in hers, and leaned down and placed her lips close to his ear. "Listen, Buster, this is not your way out. You made a promise out there and I intend on helping you keep it. I know you have probably taken care of more people than I can count, in more situations that I could imagine, but you are not through. Do you hear me? In your own words, Mister, you told me to 'tighten up babe, you can make it' and I did it because you told me I could. Now if we are ever to have a chance of a life together, then you have to beat this poison that is inside you. I love you."

Those three little words had just slipped out. The tears were dripping onto his cheeks. She kissed him lightly then sat back down in the wheel chair, still gripping his hand. Do I really love this man?

Several hours later, the nurse walked by the door and noticed that Elaine had fallen asleep with her head resting on the edge of Stony's bed. She noticed their hands, but it was not Elaine holding his hand, it was Stony grasping hers. Helen lightly tapped Elaine's shoulder, but she still awoke with a start. "Honey, sit up a minute, can you?" Elaine leaned back and immediately noticed Stony was squeezing her hand. "Look" she said, "He is actually gripping my hand."

"I know," replied Helen smiling. "This is good, really good. Up until now, we have not been able to get any response out of him. I don't know what you told him, honey, but whatever it was seems to be working." She checked the heart monitor and said, "His heart beat has gotten stronger, and he seems to be showing hints of discomfort. All good signs," she was noticing the gleam on Elaine's face and told her, "I am not the doctor. Although, I've been in this business a long time and my prognosis is that he is definitely improving. Now for you, I will have an aide take you back to your room. It looks like we need to change your IV. You can come back and stay as long as you want. Okay?"

By the time Elaine returned to her room, Helen had called her charge nurse, Marge and told her about the improvement. "Oh, here you are." Marge said as she pointed to her bed. Marge had lain out some clothes that had been on hand for the candy strippers. "I thought you might want to shower and dress. Maybe make yourself presentable."

"That would be great. Thank you, very much." Elaine was taking her robe off as she went into the bathroom. It did not take long before she was out, clean and smiling. Marge renewed her IV while housekeeping was changing her bed. "I feel so much better, thank you, again." As she looked at herself in the mirror, the only revealing signs of her experiences over the last 12 days were the IV, her face and a little slimmer body, and the cast on her arm. "I almost feel human again."

Just then, the doctor came into the room and said, "Well, I left a patient here last night, have you seen her?"

Elaine laughed and told him about going to Stony's room last night.

"Yes, I know." He said. "It is pretty much all over the hospital. However, I am here to check on you. Let me see how your arm is doing. If there are no complications, then you are free to do pretty much whatever you feel like doing." He finished the checkup, and then authorized her release as soon as someone was available to take her home. Finally, the doctor left and Elaine stood looking into the mirror. She could not believe that just a few hours ago she was not sure they would even live. Eleven days they had spent in the desert trying to survive. She could only wonder how different it would have been had it not been for Stony.

The doctor had given her free rein of this floor of the hospital. If she looked 'presentable' as Marge had said, there was only one place she wanted to be, and that was with Stony. She left the room and headed back down the hallway to the man she surely owed her life to and the one she might even love.

22

Bob had been busier than a one legged man in a butt kicking contest. The reconstruction was being set up in a vacant hanger. The temporary morgue was trying to match bodies, parts, and identification. They would face the task of placing each name on the manifest before releasing them to the families for burial.

He still had not interviewed the last man alive on the flight, if he pulled through. That would be the next thing on his To Do list. So, he started back to the hospital to check on each of them. The airline had been hounding him to allow their attorney's access to the survivors. He would or could not do that until he had all of his questions answered. The protocol was that the FAA had priority for a reasonable amount of time after an incident in order to determine any safety issues. Bob knew he needed to talk to both survivors ASAP because time was rapidly running out. He caught up with Elaine in Stony's room.

"Hi, Ms. Davis." He said. He noticed that she had gotten dressed.

"You must be doing very well. Are you hungry?" He asked. "Or perhaps I could buy you a cup of coffee?"

"Yes, to both." she replied. "Thank you for asking."

"I noticed they have upgraded Stony's condition to guarded and hopeful." Bob stated.

"I have spent most of the morning with him." She smiled. "He is responding more and his breathing is much better. The doctor says if there are no complications tonight, they will be removing his ventilator, probably tomorrow morning. I cannot tell you how thrilled I am that he's getting better, I was so scared for him."

They sat at a table on the veranda overlooking the city enjoying the meal, the company and the break from the hospital anxiety. Bob said. "Do you feel like talking about your experience?" She simply smiled as he once again took out his little tape recorder. It hummed as Elaine relived every detail she could remember for the past twelve days. When she finished, Bob turned the recorder off and said, "It really is none of my business, but I figure you both deserve all you can get. Therefore, the information I am about to give you did not come from me. Do you understand?" Elaine was looking square in his big dark eyes again and simply nodded affirmatively. "The airline will want to settle with a compensation package, trying to avoid the courts. So, make damn sure you get all you can get. You could have died out there, remember that. Okay? That's enough said."

"What about Stony?" Elaine asked. "What will happen to him in his condition?"

"Does he have any kin?" Bob queried. "Maybe they could speak for him."

"I believe he has grown children, but I don't know where they live." She was thoughtful for a moment. "Besides that, he is a very proud man, I'm not sure he would take anything! He will probably just tell them about their #@%* plane and that he will not be flying the skies with them again."

Bob laughed. "He sounds just like my kind of guy. I hope I get to know him. Maybe when you talk to them, you might even suggest a starting point for any settlement. You and he could just as easily been one of those mangled bodies lying out there in that desert for eleven days. Remember that!" Bob's beeper went off and he excused himself to talk in private. "Well, it seems our man is awake. Could you give us a little time alone before you come in? She nodded. "Thanks." Bob winked teasingly toward Elaine, "It looks like we all had a hand in saving him." He turned toward the elevator thinking, now I will interview the only man on the face of the earth that knows what happened at the crash site.

Bob and Stony spent the next six hours together. Bob did not want to push him so he waited through the medications, the sleeping, and the casual banter that formed an instant bond between the two men. They seemed to have a lot in common. Stony was retired from Naval Aviation, so they spoke the same language, he understood all the terminology used in the business.

Bob managed to get the whole story. The noise just prior to the crash that Stony had heard could explain the fuselage explosion, especially if it had been a hydraulic leak. The mist or vapor had filled the cargo hold where a spark could have blown the plane apart and everyone above the hold would have died almost instantly. Stony's description of his seating position and where he had come to rest was supporting Bob's earlier theory. Bob felt as though he had enough information now to at least confront the Associated Press and give an acceptable overview of the tragic accident.

As Bob was finishing their interview, Elaine entered the room. He noticed how their eyes had locked onto each other as she moved to his bedside. Bob stood quietly by the door and watched the two, curious more than anything else, until he realized that they did not even know he was still there.

Stony looked much better now that the breathing tube had been removed and Elaine could not help but notice the smile on his face.

"How are you feeling?" She asked.

He rolled his head in the direction of the cup of ice water, so she picked up the cup and held the straw to his lips. He took a long slow drink.

"Thanks." Stony said. "I have felt better, must have been one hell of a party. What did I miss? How is your arm? How are you?" He lay there looking deeply into those blue pools that Elaine called eyes. "Damn." He said. "Wait a second I must have died and gone to heaven. I have this angel standing here. Well, you look like one to me."

Elaine laughed a musical happy laugh and held the straw for Stony to take another drink. "Really, I am fine. Rested, nourished and even dressed in something sensible, I feel much better and safe." Now that he was awake, she did not know quite what to say to him. She wondered if he remembered the words, she had spoken to him while he was still unconscious.

After the awkward silence, he spoke softly. "Well, reckon you will be getting on your trip to California shortly. By the way, tell your sister hello. I'd like to meet her some day." His voice trailed off as he fell asleep in the middle of his thought.

Bob thought, Hell, this man could have this woman for the rest of his life. Right by his side, all he had to do was ask.

Elaine turned away from Stony with tears filling her eyes. Bob took her as she came to him and held her. "Honey, if he is everything you told me, then his concern is to see you happy and above all else alive. You realize that you have had more time to think about this than he has, so if I were you I would try to stay in touch with him after things get settled down and smoothed out. Who knows you might even need a best man someday and I have never been one of those." They both laughed a little nervously at such a personal moment, but it did brighten the atmosphere.

"Thank you, Bob, for being a friend. Hopefully you might just be one for a long time, to both of us." She left the room and walked down the hall to the observation deck where the warm breeze lightly lifted her hair from her face. Mr. Farley is right she thought, give it time, but be ready to stay in touch. Heck, she thought, I may not feel this way in two or three weeks. She looked down and noticed Bob Farley as he approached the crowd of reporters that had taken up residence on the front entrance of the hospital. They had been pointing and taking pictures of her while she had been standing there.

Bob stepped up to the microphones and slowly, deliberately said. "We have two survivors. Both of them have been through a hell of a lot. I will not give out their names until the family notifications are complete. I will tell you the aircraft crash was unavoidable due to weather, power outages and multiple problems aboard the plane. Everything that could go wrong did. These two were extremely lucky to have survived. The fact that they did survive at all was due to the damn good job performed by the crew of that airplane. The reconstruction will be ongoing for weeks, maybe more. From all I can gather now, external circumstances played a major role in this catastrophe. I want to thank all those involved in the search effort, also the media for their patience, and the thousands of volunteers that came from New Mexico and Arizona to help. I will be keeping you posted on facts as I get more details about the incident."

Elaine watched as he left the hospital, surely on the way to the reconstruction hanger to get the latest news. I wonder if that man ever slows down, she thought.

As he pulled up to the hanger a group of men approached his car. "Here we go. These have got to be the attorneys." He said.

"Hello, Mr. Farley. My name is Elijah Cooper, with Cooper, Cooper and Hawkins Law Firm." The well-manicured sophisticated gentleman's voice purely cooed. Bob immediately took a dislike to the man. He knew what was coming.

"We represent the airline and would like to have a word with you, sir." Mr. Cooper said extending his hand.

"Gentlemen," he said as he turned to include the whole group. "I will be glad to talk to you at length, but not now. I will inform you that Ms. Elaine Davis, the woman survivor will be speaking on behalf of both her and Mr. Stony Dawson. Mr. Dawson, at this time is unable physically or mentally to offer any comments on your clients concerns. That means no questions about monetary settlements, public statements he made or might make about the airline, the crash, or any other matter until further notice. You got that? I am sure the President would appreciate you full cooperation in this matter. Ms Davis will be expecting you before she leaves the hospital. She received her discharge from her doctor and is waiting, even as we speak, for her family to pick her up. So, I suggest you hurry." As the men jumped into their cars, but before the doors slammed shut, Bob added. "Mr. Dawson is not to be disturbed under any circumstances. Do I make myself perfectly clear?"

They all nodded their heads in understanding and Mr. Cooper replied, "Yes sir, Mr. Farley, you can tell the President that you have our full cooperation."

Bob laughed to himself. He loved doing that Mr. President bit. The attorneys would be scrambling to make it back to the hospital before Elaine went home. He wondered if the President had ever heard of some of his antics. He hoped no one had called to check up on him. That might be a bit embarrassing.

23

THE ATTORNEYS LOCATED Elaine at the hospital and it did not take long for the battle lines to be drawn. They all gathered in one of the staff conference rooms to have some privacy. Elaine soon had them eating out of her hand. After all, they definitely did not need pressure from Capital Hill. That would not be good for them or the airline. After several hours of haggling they finally reached an agreement somewhere around 5 p.m.

When Elaine finally came out of the conference room her sister ran up to her and it seemed like she would never let go. "I was so worried about you. I'm glad you're okay." Carol Lee said. They hugged and giggled then hugged again as they started down the hall with their heads together talking excitedly, making plans for the next few days. The sisters spent most of the next day just staying in a motel room. Elaine told Carol Lee about the infamous eleven days. She told her all about the crash, about Stony pulling her out of the airplane, and their survival. She could not stop talking about all they had done together, until their rescue. By the end of the day, Carol Lee had heard everything about this Stony character, at least all that Elaine knew. Carol Lee cautioned her not to make too much of their attachment right now. "Just take your time and move slowly." She told Elaine, "You know that situations like this make people act out in ways they would not ordinarily act upon. So, just be careful. You really do not know anything about this man."

Elaine promised she would and then changed the subject to their younger years. She knew that Carol Lee had always had a jaded attitude about relationships, and sometimes her advice did not sit well with Elaine. Rather than cause a disagreement, she let the subject drop. In the end, Elaine would make her own decision about her and Stony's future.

Elaine and Carol Lee caught up on all the old and new news. It seemed to be exactly what they both needed. They had not been this close in years. Maybe Carol Lee was right, I would take time to think. But, she definitely wanted to give it a chance and see how things went between her and Stony.

They decided they would stay in for the night and just rest. Both took showers and changed to their bedclothes. After settling on her bed, Elaine reached for the phone and called the hospital to check on Stony's condition. The information desk clerk told her that Mr. Dawson's condition was rapidly improving. "Would you like to be put through to his room?" the clerk inquired.

"No." Elaine told her. "No, not tonight, I'll let him rest. Maybe I will call again tomorrow. Thank you anyway." She sat there a long time just holding the phone, wondering if she was doing the right thing.

Carol Lee came around the corner from the bathroom and sat on the edge of her bed. "Are you okay?" She asked quietly.

"Yes, Stony seems well on his way to recovery. I don't know why I did not let her put the call through to his room. Suddenly I was just afraid to talk to him. Crazy, huh?"

Carol Lee patted Elaine's knee and said, "Honey, you do not need to worry about him. I am sure he will be just fine. He probably has a girl friend where he lives, anyway. If I know men, he will not let any grass grow under his feet in getting home to her. Why in a couple of months this will all seem like a bad dream. He will have moved on, and that is exactly what you need to be doing. In addition, we will start that first thing in the morning. Good night, I love you."

Elaine finally hung up the phone and said, "I suppose you are right. I am tired and this bed feels so good." She slipped her feet in between the fresh sheets and fell asleep almost as soon as her head hit the pillow.

The doctor had moved Stony to a private room. Stony looked forward to eating some real food. When a nurse came to check his vitals, he asked about Ms. Davis.

"She checked out yesterday, sir. I apologize. I thought you had been told." She answered.

By God, he thought, she could have at least come to say good-by. This is why he had not let down his guard. All these years, it is just easier not to be attracted to anyone. He finished his meal and flipped through the channels of the television that was hanging precariously from the ceiling. He caught a couple of news programs and soon found out he was being made some kind of hero. These were not the comments he wanted to hear. He would have no privacy at all.

He began making plans on getting out of the hospital building without anyone in the press knowing. The doctor had told him that as soon as the swelling in his leg went down, when he could walk without pain, he could go home. He definitely did not wish to be in the lime light. He did not desire to see even one reporter, nor anyone else as far as that goes. "Hell, they did not want to talk to me when I came home from that damned war. They sure as hell are not going to stick a microphone in my face now."

Several reporters had tried to sneak in that evening. The little night nurse was wise about who was supposed to be roaming the hall after visiting hours. She managed to run interference for Stony. He liked those no nonsense woman, strictly business, that kind of approach to doing things was how every body ought to be. He smiled to himself, "I have never been mistaken for someone wishy washy. I try to see things in black or white, I make my decisions based on what is right, not what is the easiest." He always appreciated that in other people. He knew it sometimes was hard, but people with character would do what was right. "Now to do the right thing," He said, "First I'll call my mother and let her know I am alive and well, but no hero." He also called his kids and reassured them that yes, he was fine and no, he would not need any help getting around. Yes, he would be leaving before long and heading for home. "By the way," he added, "Do not believe all that crap you hear or see on TV."

Stony turned off the TV and lay in the darkness looking out at the lights of Phoenix, but all he saw was a certain blonde-haired woman by the name of Elaine. Hell, he missed her already. How damned stupid is that, he thought.

Later a volunteer came by and asked if she could get anything for him. He replied. "Yes, you could get me a nice card for someone I miss very much."

"Yes, I can do that for you. I'll be back in a few minutes." Which she was and the card she purchased was very suitable for what he had in mind. He had been trying to think about what he should write to her.

Stony finally fell asleep holding the card with *Elaine* written on the top.

Elaine was awake early. She quietly dressed and slipped out to the rental car. She went directly to the hospital, stopping by the gift shop to find a present for Stony. She finally settled on a satin rose with a small vase and a card that said, "Thank you for coming into my life." She signed it simply 'E'.

Entering his room, she noticed immediately his color was almost back to normal. Smiling she placed the rose and the card on the wheeled stand next to his bed. She leaned over and lightly kissed his check, noticing the card under his hand, saw *Elaine* written across the top. "I'll look forward to receiving that card." She whispered. Turning slowly she looked back one more time and was glad she had come before leaving town.

Carol Lee was still asleep when Elaine returned to the motel room with doughnuts and coffee. She woke Carol Lee. They ate, then showered, and dressed for the trip to Los Angeles, CA. She was humming softly while packing her few belongings in the travel bag.

"Why are you so happy and bouncy this early in the morning?" Carol Lee asked.

"Oh, it is just a beautiful day to be alive." Elaine answered. She was thinking back to that moment when she kissed Stony good-bye.

The kitchen cart that was bringing his breakfast awakened Stony. Before they entered the door, he heard the clanging dishes. When the door pushed open, the hall light flooded his room.

"Damn, doesn't anyone ever knock?" He bellowed.

The woman with a white apron across her middle appeared in front of him and asked, "Would it be okay to move the flower and card over to your night stand until you eat?"

"Yes, just leave the food tray and shut the door on the way out." He growled. He lay back on his pillow. "What flower? What card?" He reached for the pull cord to the light over the head of his bed. When his eyes finally adjusted, he saw them. A little purple rose in a white bud vase and a card lying next to it. Stony sat up and swung his legs over the side of the bed.

The pain in his leg was excruciating, the scream he heard was his own.

The nurse was running as she entered his room, "I expected this a little later in the day. I meant to be here when you tried to get up and walk, you know, to give you a pain pill before you attempted this. Here, just lay your leg out straight. I'll be back in a moment with your medication." She brought his pain pill then started talking to him to get his mind off his leg. She explained that it would take time and rehab to eliminate the pain in his leg. As she handed him the card she said, "Now tough guy, the next time you need something out of your reach, there is a little red button on your remote. I have clipped it to your pillow, well within your reach so just push the button to call the desk. Okay?"

"Yea, I'm sure I will have no problem remembering that from now on, thanks." Stony lay reading his card and wiped a tear from the corner of his eye. She had not left without saying goodbye after all. When I finish taking care of my promise to Jerry, the pilot, maybe I should look her up. He smiled a broad smile as he thought of the next time he would talk to Elaine.

24

The days that followed filled him with pain and then pain pills. The desire to walk out on his own with as little pain as possible made him determined. He pushed the rehab exercises until he could barely move. When he was not in rehab, he walked the halls continually. He knew the pain would eventually go away, so he pushed, and then he rested, then pushed some more, then rested. He slept very little. The nurses talked among themselves about how strong-willed he was. "No wonder he saved himself and Ms. Davis." They would joke about if they were stranded they would certainly want someone with his grit to be with them.

The doctor told Stony he could go as soon as he felt strong enough. He did not feel strong, but he was ready! He had managed to wean himself off the pain pills, knowing that his body would adjust to the pain and it would just be discomfort to him. The older night nurse had purchased him some clothes. He had requested just an old pair of jeans, a white shirt, and a pair of loafers. He had arranged for a rental car so he could drive himself home. It was 55 miles to Coolidge. He felt strong enough to accomplish that. The rental car company promised to park the car in the back parking lot of the hospital. He knew that the media would be covering the front entrance waiting for him to exit.

After visiting hours, Stony dressed and prepared to leave. The old nurse that had gotten his clothes knew what he was about to attempt. When he slid the door open to check the hall, there she stood with a white lab coat. "They will never miss this old thing. I thought it might help you blend in with the personnel leaving at 11 p.m." She smiled and patted him on the check, "You got spunk, I'll give you that. I am not going to worry about you. I know you will make it just fine."

"I know," Stony replied, "I kind of like you too. It has been a pleasure to have you around."

"Oh, by the way, your car is the one next to the dumpster. You will not have any trouble finding it. The key is over the visor."

Stony tilted his head as if to question 'how did you know?'

"I just happened to be there when they delivered it," she smiled, "I heard you when you made your call."

Stony checked his watch, gave her a quick hug and said, "Well, I will be on my way. Thanks, for everything."

Nearing the dumpster, he began to remove the lab coat and when he passed it, he threw the coat away. He opened the door of the car, found the key and slowly eased himself into the seat, resting just a moment before he started the car and pulled out of the parking lot. It wasn't long before he was on I-10, headed for his mobile home in Coolidge. After leaving the lights of the city, he turned on the dome light to look for the location of the cigarette lighter. As he pushed in the lighter, he noticed a note lying on the passenger seat. Opening the note, he read, *'Hang in there, Tough Guy, and don't forget your friend in California.'* It was signed, *Night Nurse Murphy*. He smiled as he found himself really liking the tough old broad. Turning off the dome light he settled in for the ride in the quiet darkness of the desert night.

He slipped in the front gate of the 55+ park and most of the lights were out in his neighbors' homes. "Hey, old girl, Daddy's home," as he unlocked his front door he said. "And believe it or not, I really missed you." He crossed the living room to the small bar and poured himself a drink, then sank into his favorite chair. Sipping the dark rum and cola with a twist of lime, he closed his eyes and began reliving the past few weeks.

He finished his drink, got up, showered, and then sank into the old familiar bed. Tomorrow would be another day and he sure as hell would not be flying for a long while. The bed felt so good, he slept deeply with dreams of one adorable creature.

Morning came earlier than he would have liked, with a knock on the front door. Opening the door, he saw a man from a courier service out of Phoenix. "Yes?" He asked.

"You need to sign, sir," said the courier.

Stony did just that, took the large brown manila envelope and dropped it on the table on his way to the kitchen to make coffee. After pouring a steaming hot cup of coffee, he picked up the envelope and noticed it was from the airlines. He opened the catch and turned the envelope so he could pull out the contents, but out fell a bright shiny gold card. **Free Lifetime Flying.** Stony began laughing, "That is just what I wanted." He removed the remaining contents and gleaned through the papers when he noticed a cashiers check for the sum of two million five hundred thousand dollars. "Oh, my God!" was all he could say as he read and re-read the letter several times. "Oh, my God. All I have to do is sign the release form enclosed."

Stony sat staring at the check in disbelief. "Damn." He said, "What in the world?" The letter read that the airline would pick up all medical expenses now and in the future and pay him the two million five hundred thousand if he would agree to no future litigation toward the airlines, their affiliates, the crew or any employees there of. "Hell, I would not have considered a lawsuit anyway. But if they would like to throw money in my direction, why not?" He singed the release letter and placed it in the already stamped and addressed envelope, laying it on top of the computer, he said, "and I'll mail that on my way out."

Elaine had enjoyed the past few days, lying in the sun on the apartment deck, eating out, and visiting with her sister. They were enjoying a late morning, drinking their coffee on the deck when the doorbell rang. Elaine answered the door and immediately the courier handed her a large brown envelope. She signed for it and then sat back down at the table in the kitchen to open it. Elaine held the letter in her left hand and her coffee mug to her lips as she read. She choked on the coffee as she noticed the check for two million five hundred thousand dollars that had been folded into the letter. Putting down her coffee, she read aloud, "Free medical expenses now and in the future, here's a gold card that reads, **Free Lifetime Flying**, and a release form that states that if I agree not to initiate any future litigation towards the airline, their affiliates, the crew or any employees. All I have to do is sign the release form and all of this is mine. Do I feel guilty? Hardly, I remember what Mr. Farley told me about when it came time to settle. I am definitely signing the release form." Elaine was smiling like the Cheshire cat. "Carol Lee!" She yelled out to the veranda. "Do you know a place where we can get a very special expensive brunch?"

She signed the form, put it in the envelope and told Carol Lee, "I need to mail this on the way out." She then scooped up the remains, put them back in the envelope, and stuffed it into her purse. As they were eating, Elaine considered telling Carol Lee exactly what was going on, but decided that it could wait a while. She really needed to get her affairs in order before letting this information out. After they returned to the apartment, she told Carol Lee she needed to run some errands and would be back in a little while.

Elaine drove immediately to a near-by bank. She opened an interest-earning checking account with ten thousand dollars. Another four hundred ninety thousand went into a money market account. She then divided the remaining two million with five hundred thousand invested in mutual funds and five hundred thousand into several high-interests CD accounts. She placed five hundred thousand in a trust for her son, Evan. The last five hundred thousand went into the hands of an investment banker who would see that sponsorships were provided for exceptionally bright high school graduates. Graduates, who otherwise could not afford a college education.

Elaine left the bank feeling a bit overwhelmed. I hope I made the right decisions. I am sure not used to having those kinds of numbers to deal with, it still does not seem real to me. She window-shopped at the local mall, to kill some time and think about how different her life would be. Now she did not have to think about having just enough money to get by. "I hope I don't wake up and find this is all a dream." She said.

25

Tony was looking over the rental car before turning it in. He opened the trunk and found that Nurse Murphy had placed the rose and Elaine's card right in the middle, where he was sure to find it. As he carried the items into the house, he said, "Sorry, Marilyn, I haven't thought of you as much these last few days." He realized he had not thought about his late wife at all. Only of Elaine. "I reckon it is time to move on. The counselor said I would know when the time was right."

As he drove to Casa Grande to turn in his rental car, he was admiring the landscape of the area surrounding his home. This was so different when you compare it to the crash site. This part tamed by cultivation, irrigation and crops. Fields that looked almost manicured by the precision of the local planting and harvesting techniques. The crash site was a rugged and desolate wasteland that was dangerous and almost always deadly, and only a few hundred miles southwest of here.

He began to wonder what this area landscape was like before the Ho Ho Kam Indians first settled here. To this day, you could see where they had built canals to carry water from the mountains and irrigated their land. They seemed to have found the secret to survive, but they had eventually all moved to the north and intermarried with other tribes and then they were gone. Only the Ho Ho Kam can ever answer that mystery, so we will never know for sure.

The shuttle had returned him to the park and pulled in front of his trailer. Stony walked inside, retrieved the wallet that he had promised to return. He made sure everything was secured. He stepped back outside, climbed carefully into his truck to begin the journey back to St. Louis. He placed the wallet into the center console, pulled out of the park and wondered if he had allowed himself enough rest. "Well, only time will tell." He said.

The days' end found Stony in Texas. He had driven all day and even into the night to get to the east side of Amarillo. His head was throbbing, he was ready to stop and get some rest. It did not take long before he managed to find a suitable motel. Shortly he would feel much better, after a good meal, a hot shower and a comfortable bed. That is exactly the order they came. The throbbing headache was gone after the good meal, the aching and stiff body was gone after the hot shower, and the tiredness soon ebbed out of his body as he drifted off to sleep in the comfortable bed.

When Elaine arrived back at the apartment, she thought they would spend the evening at home, but Carol Lee had decided that what they needed was a night on the town. "Don't you think a little night life might be in order? How long has it been since you've gone out and just had fun?" Her sister asked her.

"Well, it has been a while." Elaine answered. "Just a little fun, right?"

"Leave everything to me." Carol Lee smiled then went to get dressed. "You might want to change into something with plenty of sway. You will probably be dancing until dawn."

After a light supper, Carol Lee told Elaine, "You will get a few drinks with me as the night progresses, won't you? Besides it might help you relax, forget about the last two weeks. Maybe even help you think straight when it comes to this Stony character." Carol Lee had heard about this Stony person for the past three days and her hopes were that Elaine would meet someone to take her mind off all that. Elaine had agreed to come with her tonight just to appease her. Carol Lee knew that, but it really might be good to get her out of her comfort zone for a while.

They ended up in a favorite haunt of Carol Lee and her co-workers. it was the typical nightspot, dark and loud music, not good music, but it was loud. They turned up the music so you will dance, then you have to yell to be heard. Elaine noticed that every variety and type of person that you could imagine was standing elbow to elbow at the bar. The dance floor was not any less crowded, "I think we have come on the wrong night. You could not get out there and dance if you wanted to." Elaine shouted at Carol Lee.

"It will be alright, you'll see." Carol Lee shouted back. She then introduced Elaine to some fellow whom she worked with and he almost fell over the table during the introduction. Elaine thought, "Oh man, I hope this idiot doesn't ask me to dance. He can't even stand up.' Nevertheless, of course, he did. With each introduction and subsequent dance, the evening slowly became smothering for Elaine. After the fourth dance, Elaine quickly excused herself and told Carol Lee that she was going to call a taxi to go home. "You stay, have some fun. I'll be fine."

She used the house phone and the taxi was waiting when she walked out the door. Thinking about the past few days, all the way back to the apartment she realized this situation would never work. She and Carol Lee were just too different. Carol Lee loved what she thought was fun. However, to Elaine it looked like just a bunch of middle-aged juveniles trying desperately to look like they were having fun. <u>If</u> she wanted a man at all, she knew where there was a real one, and it was not in California.

Elaine striped her smoke filled clothes and tossed them into the washer as soon as she walked into the apartment. After showering, washing her hair, she put some very mild linen scented spray cologne. She wanted a fresh smell, a fresh start, and a fresh new location. When she passed the coffee table, she noticed a travel book. Picking it up, as she sat down on the couch she curled her legs under her. Glancing through the magazine her eyes landed on a Belize advertisement. Oh, they have wonderful places to snorkel, it sounds wonderful. She thought. Some day I may just go visit there. I have always wanted to see other parts of the world. She had never been outside the U.S., but she had dreamed among other things, that maybe some day it would be possible.

Without thinking, she called the operator for Coolidge, AZ and got Stony's phone number. When she was connected, she listened to the familiar voice saying, "I am not available right now, leave a number and a message and I will return your call as soon as I can." Beep! Elaine did not speak. She hung up the receiver and went to bed.

Elaine had no idea what time Carol Lee came home, and she did not really care. She was wishing now that she had stayed in Phoenix. It was amazing, she thought, how much you could learn about someone in a situation like the crash and following survival. If asked how would you describe Stony, what would she say? Elaine thought about the question for quite some time. I would say that he was a very strong willed man of few words. He was independent, led by doing and not by talking. He did not require much, was not frivolous, she saw no need in him to 'keep up with the Jones'. He made his own decisions about what he wanted. She could imagine his home. He probably had very little except necessities. His vehicle would probably be older, but would function flawlessly. He probably owned the best in fishing and hunting gear. Those things were important to him. He was also considerate to others. After all, he had been with his children and his mother before the flight home. Moreover, that seemed to be a yearly event. That is what I would say, she thought. Not bad qualities if a woman was looking for a man.

Morning came and she did not even get out of bed until Carol Lee left for work. Elaine thought Carol Lee would at least check in on her, but she left without saying a word. When things did not work out as she planned, she always kept quiet. Elaine never knew exactly if it was because she was upset or because she thought you were upset.

Elaine ate a small breakfast then washed her dishes, dressed for a busy day. She had made plans last night and there was much to do.

The door to the travel agency swished closed behind her and she smiled knowing she would be leaving on a cruise to Hawaii for 15 days. She felt there would be plenty of time to figure out what direction her life would be taking. This was totally out of character for her, but she found the idea exhilarating.

Packing her small bag once back at the apartment. She thought, now I have a reason to buy some new clothes. She was sure that would fill the next three days before she was to sail. Writing Carol Lee a note, she explained the need for time alone and she felt this trip would help. Telling her not to worry, she would be contacting her within a month. Elaine felt that would be enough time for her to figure out things for herself. I know you want only the best for me. Wish me luck. Elaine signed it with I love you, thanks for everything.

She called a taxi, chose a hotel close to the cruise lines where she could walk to the nearby shopping mall. The physical activity would help make her stronger and buying new clothes, shoes, and accessories would keep her spirits up.

26

Stony had reached the edge of St. Louis by 8 p.m. on the third day of driving. He checked in at a local inn, took his bags to the room and literally fell across the foot of the bed and closed his eyes. Stony was physically drained and bleary-eyed after three days of driving. Tomorrow he would have the pleasure of doing what he had promised Jerry, the pilot. Meeting the grieving family would be hard, but he thought they would be proud to know that Jerry's last thoughts were of them.

When he finally awoke the next morning, he could hear the sound of rain and wind. Oh great! He hated rainy days and did not like having to get out in them. The memories always seemed to flood back into his mind, and of all days, he had to add one more sorrowful thing to the rainy day list. He called information to get the phone number for the Jerry Bradford residence. He explained to Jillian why he was in town and wanted her permission to come to her home to meet with her and her children. She was hesitant at first but soon realized that Stony had information that came from Jerry himself. "Yes, please come. I would like very much to talk to you. Can you be here by 10 a.m.?"

"Could you give me your address? He wrote it down while he listened to her, and slipped it into his pocket. "Yes, I should have no problem being there by that time." He replied.

"Thank you for calling." She sounded almost grateful. He then headed to the lobby and the inn's continental breakfast. Finishing his last cup of coffee, he checked the address on the notepaper he had placed in his wallet. He then picked up a city map at the front desk and quickly found the closest route to get there. His first stop was at a neighborhood discount store where he bought two of the biggest stuffed animals he could find.

As he drew close to the address, he could not help notice the wide landscaped lawns of the upper-middle class neighborhood. The houses looked like they could be on a postcard. Beautiful and yet very welcoming, the kind of community where you would feel comfortable raising your children. He understood even more about what kind of man Jerry Bradford had been and his need to provide the best for his family.

"I'm glad I came." He said as he pulled into the circle drive and stopped when he reached the front door. Stony put Jerry's wallet in his pocket and then reached into the back seat to retrieve the soft over-sized animals.

The front door opened as Stony reached the house. A petite woman with strawberry blonde hair met him. She was dressed very casually in jeans and a pastel green cotton blouse. He liked her immediately as she smiled openly and welcomed him into her home. "Oh, my, you have your hands full, let me help. What a miserable day in Missouri for a visit. Please come in out of the rain."

Handing one of the animals to Jillian he said, "I'm sure you've guessed these are for the girls, I'll let you decide which one goes to whom."

"This is very thoughtful of you. Mr. Dawson. Dawson?...Isn't that right?" She asked.

Stony simply nodded affirmative.

"Girls, come in here for a moment, there is a surprise for each of you." Two of the cutest little girls he thought he had ever seen came bouncing into the room and straight to their mother.

With difficulty, Stony squatted down so he could look both girls in the eye. "Your dad wanted you to have these. He loved you both very much."

"Is it okay, Mommy?" The eldest looked up at Jillian with pleading eyes. "Can we keep them?"

"Yes, I think it would be fine for you girls to keep them. Your Daddy wanted you to have them. Now, what do you say?" Jillian spoke softly and when Stony looked up, her eyes glistened with unshed tears. The girls in unison said, "Thank you." then turned and ran toward the back of the house, presumably to their playing area. "Would you like some coffee, Mr. Dawson?" She asked

"Please, call me Stony. Yes, if you have some already made, I would love a hot cup of coffee." He followed Jillian into the dining room and sat down at the table, while Jillian poured two cups of coffee. She then joined him, sitting directly across the table from him. Stony could not help noticing all the envelopes piled in the middle of the table, all with windows in them.

"Is it getting tough?" He asked.

"Yes, it will be very tough," she lowered her head, "I am sure it will not take long to go through what savings we had. Nevertheless, I am sure we will manage. I can downsize to a smaller house and I am capable of going back to work. Thank you for asking, Stony. My family, our church, and all our neighbors have been wonderful."

"So, let me get right to the point." Stony sipped his coffee and continued, "I am sure you have wondered why I am alive and he's not." She started to speak, but he held up his hand. "It's somehow unfair for your husband to be the one that died instead of me. I feel guilty for that. My children are grown. I have fought in a war where I should have died, although now he is gone and I am still here. Its okay, I've also lost a spouse and I know what thoughts can pass through your mind." He let her think about the comment for just a moment, again raising his coffee cup to his lips. He then began telling Jillian the story about the flight. He explained how Jerry had reacted very professionally over the intercom.

"Keeping people calm is half the battle in these situations; he did a good job of that, but in the end it didn't matter." He went on to paint a picture about the condition of the cockpit, and finding Jerry still alive. How he had held on as long as he did had been a miracle. "Seemingly, long enough to convey the message he wanted delivered back to you and the girls. He told me to tell you how very much he loved you all, shortly before his passing."

Stony reached in his coat and handed the wallet across the table to Jillian. She took it and held it to her breast with tears streaming down her face. After a few minutes, she ran her hand across the smooth brown leather exterior of the tri-fold. It seemed very familiar to her and she said, "I gave it to him for Christmas last year." He instantly pictured the simple yet joyful Christmases that had passed in this house, and a warm smile came to his face.

Jillian spoke, "Thank you, Mr. Dawson… Stony, for keeping your promise to Jerry. I know that you bought the gifts for the girls, but I do appreciate your kindness."

"There is no need to thank me. He asked me to make a promise and I kept it. That is all there was to it. By the way, you might want to check out the contents of the wallet. He made a comment about some insurance policy that you did not know he had. I believe it's written on a piece of paper that is there. Before I leave, I just want you to know your husband died a very brave man, with you and the girls on his lips and in his heart." He smiled, then said, "Now, I've done what I promised, do you have any further questions? If not, I will be on my way. You, my lady, have a lot to do and I will not detain you any further. I think that by days' end you will see a light at the end of your very long tunnel. I'll let myself out. You have things you'll need to get done."

Jillian stood, came around the table, grabbed Stony around the neck and hugged him tightly. "Thank you so much for all your trouble. I wish you only good luck and happiness."

Stony had driven several miles before he recalled the feeling when Jillian hugged him. No wonder Jerry fought so hard to stay alive!

"Well, now that is over and I hope someone hits me in the head with something if I ever make another promise to anyone." He smiled with the thought of how Jillian and the girls would be able to live when she found out there was a $750,000 policy waiting for her to claim. With what he already had through the airlines, she could live very comfortably until the girls were grown and she decided what she would do with her life.

Many, many, hours later, Stony was having trouble remembering the last fifty miles. "I'm about to get road hypnosis, I need to stop and at least stretch my legs and get my head clear." He spoke aloud so he could at least hear something beside the hum of the engine. Stopping for gas, he asked the attendant, "How far am I from the Oklahoma line?"

"Are you headed east or west?" The attendant answered without even looking up from the gas hose.

"I'm headed west." Stony said.

"Coming from Missouri?" The attendant asked.

"Yes, why do you ask?" Stony queried.

"Well, you passed the Oklahoma/Missouri line about 35 miles back. Have you been on the road awhile?" The attendant finally looked up at him and said, "No need to answer, I can see your eyes. We got coffee inside if you'd like a cup."

"You got a place where I can wash up?"

"Yep, go inside… turn right."

Stony turned and walked into the convenience store, turned right and found the restrooms. After using the facility, he washed his face to wake up. He finished drinking a cup of coffee, then he got back in the truck and began again. Oklahoma passed, then Texas came, he found a small motel on the outskirts of Dalhart and spent the night. The miles came and went the next day as they had yesterday, through Texas, New Mexico, and then finally Tucson. He perked up a little. He knew he was almost home. An hour later, he saw the Eloy exit on I-10 toward Coolidge. Boy, he thought, I'm sure glad I left the air on at home. It had taken him three days to get to St. Louis and two to get back. He probably should have stopped one more night in there somewhere. But heck, he could rest when he got home. When he saw the entrance to the park, he almost laughed, "I don't know why I thought I needed to get here so quick. Why the hell was I in such a hurry to get home to no one? Maybe I need to get a dog."

Standing in the shower, he felt the miles begin to slip from his body. I will fix a drink then go straight to bed, he thought. It is still a little early, but I could use the rest. Before he sat down holding his dark rum and cola, with a twist of lime, he put on his favorite soft jazz CD. He relaxed, really relaxed for the first time in over a month.

His mind took him back to the mountain oasis pool and Elaine standing with her backside to the sparkling fire. The light had danced over her curves, and even in the semi darkness, he made out the hourglass figure. Her legs were probably the most perfectly formed legs he had ever seen. As she stood up in the water, the firelight caught the droplets as they rolled down her delightfully slim back. God, she had been a vision, standing there not knowing that I was anywhere around. She did not seem to be timid or shy about her nakedness. Stony could not shake off that image that was frozen forever in his brain.

He got up to fix another drink and noticed the answering machine message light was blinking. Pushing the button to hear the message, there was nothing. There had been six calls and they had not uttered a word. He checked the caller id, but did not recognize the numbers. Nevertheless, wanting to see if it had been something important, he called the first number back. He had not even so much as glanced at the time and was surprised to receive the following answer, "This had better be important, it's almost 2 a.m. and I have to work tomorrow!"

"I am so sorry. I did not realize it was this late. I was just returning a call to the number that was on my answering machine." Stony said apologetically.

"Well, I haven't made any calls, but I'm sure my sister did. And, she has left for parts unknown. Sorry." Carol Lee then hung up the phone.

Stony stood mulling this information over in his mind. Why would she call me then not say anything? She apparently has not told her sister where she was going. Where was she going? On the other hand, maybe she had already gone.

I am going to bed. I will have to think about this when I have a clearer mind. He traipsed off to bed and some much needed sleep.

Elaine spent the entire next day buying a wardrobe and enjoying every minute of it. For the first time in her life, she did not think too much about the prices or if it was functional. It was difficult trying on certain outfits because of the cast still on her arm. She just bought for the upcoming cruise, so there were only a couple that she had to see if she would be able to maneuver the tops over her arm. Several times through the day the thought would come, she was being far too extravagant. "Please, just enjoy the experience." She told herself, "For the first time in your life don't be so practical and thrifty!" Her attitude gradually changed as the day progressed and even found she was glancing in the men's department. A display model's clothing would catch her eye and a picture of Stony would appear in her mind. "I think he would look good in that." She even said aloud a couple of times. Oh well, this was a day of freedom for her and she felt entitled to let her mind wander where it wanted.

The last purchase of the day was a small set of luggage in which she would carry her new wardrobe. Never in her life had she owned a matching set of suitcases. My, my, she thought, how quickly I have learned. Returning to the hotel with her load of purchases, the door attendant just snapped his fingers and a bellhop appeared seemingly out of thin air.

Elaine never thought twice about accepting his help. She was glad when she gave him a tip big enough that he smiled and said. "Thank you very much, ma'am. Have a nice evening."

She decided to call room service for a light supper, then a hot shower. Afterward, still wrapped with the hotel bathrobe, she picked up the phone and dialed the number that automatically came to her fingers. "Hello?"

Oh, it is not the answering machine. What do I say? She hesitated.

"Hello? Elaine? If this is you, please say something." Stony spoke softly.

Just a second more, she spoke the words that came out naturally. "How are you?" She asked.

She could hear him let out the breath he had been holding. "I'm doing pretty well. They finally released me from the hospital. I drove myself home, rested for one night, and then made the trip to St. Louis. I got back yesterday evening. Now I will be taking it easy for a while. How are you doing?"

Elaine was afraid that he could hear her heart beating through the receiver. She could not believe that she had missed him so much. "I'm feeling fine, thank you. I've had the most wonderful day of shopping that I've ever had in my life." She told him about her time with Carol Lee, and how she had decided that time by herself was probably what she needed right now.

"Yeah, I know what you mean." He told her a little about meeting Jerry's wife and two little girls. "I think that's what I need now, a little time alone in my home to get my mind straight."

"I'm going on a slow cruise to Hawaii." She laughed lightly, "I guess I didn't get enough sun in the desert, so I'm going out for more."

They bantered back and forth until there seemed nothing more to say. There was no indication from either one about what they were actually feeling. They were like teenagers after a first date. Both full of excitement, but lacking the confidence to talk about what might be too personal and thus, revealing.

"I guess I'd better let you get some rest. I know you've got to be tired." Elaine told him in closing.

"Yeah, you too," he said, "I am glad you called while I was home, otherwise I might never have known it was you." He laughed, and then said, "I am sure we will talk again. Bye." Then he was gone.

27

STONY GOT UP the next morning with a boost of energy that he had not felt in ages. He cooked a big breakfast of bacon, eggs, and toast. He cleaned his home and then decided he would take his truck down for servicing. "I might even be up for a game of pool with the old timers in the park."

Elaine had packed after talking to Stony and this morning was excited about getting aboard and beginning the cruise. After the bon voyage party, she soon was enjoying the ocean breeze as it blew her hair lightly from her face. "This is going to be wonderful." She spoke to no one in particular and yet, to everyone on board. Elaine felt as if she had awakened from a long, long sleep. Everything seemed to burst with colors this morning that she had not noticed for many years. This is the first day of the rest of my life, she thought, and I am going to enjoy it this time. She found a lounge chair and sit back to take it all in. You could hear the rumble of the engine turbines vibrating if you listened close enough. The sea birds were gliding effortlessly above the fantail of the ship.

The thoughts soon turned to the conversation she and Stony had last night. I thought there might be some indication of how he actually felt toward me. Maybe I am hoping for something that is not there. There were times in the desert and on the mountain, that she was sure that he had feelings for her, but he had tried so hard to hide them. I suppose it is possible that I just misinterpreted some of the looks and the reactions that I saw in him. The conversation they had held the night before the snakebite, he might not even remember. However, for now, I am going with my gut feelings. There was too much chemistry between us, she thought, I know he felt something too.

She had fully intended to let him know one way or the other that she would welcome his inquiries about their future. However, he had not given her any openings and she had not given any openings to him either. Elaine hoped that after this trip and after she had time to consider all possibilities, she would have an answer.

Stony had been a ball of energy all day, he just could not seem to quit. After cleaning the house, washing the truck, and sprucing up the yard he still was not done. He had made a few phone calls and found painters to paint the interior and exterior of his mobile home. The painters turned out early the next morning and the painting turned out so good, he then decided he needed new carpeting and tile, so off he went to the local carpet store. Who knows, he thought, I might be entertaining one of these days! It took a couple of days but after the carpeting and tile was in, and it looked so nice, Stony decided he might as well go all the way and buy new furniture, new bedroom sets, new living room ensemble, and new dining table, chairs, and hutch. The furniture salesperson had asked what color were his carpeting and drapes so they could pick a color that would compliment "Drapes?" He questioned, "I guess new drapes, new shades and new curtains must be added to the inventory list."

"Damn, if I didn't know better, I'd think I was in the wrong house. This old baby looks pretty good." Stony was especially pleased when he looked in the guest bedroom. The curtains were somewhat frilly for his taste, but he was sure that Elaine would like them. He had become somewhat concerned because he had not heard from her for four days. When he recalled the last phone call, he thought her number should still be on the list of contacts. Making sure of the date and time of the phone call, he immediately pushed send and waited for the ring.

"Sunny Days Hotel, how may I help you?" The desk clerk sounded like she wanted to help.

Stony stammered around, finally asking about a guest of theirs by the name of Elaine Davis. "Is she still there?" He asked, hopefully.

"No sir, I'm sorry but Ms. Davis checked out three days ago for a cruise, to Hawaii, I believe. I understand she will be back in two weeks, sir, would you like to leave a message?" The helpful clerk replied.

"No," Stony said, "That's okay. I'll catch up to her later. Thank you for your time." He hung up the phone. "Damn, I should have told her, I really screwed up this time. I should have told her I think I am in love with her. She will probably meet somebody on this cruise and then she'll never want to hear from me again." He spent the rest of the day moping around like a kid that had crashed his favorite bicycle.

Suddenly it registered that Elaine had told him she would be gone for a while. What had the desk clerk said? Back in two weeks? Maybe she wanted him to know. "Hell, how hard could it be to find out which cruise line she used? Don't they have manifests of their passengers?" Stony picked up the phone and begin calling travel agencies in Phoenix until he found one that knew the schedule of cruises. "I need the name of the ship that left three days ago from Los Angeles."

"Hold on, sir, and I will transfer your call to the cruise line's office located in Los Angeles. They will be able to tell you what you want to know."

"Thank you, thank you, very much." Stony said excited now that he was about to find out how to get to Elaine. Lady luck was being good to him today. The agent that answered the phone was the same one that had helped Elaine book her trip.

"Oh yes, I remember the lady with a cast on her arm, she was in a hurry to leave as soon as she could. Is there a problem, sir?" She asked.

Maybe this is a sign, he thought.

"No, or at least I hope not. I was just a friend, but now I have found that I have fallen in love with that young woman. I think that is why she took off so fast, we haven't really gotten a chance to talk about how we feel. Is there any information that you could give me? I really need to find her." Stony knew they probably would not give him much, but he had to ask.

"Are you the man she was stranded in the desert with?" The agent inquired.

"Yes ma'am, I am. Maybe you've heard it on the news?" He asked.

"No sir, I didn't. She told me about you when she was in the office. I think she might be pleased if you 'found' her. I booked her through to the Hawaii Holiday Shores on a fifteen-day cruise."

"Oh, thank you very much, Ma'am. I shouldn't have any trouble finding her."

"Sir?" The agent spoke just as Stony began to replace the receiver. He pulled it back to his ear. "I can book you into the room next to hers at the Holiday Shores, if you would like. There are two flights leaving that would get you to the islands before her. Would that be acceptable?"

"Absolutely, book me on the first flight that you've got. Wait, when will it be leaving? I'm in Phoenix right now."

"That's not a problem sir, I will book you through the Sky Harbor Airport and your flight will be leaving day after tomorrow at 10:05 a.m. Is that acceptable as well?"

"I can't thank you enough. If everything works out, I will be dropping by your office to thank you personally. Thanks, again."

Stony hung up the phone and was already thinking about how much he should take with him. Just the necessities, for now, he thought, I can pick up some things when I get there. It will be a few days before Elaine's' ship will dock. He would be there long before she arrived. It was his intention to be there and waste no more time, straight to the point. She would either accept him or not, but he had to know. His heart was singing, 'Go get it' it seemed to say, and his head was thinking about the rejection, maybe even embarrassment if she did not have any feelings for him. "All I know is how I feel now that I'm not with her. It might be worth it just to be able to see her one more time." He muttered as he packed his shaving kit.

Elaine had walked over the entire ship, astonished at the size of just the top deck area. It had a wide variety of stores on board, it was like a traveling city. Every kind of service that you could purchase was available somewhere on the ship. She never dreamed that one day she would be doing something like this. Yet here she actually was, on her way to Hawaii! She wondered how different it would be if Stony were here to share these new experiences. She found a lounge chair and lay back imagining her and Stony dancing under the stars, holding hands walking along together on the promenade deck. She saw others as she lay there and they reminded her of a fascinating little dream she had the other night.

In her heart she knew that she had fallen in love with him and she wished now that she had said so, she felt sure that he would be afraid of commitment. It had been so many years since he had been in love with his 'Marilyn'. However, if he had known that she had feelings for him, it might make a difference. The choice would be his to make, acceptance or rejection. 'When I arrive at my room at the hotel, I will call him." She whispered, determined that he would know the truth. "I do not intend to let him get away thinking that I don't want him." Maybe at our age, she thought a little push might be good. He was not getting any younger and neither was she, they did not have time to waste. The plane crash had taught her that much. She turned in early and lay for a while thinking of all the possibilities, and how much their lives could be changed. She could hardly wait to get to the hotel to make that call.

Stony did in fact arrive a day before Elaine at the Holiday Shores, he checked in at the front desk, and then inquired to the dark Polynesian clerk, about Ms. Davis' reservation.

"Yes, sir," answered the clerk, "the ship appears to be on time and should arrive in dock tomorrow around 9:45 a.m. That will put Ms. Davis' check-in at approximately 10:30. The room reservation is for the room next door to yours, sir."

"Thank you for your help, sir. I'm planning a little surprise so if you don't tell her anyone was asking, I would greatly appreciate it."

"Yes, sir, that won't be a problem. The traveling agent with the cruise line has already called and prepared us." He answered smiling broadly with a mouth of snow-white teeth. Stony smiled as well as he turned his bags over to the bellhop and started for his room. After rummaging through his bag, he pulled out the card that the candy-stripper had gotten for him at the hospital. He sat down and finally began to write something in it, he talked to her straight from his heart, not from his head. He sealed it and took it back down to the desk clerk. "Would you see that Ms. Davis gets this when she checks in?"

"Certainly, sir, I'll see she gets it personally." The desk clerk tucked the card into his inside breast pocket as he turned to another guest.

He waited until the clerk returned to him to hand him a list. The list contained several scenarios that Stony would like to stage. He needed all the help he could get.

"Yes, sir. We will see that the director of activities gets this. If he has any questions, he will call you." The clerk assured him.

Stony handed him a twenty. "No turning back, now." Stony smiled and went in search of just the right shop. He wandered through the maze of shops in the hotel, thinking of the possibilities that he and Elaine had in their future, if she would have him.

Finally, finding a jewelry shop, and looking at every item they had in their front windows, he went in the open double doors. Several items caught his eye, but he knew that he would know the 'right one' when he saw it. As he made his way to the last counter, he saw it. It seemed to shout to him, 'here I am, I was made for her' from under the luminous lights. The ring was a traditionally cut emerald ring, the emerald shone brilliantly surrounded with a single row of perfectly cut diamonds. Each diamond sparkled intensely, as the sales clerk took the ring out of the jewelry case and Stony took it in his rough calloused hands. His first thought was how beautiful it would look on Elaine's' dainty feminine hand.

"It would look beautiful on her hand." He said aloud glancing up at the clerk. "I'll take it."

"Don't you want to know the price?" Asked the clerk surprised that he hadn't ask for himself.

"I don't really care what it costs," Stony answered. "It's perfect for her."

The clerk rang up his purchase after putting the ring in a black velvet case with white satin lining. Stony took the ring box and receipt and began to make his way back to his room. It took him a little longer than normal because he kept stopping to open the box and stare at the brilliance of the stones. Even entering the room, he sat on the bed next to the lamp, opening and reopening the ring box. "Damn, I wish she was here now. I can't wait to see her eyes when she opens this box." He muttered repeatedly.

He had been planning since he had hung up the phone after talking to the travel agent. He would check later to see if everything he had asked for, could be accomplished. In the meantime, he needed to make a few changes himself. He wanted a nice sport coat, or maybe he should get a suit. No, he thought, I couldn't do that to Elaine she will be dressed casually, okay, a sport coat it is. Now which one? He entered a men's shop next door to the jewelry store. After trying several coats, pants, and ties, the sales clerk approached him and asked, "Is there anything in particular that I can help you find, sir?"

"Well, yes, now that you mention it. What I would like to find is a white sport coat, black pants and perhaps some patent leather shoes."

The clerk's eyes got big, his eyebrows shot up and before thinking said, "Sir, you are really showing your age." Recovering quickly, he added, "But, I think I might have just what you need. Let me check the inventory. I'll be right back." He disappeared behind the curtain that, presumably led to the stock room, leaving Stony time to reconsider his option. He began again, looking through the racks of clothing.

When the clerk returned, he was smiling, "Sir, you are in luck, look at what I have found for you. A white linen sport coat, charcoal gray gabardine trousers, and black patents. What do you think, sir? Will these be satisfactory?"

"You mean you actually had some back there?" Stony seemed surprised that the clerk had produced exactly what he had envisioned. "Now, I need just the right shirt."

"Yes, sir, I thought you would." The clerk reached behind him and held up a pastel pink shirt with a striped tie that held the exact shade of pink, gray and black. He smiled expectantly at Stony. Stony did not disappoint.

"Those are perfect!" He said with a sparkle in his eye. Already imagining the look Elaine would have when she laid eyes on him. "Let me put them on. I am sure there will be a few alterations."

"Yes sir, let me call our tailor." The clerk was very pleased with himself.

"Can we get those done by this evening?" Stony called after the clerk as he went in search of the tailor.

"Not to worry sir, they will be finished and waiting for you by 6 p.m."

Stony left the men's store and found a small café for a bite to eat. He managed to get around to some of the other stores and made a few small purchases, before going back to his room to wait for the alterations.

He left his room by 5:30 p.m., and approached the front desk first.

The clerk recognized him immediately and asked. "Sir, would you like to check the progress of the arrangements?"

"Yes, I would. Do you have time now?" Stony asked.

"Just a moment sir and I will call the concierge. He will have a key." The clerk dialed his phone and spoke softly into the receiver. The concierge came from across the lobby and asked, "Would you follow me to the room, Mr. Dawson?"

The florist had filled her room with small purple roses. He had chosen a single pastel pink rose for her pillow. He had purchased a bottle of Rose Mateus, the same as they shared in the desert, and had asked the bellhop to attach a cord and hang it on her side of the door that joined their rooms.

Attached to the door was a note.

Open this door very carefully. There is something waiting on the other side that could change your life forever. Please use caution!

"Your hotel staff has performed above and beyond, sir." Stony shook the man's hand vigorously. "I want to make sure they are all rewarded appropriately."

"By all means, sir, would you like the hotel to add the proper amount to your bill? Or, as an alternative, would you rather do it personally?" The concierge inquired.

"I think I would rather do it myself. Thank you, sir. You should be very proud of your employees and their excellent efforts. Now, let us hope that it works like I imagined."

The concierge had reached the door, but turned to say, "I feel sure the lady will be quite impressed, sir."

Stony made the 6 p.m. pick-up time and was very pleased with the results. Boy, I hope this is an omen, he thought as he headed back to his room. Everything is working out almost too well.

28

The ship docked on time the next morning and Elaine waited for the shuttle that would take her to the hotel. She felt right at home on the island in one of her new sundresses. This particular one was white, trimmed in an aqua blue scalloped piping. She wore white sandals and had her blonde hair pulled back into a French braid. While on board, she had taken the luxury of a manicure, a pedicure, and a facial. The services she had provided so many times to her customers. She had thoroughly enjoyed the shampoo and the pleasure of someone working on her hair. She looked into the full-length mirror one more time and decided she would pass the tropical test.

About twenty minutes later, she was checking in at the front desk. The Polynesian desk clerk welcomed her to Hawaii and handed her an envelope from the inside pocket of his vest. She immediately pushed the envelope into the top of her bag.

"You might want to read it in the elevator, ma'am." The clerk spoke to her as she turned to leave.

The bellhop had her bag and she headed for the elevators, finally registering what the clerk had said. What could be so important that she needed to read it before she got to her room, she thought. Besides, I need to make a very important call first.

However, there was a line waiting to board the elevators and she would have to wait a few minutes anyway. She pulled the envelope out of her purse. She glanced back at the front desk and noticed that the employees were all watching her. Turning toward the concierge station, he was looking directly at her as well. She touched her hair thinking it must be windblown, then continued tearing open the envelope. As she pulled out the card, she immediately recognized it from Stony's hospital room. Letting out a small gasp, she began reading. *Elaine, I really don't know how I feel except that everywhere I go, everywhere I look, I picture you beside me.* Tears began rolling down Elaine's cheeks. The concierge was there instantly with a tissue. She looked to him in surprise and wondered why there was a small smile on his face. I am crying here, and he is smiling? Her eyes went instantly back to the card. *I feel like a teenager, so much emotion and yet afraid of driving you away. I have been a lonely man for many years. The kids say I am hard to live with, but maybe together we might prove them wrong? I will be waiting for your answer, please do not make my agony last much longer. Stony*

Elaine shakily tried to place the card back into the envelope, finally giving up she shoved both back into her bag. Her heart was beating wildly as she looked around the lobby. He can't be here, what am I thinking. He does not have a clue where I am. The tears still streaming down her cheeks, frantically looking around, she now sees everyone looking at her. Turning finally to the bellhop she said, "I need to get to my room for some privacy. I can carry the bag myself."

"No ma'am that is why I'm here. Please, let me help you. I know you have one good arm, but this is my job. Believe me; I've seen worse things than a little crying."

"Okay I guess you are right. It's not that big of a deal." Elaine conceded.

"Yes, ma'am, right this way. I wouldn't miss this for the world." He muttered carrying her bag into the elevator. He felt the pocket of his vest, fingering the hundred that Mr. Dawson had given him earlier. If for no other reason than the bill, he wanted this to come off as planned. Elaine noticed that the other passengers had already cleared the lobby. They were on the elevator by themselves.

She was confused as to how Stony could have gotten the card here. How did he even know her hotel? She was not thinking straight at all, glancing at the bellhop she noticed he was smiling like the cat that stole the canary. "Is it a job requirement that you all smile when there is a guest around?" Elaine asked.

"Yes Ma'am." He replied as he led her to her doorway and unlocked it with the passkey. "Would you please stay in the hallway until I check your room and open the doors to your balcony?" He asked politely.

"Yes. Yes, of course. Thank you." Elaine stammered. She had no idea of the services that hotels offered, it seemed feasible that they would want to check and make sure everything was in its place. She stood patiently in the hall as the bellhop flipped on music and she heard the music of Don Ho. She heard the door click and could feel the soft island breeze drifting through the doorway and into the hall.

Fully opening the door, the bellhop stepped into the hall and bowed to her indicating with his arm that she could now enter her sanctuary. This is just like the movies Elaine thought as she turned to the door and stepped into a room full of purple roses. The fragrance was almost overwhelming as she just stood for a moment right inside the door. "This is unbelievable." She said taking in the beauty of the moment.

"Oh," she reached for her purse, "I almost forgot. I need to tip…" However, the bellhop had already disappeared and the door closed. Elaine looked for a card among the flowers but there was none. Surely, the hotel does not do this for every guest. She thought as she turned to survey the full room. Her eyes fell on her pillow and the one single pale pink rose. "Oh, this is stunning." She picked up the rose and placed it to her nose. "Mmm…. like heaven." Elaine started to sit on the edge of the bed when she noticed the floor beneath the adjoining room door. A small piece of red carpet was sticking out about four inches. Then her eyes moved up the door noticing for the first time, the bottle of wine that hung there. "What in the world?" She was mystified as to what was going on. It was then she saw the note attached to the door under the bottle. "Okay, now I'll know exactly what all this is about."

As she neared the door she recognized the wine was Rose Mateus and there was a white ribbon tied to the neck of the bottle. Comprehension dawned on her, but "It can't be. This is impossible. There is no way…." She bent to read the note. *Open this door very carefully. There is something waiting on the other side that could change your life forever. Please use caution!* Elaine grabbed the dead bolt with her good hand and still held the pink rose in the other. She pushed open the door, as it swung open her eyes fell on a little black box tied with another piece of the same white ribbon that was on the wine bottle. On the ribbon was one word 'Elaine'. She removed the box from the ribbon and slowly opened it to find the most gorgeous, brilliant unblemished emerald and diamond ring she had ever laid her eyes on.

Glancing around the room for Stony, all she saw was a path of purple rose petals that led to the balcony door. Quickly stepping into the room, she followed the path of rose petals and slowly pulled open the balcony doors. There he was! He was standing behind a table set for two. At last! He was standing there with his graying red hair, his face actually glowing with sunlight. She could not help thinking how handsome he looked and how vulnerable.

"You look very nice." Elaine said, "Are you expecting someone?"

"Only an angel," he replied softly, "I met her once on a mountain." He slid the chair back and asked Elaine, "Would you care to join me? By the way our glasses are empty, did you bring the drinks?"

Elaine did not say another word and with tears in her eyes, she slowly walked toward Stony placing the pink rose in his lapel. He stepped away from the table and toward her, "God, you look more beautiful than I remembered." They met with a kiss, their lips hungrily searching, their arms wrapped tightly around each other in an embrace that was like two heavenly bodies locking their selves together after colliding in space. The light show was spectacular! The instant passion for each other left them both breathless. This was the moment! They both had lived their lives waiting for this very moment in time. It seemed their very souls had combined. Is this what they meant when they said soul mate? Elaine tried to speak but no sound would come out. Stony seated her at the table and walked back into the room to retrieve the bottle of wine.

When Stony left the balcony, Elaine inhaled deeply to absorb the smell of his cologne. A wonderful light sensual fragrance maybe was what made her light headed. Her body seemed truly to come alive with desire. "Oh my, I should go carefully here. My heart is beating out of my chest."

Stony had stepped from the balcony to put a little space between him and Elaine. He had held her body next to his and suddenly the whole world had vanished. It had been just him and her again, but now her touch had been more powerful than he could have imagined. The softness, the smell of her shampoo and light airy perfume, he had wanted to lift her to him and disappear into her body. "Okay boy, get a grip. Don't do something stupid and blow this."

He appeared back on the balcony with the bottle, opened it and poured two glasses of wine. He sit down at the table and looked at Elaine, she was already looking at him. They sat silently and just absorbed the feelings, each thinking their own thoughts.

Elaine finally asked, "What is that cologne you are wearing?"

"Why?" Stony looked up surprised and asked immediately, "Is it too much?"

"No, it's just right." She smiled at him and said. "It's absolutely perfect, I like it very much."

She laid the little ring box on her napkin and said, "If you want me to have this then I need to know if it's a proposal or a gift."

Stony got up and moved around the table. He reached and opened the box, then going down on one knee; he picked up Elaine's hand and said. "I'm not good with flowery words, but if you will accept this as an engagement ring you would make this old fool a very happy fellow." He hesitated and started to say more, but Elaine gently put her fingers on his mouth and answered.

"Yes, I will accept this ring with the intention of marrying you in the future. After all, we have to prove the kids wrong, don't we?"

Stony slipped the ring onto Elaine's finger. "It's Royal Denmark. I have worn it for many years. I'm glad you like it." Elaine looked at him puzzled for a moment. "The cologne, it's called Royal Denmark."

"It really does suit you quite well." Elaine said as she smiled into his eyes.

"I might add I like yours as well." There began a conversation that lasted for hours. They were full of questions about their lives before they met that fateful day in the desert when he rescued her from the wreckage. First, it began with 'How many children do you have'? Then came questions about marriages, careers, even religion and finally futures were lightly discussed. Opening with their children and grandchildren's dreams and hopes, and then their own perspectives on what they wanted for their life together.

Stony ordered room service and there they sat at the table, eating their meal (neither one could tell you now what they ate) and talking. There was much happy laughter, then seriousness discussions, then laughter again. They tried to consider anything and everything that came to mind and before they stopped long enough to notice anything outside, the sun was beginning to set.

Stony suggested a walk on the beach, "But first let me take off my coat and change my shoes. Do you need to change?" He asked.

"No, I'll be fine. I will just carry my sandals when we get there."

Consequently, off they went holding hands, stopping occasionally to exchange a small embrace and light kisses, still talking as they headed to the sandy shore. Chatting until they were out of sight down the beach. Eventually Elaine noticed it was night and they had been walking in the dark along the waters' edge. She stopped and asked, "What time is it getting to be?"

"Would you believe 3:15 a.m.? When you are lost in conversation how the time flies by. Do you think maybe we ought to get a little sleep tonight?"

They held hands as they turned toward the hotel. They were silent now as they walked side by side, comfortable and content to be in each other's company. Elaine thought I feel like I have known him all my life. She squeezed his hand and arm as she laid her head on his shoulder while they made their way to their rooms. Once inside her room they kissed goodnight, Stony stepped into his room and with a backward glance, smiling, said, "I'll see you later this morning. Don't go anywhere without me."

The adjoining door never closed as both slipped out of their clothes and into their own beds. Stony and Elaine slept that night the most peaceful sleep that either one had experienced in years.

Elaine awoke about 10 a.m. and lay there thinking about what her future would be with this man. There is one thing for sure she thought, I'll never be bored. Finally getting out of bed she brushed out her hair, showered, put on some light makeup and then went in to check on Stony. She noticed that the bed covers were still smooth except where he lay. He must not have moved all night, he still lay flat on his back.

She moved around to the side of the bed and leaned in to kiss his lips. Suddenly his arms were around her, he pulled her down on the bed and said, "Let's make this a shared experience. What do you say?"

Elaine smiled up at him and replied, "I didn't mean to wake you, but since you are, then we both can enjoy the kiss."

Stony leaned up on one his left elbow and with the lightest of touches, he lifted the bathrobe up and away from her breasts. Looking at her naked body, he made a low guttural growl, sounding as if he was in pain. Elaine felt the same desire as his fingers began touching her skin. She looked into his eyes and saw the gaze of love. She had never seen this look before on a man's face, and suddenly she knew.

Just a kiss would not satisfy her body's desire. "Oh, my God," she whispered, "I have never felt feelings like this. Would it be wrong to tell you I want you? No! Not want… I need you. Stony, I need you now."

Stony did not say a word. He simply rolled toward Elaine, kissing her lovingly, lovingly, his hands beginning to explore her body for the very first time.

They both became lost to the outside world, each needing the fulfillment that only the other could give. When they became one there was no self-consciousness, no hesitations, only the feeling of being engulfed with passion and desire that neither had known existed in this world. The next hour was unbelievable. Their bodies with a mind of their own hungered for nothing but total responsiveness to their partner. The height of passion came and went multiple times for Elaine, each orgasm more intense than the last. Stony seemed to know exactly where to touch her body for the maximum response until this pinnacle became almost more than she could bear, realizing the reason was because he was experiencing it the same time as she.

When the final waves of desire subsided and the tremors that shook their world eventually stopped. They lay wrapped in each other's arms so tightly they felt each little shudder.

As they lay together, reliving what had just happened to them. Both realized that love had finally entered their lives once again. After all the years of sadness, loneliness, and sometimes even being close to desperation, both had concluded that true love was impossible. Now it seemed to fill the room. They knew what they had just experienced could never be experienced with anyone else. This cocoon of desire for commitment, honesty, communication, love and passion had been created by and now covered Stony and Elaine and would forever protect them from the outside world.

They lay unashamed and unembarrassed very naked and thoroughly captivated in each until long after noon. Enjoying the silly laughter, the light banter and the playful teasing, they were aware of every moment shared. Elaine slowly sat up on the side of the bed and said wondrously, "This must surely be what they mean when they say 'Heaven on Earth', that's what it feels like, and looking out the window only confirms it."

"I wonder do they get hungry in heaven." Stony asked. "I'm starved. Let's rent a car, and then we can find something to eat. How do you feel about a tour of the island later?"

"That sounds great, I'm hungry myself. But I need to do a little shopping later."

Soon they were on the road to nowhere in particular, until Elaine spotted a swimsuit shop. "Here's where I need go. Do you want to help me pick out a suit?"

"Absolutely, I wouldn't mind watching you model a few swimsuits. Promise me you won't choose one too quickly, okay?" Laughing as they entered the shop, Stony found a seat close to the dressing rooms to rest and enjoy the show. Elaine and the shop clerk went through nearly every suit in the store, but he had no complaints. He smiled as he watched her come out of the dressing eager for his opinion on each suit. "How can I decide?" He pleaded. "You look beautiful in every one of them. You get the one you want, I'm sure I'll like it."

"Okay, I've got just a couple more. It won't take much longer."

Hell, he thought, I could sit here all day. "Take all the time you need."

She stepped behind the door once more and then appeared in <u>the</u> perfect suit. His eyebrows come up and he was nodding his head. "Yes, that's it!" He said before she had a chance to ask what he thought.

The suit was a baby blue one piece that had fish net in a deep V down the front and a very low cut back. Stony was not sure whether it was her eyes that matched the suit or the suit matched her eyes, either way, it was a perfect 10. Elaine could tell by the far away look on his eyes and a smile that went from ear to ear. "I'll take this one." She told the clerk, and then returned to the dressing room to change back to her street clothes. Once she was in the dressing room, Stony paid for and was holding the suit along with another purchase by the front door when she caught up to him. Heading up the coastal highway once again taking in the scenery, Elaine chatted about first one thing and then another.

Spotting a secluded spot where the breakwater mellowed out into a deep lagoon, Stony cut into a cove with a beautiful little beach. His quiet demeanor bothered her; He had not uttered a word since they had left the store.

"Are you okay?" She asked as he shut off the engine.

"Why yes, I'm perfectly fine." He replied.

Stony opened the car door for her then reached in the back seat and pulled out the blanket he had bought and started down to the edge of the water. Finding just the right spot, he spread the blanket and patted a spot indicating for her it sit with him.

Elaine said, "You've been unusually quiet since we left the shop. Anything you want to talk about?"

Never taking his eyes off her, he said, "I want you to know you are the most enchanting woman I've ever been with, you absolutely captivate me and it seems to take no effort on your part. I have never been around anyone like you before, and I am crazy nuts about you. Nevertheless, there is a story to tell, one that may bother you. I am just not sure how you will take it."

Elaine reached over and patted his hand then replied, "I would like very much to hear your story."

Hesitating just a moment, seeming to want to get the words just right, he began to relate a tale he had never told anyone before.

"My crew was flying out of Cam Rahn Bay, Viet Nam. It was February 1969, but the war was still hot and heavy in that area. We were flying way too many hours. The strain of our schedule was stressing all of us out. We were all so tired, very, very tired, performing our duties strictly by memory, because none of us could think straight. No one knew what was really going on in that war. We could not understand what was happening back in the states, the people marching in streets protesting our even being there, upheavals on college campuses, movie stars siding with the Viet Cong. What the hell was happening in our world? To say the least, it was an extremely confusing time.

You know that I loved my wife, she was my life at that time, and she was what I was holding on to trying to make sense of our situation. However, something happened after we landed one night after a 12-hour flight. We had been in the North China Sea patrolling Hinan Island. Our crew had undergone debrief, and then we all just sat outside the barracks on the bunkers having a few beers watching the lightshow that was the F-4s dropping napalm and some phosphorus flares in the valley across the river from us. Finally winding down a bit, we filtered one by one back into the barracks. I had crawled into my bunk, trying to catch some sleep before our next flight." Stony hesitated once again and Elaine almost hurt for him, she knew that whatever he wanted to say was terribly hard for him.

"Since childhood I have never dreamed crazy, wild, make-believe world stuff. It has always been about real things or events. Things that had happened or were about to happen, maybe I would not even remember them until they occurred then I recalled that I had dreamed it." He searched her eyes, making sure she would comprehend what he was about to tell her.

"Go on, it will be fine, I promise." Elaine patted his hand, encouraging him to keep talking.

"I think I had been asleep maybe thirty minutes, when this dream… this experience… maybe it was a vision… call it what you will, occurred. This woman appeared to me. She was wearing a pale blue 'teddy'. I did not know back then what they were called. I had never seen one. You see them all the time now in stores.

She came into my bed and we made love that night unlike

anything I had ever experienced or imagined in my wildest fantasies. I remember everything about her, the shape of her body, her legs, the color and the feel of her skin, her breasts, and every part down to her toes. I can remember the taste of her… her smell… the scent of her lingered with me for days afterward. When I awoke that is the first thing I noticed, her scent was all over me. I was sweating profusely. My bed was wet from our lovemaking. I thought I was losing my mind. I got out of bed and practically ran to the showers, hoping that no one had heard any sound that I might had made while with her. I threw away my underwear, and stood in the shower for what seemed like an hour, trying to clear my head of this…this…whatever it was. Standing in the shower it dawned on me I had never seen her face, every part of her except her face. I could only imagine what the shrinks would make of this so I never told anyone, until now.

I experienced something that I never had before or since then. How could a person have fantasized about something that he didn't even know existed? Hell, I have never even read about anything like it, I sure as hell had not known love like that at the time. I have wondered for years. Why? Why then? Why there? Why me? I have carried it with me all these years, halfway looking for her or someone like her, but I never found her. There were a couple of times when I thought maybe, I was that close to believing it was her. However, something was just not right. It just was not the same.

This morning when you stepped out of that dressing room with that blue swimsuit on, I just about fell off my chair. It was you! I never expected to find her…you… ever. And yet, there you stood and it instantly all came back to me. Do you remember the kiss on the balcony? When I stepped back into the room and away from you? There was something unsettling about your smell, but I had pushed that memory so far back it didn't come then. Seeing you in that baby blue suit, it hit me like a ton of bricks. It was no wonder our lovemaking had seemed so comfortable, so right. We had done it before. At least I had made love to you before.

The reason I was so quiet, I think I understand now why. Maybe God had been showing me a peek into a brighter future than the one I was heading into. That was something I had held on to hoping all this time it might really be true. Maybe happiness would eventually find me. It had been so many years, I had given up thinking it would happen. Now, I think it has. Now that I've found you."

Stony sat calmly, waiting for a response. "You probably think I am nuts, and now you're having second thoughts?"

"No, I don't think you are crazy." Elaine said, "I feel very much honored that you shared that with me. So…I take it you like my swimsuit?" She leaned close and kissed his lips. "I'll remember to keep that color in mind for my future wardrobe."

They both laughed then tenderly Stony kissed her and said, "Hon, you would look good in a burlap bag. I think you are the only woman on the planet for me. It took one hell of a long time to find you!"

Elaine had brought a plastic bag from the hotel knowing she would be swimming later in the day, so Stony taped it over her arm to keep her cast dry. He sat admiring her gliding effortlessly through the blue of the ocean. He recalled the event of the morning and now he began to realize that his dream of so long ago had a purpose after all. Well, some things were worth the waiting, he thought. Remembering all those lonely years, times of passing up a drink with the boys or the weekend fishing trip because he had a school function or homework to check or clothes to wash. It all made him appreciate her even more. In his mind, the crash seemingly caused by higher powers controlling the events of that day, it was destiny. He fully intended to spend the rest of his life in the company of one Elaine Davis. Some day she would be Mrs. Elaine Dawson, if he had anything to say about it.

Returning to their hotel later in the afternoon, Stony's new best friend, the bellhop met them in the parking lot. "It's not good, Mr. D. The reporters have been here all afternoon waiting for a story. If you will follow me, I can get you two up to your rooms through the service elevator."

"Thank you." Stony answered, "We are not quite ready to meet with them yet."

"I took the liberty of ordering dinner in your room tonight at 7:30 sharp. I hope that's not an interference in your plans." He turned to look at Stony for confirmation.

"No, that's very considerate of you and we do appreciate your effort." Stony answered. When he had led them to their rooms, Stony had folded up another hundred and very discreetly pushed it into the bellhop's vest pocket. "Thanks, again."

They had enough time for each to shower and change for dinner, which arrived precisely at 7:30 and served on Stony's balcony. While Elaine was finishing with her makeup, he poured them both a drink of his favorite, dark rum and cola with a twist of lime.

29

As they ate dinner, they both watched the people at play on the grass below them. With their stomachs full and drinks in hand they sit back to take pleasure in the sunset. They discussed the reporters and wondered how long they would try to get a story.

"I think I will try to meet with them." Stony said. "Maybe I can satisfy their curiosity enough for them to leave us alone to enjoy our trip."

"I agree," said Elaine, "If anyone can handle the situation, I believe you can. Do you think I should go with you?"

Stony went into his room, picked up the phone and asked the front desk if there would be any problems arranging a press conference for 9 p.m. "No problem? That is great. Would you please let them know that Elaine, no. Ms. Davis, will be there, but under no circumstances will she be answering any questions." His voice became icy and he repeated his words. "Make sure the reporters understand that. No questions for Ms. Davis."

"Yes sir, we will make sure the press mind their manners while in the hotel. Security will be standing by in case of any breach of etiquette. Will there be anything else you will need, Mr. Dawson?" The desk clerk inquired.

"No! That should take care of the situation." Stony replaced the phone and turned to Elaine, "I hope."

Elaine looked at Stony's jaw muscle twitching and the seriousness of his eyes. "That was very well said, Mr. Dawson."

"We might just as well get this over with." Stony softened a little, but he knew how vicious their questions could be. They entered the lobby at 9 p.m. sharp into a sea of reporters and blinding flashes from the cameras. Stony stepped through the maze of bodies to the dozens of microphones, and then cleared his throat. He told them about the flight and subsequent crash, about how he did not believe they would have made it if it had not been for the ability of the pilot. "He is a hero in mine and Ms. Davis' eyes." Stony was hoping to swing the attention toward the airlines and get them out of the spotlight. When he finished, the questions came hurtling at him all at once. Each reporter was shoving and yelling to get the first answer. Stony held up his hand and said, "Hold it, just a damn minute." The booming voice got everyone's attention. He said, "Now I came out here tonight to give you our story hoping there might be some reciprocation of courtesy. I know you have a job to do. But, if you think, I will stand here and answer stupid ass questions about how the two of us survived a crash. Then how we spent eleven days surviving in a damn desert, so you can go back to where ever it is you go and put some stupid spin on it, or twist our words to fit your story, you are absolutely mistaken. Now, if you are ready to ask real and useful questions, then by all means, proceed."

You could have heard a pin drop in the room, but for the next fifteen minutes, he answered intelligent questions concerning the crash, their survival and the condition of other passengers and the extent of their injuries. Then somewhere in the back a voice asked, "How is it that the two of you end up here, together. You want to tell us exactly what went on up there on that mountain?"

Stony turned to face the direction the question had originated. "Who the hell wants to know?" Stony asked coldly. The group of reporters parted like the Red Sea for the Israelites. The sleaze ball reporter stepped forward to the rope barricade and identified himself as with one of the supermarket tabloids. "Would you care to ask another question?" Stony inquired without emotion. Elaine as well as security stood to one side ready to step in, if necessary.

"I understand you are a Viet Nam vet. It is my guess that you are just trying to grab a little limelight for yourself. So, tell me, Mr. Vet, just what went on between you and your little gal pal on the mountain. Why doesn't the little woman answer her own questions?" He never really got out the word questions. Stony was over the barricade and no one is quite sure if his feet hit the floor before his fist hit the guys' face. They all heard the sound of broken bones, saw the blood fly and heard the thump of the body hitting the floor. Security had started in when they caught Stony's movement. However, not fast enough to stop any of it, which is how quickly it happened.

Elaine yelled for Stony to stop as he bent to pick up the man by his throat. A hush fell over the room. Blood trickled from the man's nose and down over his chin as Stony said, "I have nothing else to say to the likes of you. I suggest you crawl back under the rock you left to come here, or I will forget that we have a lady present. Not a 'gal pal', not 'the little woman'. As for being a 'vet', I served 20 years for this country and I will not tolerate any smart-ass lip service. Do you comprehend what I just said?"

Stony dropped the man in a heap, stood straight and announced that the press conference was over. He somehow managed to step right on the man's fingers as he turned to leave the room.

Security ushered the media out of the room and Stony out to the local law enforcement officers waiting in the lobby, who promptly put him under arrest for assault.

Elaine, along with the concierge, followed the officers in a hotel courtesy van, down to the police station where the hotel paid his bail.

On the way back to the hotel Elaine asked, "Is this the way you always handle yourself in situations where you get angry?"

Stony finally spoke, "No, not normally. I usually just walk away, but when that sleaze bag started his insinuations about us…you, I could not walk away. Maybe it was something I needed to have done a long time ago."

They arrived at the hotel and after thanking the concierge and the hotel for their intervention, they went straight to Stony's room without another word. He took off his shirt, went to the bed, then turned and lay across it.

"Okay, that's it, no more hitting anyone." Elaine said from the doorway between their rooms. "Agreed?" Stony nodded in agreement, rolled over on his side and shortly fell to sleep. She stood watching him for sometime, wondering if he really could control his temper. Nevertheless, at the same time she felt protected, safe and defended. She would never doubt that he would be there for her. Besides, the reporter really did deserve what he got.

She lay down beside Stony and soon was sound asleep herself.

30

ELAINE AWOKE TO the incessant ringing of the phone in her room. Jerking herself out of sleep, she walked into her room and answered. She told the person on the other end to give her a few minutes, and then she would be right down. She thought she had just fallen asleep, but the night had flown by. Still groggy she washed her face, combed her hair and brushed her teeth. Pulling a pair of Capri's and a cotton blouse out of the closet, she changed her clothes. She stepped into her sandals, went to the adjoining door to check on Stony and then slipped quietly out into the hallway. Checking her watch, it had only taken her twenty minutes to get presentable and start to the restaurant.

She spent the better part of the next two hours talking with three people, Mr. Kenneth LeTier, Mr. Drew Raglan and Mr. Anthony 'Tony' Anson, all of them with the MGA Studios from Burbank, California. Mr. LeTier had contacted her when she was in California with Carol Lee. She had not thought anything serious would come of it. She had been surprised when she got their phone call this morning. What they were after was a true-to-life biography combined with a love story. There would be nothing tawdry, just the true story of the crash, their survival and their falling in love. It would be a great Hollywood material, maybe a made-for-television segment. It would be nice if people knew what a wonderful man Stony was. "There will be one stipulation," she said toward the end of the negotiations, "Every bit, every line, the complete screenplay would have to be approved by myself and Stony."

They were all in agreement that would not be a problem. Mr. Raglan told her, "You and Stony will soon receive a contract by courier directly from our attorney's office. I am sure you will want to consult your attorney to handle all the details. When those details are finalized, we will arrange for the two of you to tell your complete story to a screenwriter. That is when production will begin." Mr. Anson asked, "Do you have any further questions?" He handed her his card and said, "If in the future you do find that you need answers, please feel to contact me at this number."

"Thank you all very much." Elaine replied almost overwhelmed with the magnitude of the moment. After the three had walked off, she noticed an envelope on the table with her and Stony's names on it. She opened it and found a fifty thousand dollar check advance with an attached note.

More to come.

She sat holding the check when Mr. LeTier returned to the table and told Elaine, "Please inform Mr. Dawson not to worry about the assault incident. We will make a call before leaving the island. Ms. Davis, thank you for your confidence in our studio. You will not be sorry. You and Stony enjoy the rest of your vacation it is on us. If you have any further trouble with the press, feel free to refer them to Mr. Anson. I assure you, he will take care of the publicity. You should be hearing from us within the month. Now, have a nice day."

Elaine left the table and was on her way back to her room when she noticed a big poster on the travel agency's window. There were two people in a canoe paddling across a tranquil lake. The top caption read 'Visit Belize the Land for Lovers' and on the bottom 'Get Away From It All'. She went inside and after a few minutes, she had returned and was letting herself back into her room. She looked immediately to the bed and knew that somewhere under all that cover was her soul mate. Laughing happily, she jumped in the middle of the pile. Finding Stony, she planted a big kiss on his lips and exclaimed, "Get up big boy. We have many things to do. I have a story to tell you." After explaining what had transpired this morning, she showed Stony the check, thrilled with their good fortune. Stony was not as enthusiastic as Elaine was, but because she was so happy he agreed that maybe somebody out there might be interested in their story.

"Well," Stony said, "I've got a court date coming up you may not be so happy about."

Elaine laughed. "No I don't think so, but you should call and check on it anyway."

Puzzled, Stony called the courthouse and after several transferred calls, the clerk informed him of the dropped charges. He was free to leave the island anytime he desired. He sat completely confused, "What in the hell….Did you have anything to do with this?" He turned toward the door just as Elaine was stepping out of the shower. She bent forward to dry her hair with an extra towel, unaware that he was off the phone. He walked slowly toward her, taking in the clean scent of her body and hair. She stood and he was standing directly in front of her. He reached out and loosened the belt of her robe, pushing it over her shoulders to fall to the floor, he whispered. "If this is a dream, I don't ever want to wake up."

Stony slowly lowered his face to hers and began kissing her softly, then harder, then hungrily. He lifted her gently into his arms and carried her back to his bed. Elaine began unbuttoning his shirt just as he walked, she managed to remove his shirt and toss it casually across the room. He placed her on the edge of the bed and she was instantly up on her knees in front of him. She was unfastening his belt and front snap as he tugged at his slacks. He dropped them, and then stepped out of them. He lay down on the bed, pulling Elaine to his side.

Once again, they were the only ones that existed as the earth trembled and time seemed to stand still. Their desire for each other was like famished bodies, vying for the last morsel of life-giving sustenance. Their hunger to feel, really feel, after all those long empty years. Clawing, groping, clamoring for a hold that would bring them together, and feeling like they truly needed to become 'one'. Driven by the animalistic urges that were now as natural as it must have been in the Garden of Eden with Adam and Eve. Every sense in their bodies was in tune with a rhythm that was basic as life itself, and yet in all their years neither had ever experienced.

They lay spent. Exhausted and entwined in each other's arms from the ultimate orgasmic waves that faded into peace and contentment. They slept deeply wrapped in the embrace until awakened by the ringing telephone. It was the travel agency confirming Elaine's reservation and relating the details of the tour. She hung up the phone and rolled back over to face Stony. He was staring and said, "You have to be the most beautiful woman on this earth." Leaning close, he kissed her lightly on the forehead. Elaine smiled and thought I could probably get real used to this, old boy. She kissed his lips and then each corner of his mouth. She found herself looking in his eyes and trying to remember making love with anyone in the past. It was all but gone, wiped out by her commitment to this man. "There will never be anyone for me except you." Laughing her melodic laugh, she hugged Stony so tight that she could hear his heartbeat.

They rose from the bed and took showers, dressed for dinner in the hotel restaurant. Elaine intended to tell Stony of her reservation plans for Belize over their meal. It would make a wonderful surprise.

Sitting at their table the two had only eyes for each other. They talked leaning close to hear every word. They smiled and laughed with the happiness of finding each other. Silence only came in those moments when their hands touched across the table and they were spellbound in the wonder of it all. Glancing occasionally around at the closer tables, trying to make sure their conversation was not overheard.

Stony said, "I can't imagine life anymore without you." Elaine had never experienced the longing she was feeling tonight. He went on, "I never want to be alone again." Where has he been all my life? This is what love is supposed to feel like. Her head was spinning, her spirit soaring so high she never wanted to come down to earth again. Louder than she intended she blurted, "Stony, I love you!" Every head in the restaurant turned and looked their direction, realizing that she had been heard, her face turned crimson red and she dropped her gaze to the table. Stony saw how embarrassed she was and taking the natural step of protecting her, he stood. Holding his wine glass, he tapped it with a spoon. "Attention! Attention, everyone! I would like to introduce to you my future wife. That is if she will have me. I could use some help convincing her, could I hear an applause if you think she should marry me?"

The room absolutely exploded with applause, men filled the room with catcalls and cheers, and women simply smiled at Elaine and mouthed the words. 'Honey, just say yes'.

Elaine stood and raised her glass toward the man that would soon be her husband. Cheers and the applause continued and well-wishers surrounded the couple. No one seemed surprised that the dining room had suddenly become a party room. Tables pushed together. Champagne chilled in big silver coolers began to fill the room. Musicians had been hustled out of the piano bar to play for the impromptu engagement party.

As everyone paired off and began to dance the night away, Stony could not help thinking about how everything had worked like clockwork. He scanned the room and soon spied the bellhop smiling like the cat that had swallowed the canary, and when he caught

Stony's glance he gave him a thumbs up signal. Making his way across the room, he Stony confirmed his suspicions.

The bellhop explained how the hotel had expected this to happen and the whole staff was to be ready at a moment's notice. Stony tried to hand the boy another bill, but he pushed his hand away, "This one is on me, Mr. D." he replied.

Elaine had slipped up behind them as they talked and she overheard the boy's comment. She grabbed his hand and pulled him to the dance floor. Stony stood admiring the woman that was soon to be his wife, and then turned to thank the whole crew and staff. Couples with prior plans for the evening began filtering out, but Stony did not notice them too much, he only had eyes for Elaine. The party lasted until after midnight, when the staff began to clear the room. Stony and Elaine stood together by the door and getting the staff's attention, "Before we leave we want you all to know that you have made this night unforgettable for us. Thank you from the bottom of our hearts."

After exiting the hotel, they kicked off their shoes and headed down the beach discussing what a memorable night it had been. Silence finally came when both became lost in their own thoughts. They walked on for several minutes enjoying the clean fresh night air. Elaine stopped. Stony took one step, then stopped and turned to her. "What?" He asked.

"I'm ready to open up my heart, my life, my very soul to you. You're not going to hurt me, are you?" She looked directly in his eyes, knowing the answer would reveal itself there.

Stony took Elaine into his arms, kissing her deeply. They both felt the current like electricity pass through their bodies. "I would never, ever hurt you intentionally." He replied. His eyes filled with tears and eventually spilled down his cheeks.

He pulled Elaine closer and she felt the tears on her own face. "Why are you crying?" She whispered.

Stony turned his gaze to the heavens and answered, "I loved

Marilyn so much that I just knew I had had my one chance at love. I never thought I would ever find happiness again after she died." His voice trailed away almost apologetically. "Until I found you! Tonight I give my heart and soul completely to you. There will be no second thoughts, no doubts about our being together, my life is yours."

Elaine knew this admission had been hard for him. She had learned in the desert just how much he had loved his wife. She had gotten her answer straight from his heart. They stood just holding each other until they felt the ocean tide began washing around their feet.

She quietly spoke, "I have a little surprise for you." He did not answer; he was still holding her and enjoying her aroma. "I've found a place that's advertised 'just for lovers'. I felt we qualified for that so I made reservations. I hope you do not mind that I did that without asking you first. Have you ever heard of Belize? It is in South America. They guarantee fun, fresh air, fishing, snorkeling and no disturbance from the outside world. You think you might like that?"

"When can we leave?" He asked. "Can we leave today?"

"As a matter of fact, 2 p.m. this afternoon, is that soon enough?" She laughed that magical laugh that said 'I am happy'.

"You have no idea how long it's been since I've gone fishing. I used to go all the time, I loved it, but I haven't even thought about it for years. Now, I'm the one getting wound up." Stony was almost babbling he was so excited. Before they got back to their rooms, they discussed snorkeling, kayaking, fishing, and swimming. Both making plans for their time in Belize.

31

Bob Farley had just put the final changes on his report to Washington concerning the plane crash. His findings coincided with the two eyewitness accounts. The high-pressure line to the hydraulic reserve had blown off during the emergency descent. The cause was a $28 control valve that had never failed before. With the monsoonal conditions in Arizona that had temporarily blacked out the airport and caused the loss of the central control grid to Phoenix. The chances of this all happening in the same time period were astronomical. The temporary power failure and the seconds it took to get the emergency generators on line to bring the grid up and in full operation had caused the tower to lose track of an aircraft that already had problems.

It had taken most of the last two weeks to finalize the report. He sighed with relief thinking, it is a miracle that we did not have a mid-air collision during this horrific set of circumstances. He closed the folder, leaned back in his chair reflecting back to the little oasis on that mountaintop where two people had managed to survive for eleven days.

Thinking about Stony and Elaine he smiled, "I'll bet those two have been dodging the press and the public since leaving the hospital. And if I know Stony half as well as I think, he won't put up with it very long."

Bob stood from his chair, crossed to the door and flipped off the lights as he left his office. He headed to the cafeteria for a hot cup of coffee and Danish. He saw the newspaper even before he sit down with his coffee and roll. "Oh my! Look here! That's Stony's picture on the front page! What's happened now?" He exclaimed as he made his way to a table so he could read the details. The press had plastered Elaine and Stony's picture of what appeared to be an excellent right cross to somebody's chin by Stony himself. "I figured it wouldn't take long. Good shot, my man!" Bob chuckled, as he viewed the next picture showing the man lying in a heap on the floor. After finishing his third cup of coffee, he headed back to his office. Hawaii…and together… So, that is where they went. He finished the article at his desk making sure there was nothing detrimental concerning the crash or might have an effect on his report to Washington, D.C. There was only the story of a romantic rendezvous, and one reporter that wanted to make it seem iniquitous. Hell, Bob thought, I have wanted to smack a reporter hundreds of times, this old boy actually did it. Somebody should give him an award. Bob laughed aloud as he threw the paper onto his desk. He pictured the scene in his mind, "I'm really beginning to like this guy."

32

THE AIRCRAFT TOUCHED down in Belize without incident and the passengers began to come ashore. A taxi took Stony and Elaine to a resort that was surrounded by little grass bungalows and each with its own golf cart. After checking in, they were met by a dark-skinned black-haired native, speaking fluid English, with an exotic accent and a million dollar smile sitting in an extended cab golf cart. Stony's first thought was that Belize should have this guy on the front of their brochure. He fit the part perfectly.

As the driver unloaded their bags, he handed them the key for their golf cart. He then presented them with a list of planned activities, which they were not required to attend. Then a sheet of resort rentals that was available for their use, everything from golf clubs to water skis. "If there is anything you require, just call the front desk and it will be delivered to you." Stony passed him a healthy tip, thanked him, and then watched while he drove away, smiling and waving.

He turned to Elaine, "I'm not sure we ever left Hawaii."

"Oh, don't be silly, of course we have. The air smells different. I'm going to unpack."

"Don't do that just yet. Let's go for a spin in our limo." They toured the resort grounds, made a quick trip down to the beach and then back to their little grass bungalow. "I just wanted to know where everything was located. Now we can unpack." Winking at her, as if he knew something she did not.

When she had finished unpacking her suitcase, she noticed that Stony was nowhere to be seen. He must be out doing more sightseeing, she thought. I could do with a shower and maybe a little nap while he's gone. Their shower was located outside the bungalow with thatch roofing and three walls, the door facing the bungalow. She was soon standing on a cocoa grass mat enjoying the calls of the exotic birds, feeling the sea breeze on her body wet with the warm light mist that was washing over her. Suddenly she felt something touch her back, thinking there were probably exotic bugs as well as birds, she screamed and whirled around trying to get it off her back. All she could see was a huge bouquet of flowers in the doorway of the shower, but it had Stony's feet under it. He lowered the flowers to peer over the top of them to her face. He was smiling insanely, "What are you so happy about?" She laughed as she leaned to smell all the beautiful flowers.

"Oh…you, this place, that it's Tuesday, the year of our Lord 1987, or you could just face the fact that I am a raving lunatic recently escaped from the asylum and I'm here to do you in." Laughing wildly he jumped into the shower fully dressed. Elaine shouted, "Don't get the flowers wet!" She grabbed the bouquet and ran into the bungalow. He caught up with her, took the flowers and laid them on the bed.

"I think you are absolutely nuts." She laughed. "But I'll be able to tolerate your actions as long as you promise to stay spontaneous, at least for the rest of our lives. I love you."

Stony said, "No, I love you."

Elaine started for the door, "I'm going to finish my shower."

Stony changed into dry clothes then lay down on the bed, waiting for her to finish. In just a few minutes, he was sound asleep with a smile on his face.

When her shower was complete, Elaine came in to find Stony asleep so she sat down at the small table where she could look at him. While in the shower, she had begun thinking about her new life and her past marriage. All the emotions she was experiencing with this man of many faces, she needed time to understand all that was happening to her. He seemed always say the right words for what she needed to hear. He could so easily open the doors that she had held shut all these years. It was almost dreamlike, too good a thing to be true. She was excited and liked the fact that he was sweeping her off her feet, but it scared the hell out of her as well. She knew that this was a complex man and there were many things about his past she had yet to hear. She just prayed that she could handle his past without it becoming something to influence their future together. Elaine hoped that nothing would ever change. She wanted to look forward to the new life she believed she had found.

Later, they met and mingled with the other guests, ate dinner, then quietly slipped away to walk the beach and talk. And talk they did, unaware of the time, they just walked and talked. The moon twinkled on the water of a tiny bay where they finally stopped and sat. Two histories, exposed for the first time. Each talked about what was important to them and then what they thought might be important to the other. It was a night of learning, of sympathy, of comprehension, of compassion, and finally of commitment. They opened up their lives and lay everything out for the other to see. There would be no surprises in their future.

Stony's father had been ill as far back as he could remember, and he worked harder than most kids his age. Chores were finished by the time Dad got home so there would be more time for them to go to the woods, or fishing, or just spend time together. His mother had worked full time and they never got as close as he and his father. He had joined the Navy at age 17 mainly, to get away from home and the mundane life that faced him if he stayed after high school.

He had not been a perfect husband or father. He had been a man, who during the war had thought he would never return home. So he had lived like there was no tomorrow. Elaine learned of the atrocities Stony faced in the war, of the love he had for his wife and his children. His word was his honor, if he said it he meant it. A promise was just that, an oath, not to be taken lightly. She knew him to be considerate, caring and protective. He assessed a situation quickly, made a decision and then followed through totally without fear. What he thought was right, was right, to him.

Stony found the story of Elaine's childhood inexcusable. Her family had been dirt poor and she had struggled with neglect and abuse. She had taught herself about what families should be, about love and the responsibilities that came with it. Life and the world became real to her through literature. He knew from the desert she did not complain, she never gave up, her nature was to put everyone else's needs before her own. She was always thankful for what she had. How many times in the desert had he heard the words 'well, it could be worse, we could have nothing'? Now he knew what that truly meant. She was a private person and mostly kept her thoughts to herself. However, the most wondrous thing was that she had no idea how beautiful she was, not only outwardly but inside as well. He promised himself that he would take care of the woman the rest of his life. He wanted more than anything in this world, for her to be his. He loved her so much right at this moment he felt his chest would explode.

The sun was creeping up over the horizon. They stood and started back to their bungalow, exhausted but not sleepy. Stony's leg had gotten stiff while they sat. He stumbled and fell, pulling Elaine with him. He turned as he fell and caught her in his arms and slowly lowered her to his chest. "I love you. I have for awhile, maybe as far back as the mountaintop." He went on, "I give you my heart, and I'll continue to give you all that I have for as long as I have it to give. I just wanted you to know that." Elaine watched his face and knew she had entered a space in his heart that would forever be hers and hers alone. Sometimes the honesty was too open for her to absorb. She wanted to be open with him as well so she whispered, "I know you do. I am not sure exactly when I realized I loved you, maybe when I thought, I was going to lose you forever. My heart is yours, to do with as you please. I trust you with my very life."

The embrace lasted for a while longer, and then they both began to laugh with a happiness that would be with them forever. Then tears of liberation for the vulnerability of their hearts they knew the other would protect with their love.

Stony and Elaine spent the rest of the week exploring Belize' fishing spots. The sun and sand was doing wonders for Stony's leg and Elaine's arm was getting itchy. A good sign, it was healing nicely. Elaine noticed that Stony was waking up smiling, bouncing around like a young child. The hard lines in his face had faded dramatically and were replaced by a softness that he surely had not had since he was a young man. He was like a man reborn, suddenly alive and enjoying every minute of life. His shadows slowly forgotten as each day passed. The nightmares and night sweats had all but disappeared.

This morning was no different! She awoke to his singing in the shower, off key and quite loud. She lay in bed listening to him, liking very much what she was witnessing. He had placed her on a pedestal and told her he intended to keep her there. She smiled thinking about what he must have been like while his wife was pregnant. I'll bet he was a real pain, worrying about every little thing. Suddenly she understood what a loss her premature death had made in this man's life. He probably worshipped the ground she walked on and suddenly he was thrown into a chaotic world he could not survive. I have only experienced his full attention for a few weeks, I cannot imagine ten years. The love she had only read about in books actually did exist. For the first time in her life, she believed in true love. There was love so intense that it was impossible to live without. She had come to realize the fun of love, letting your hair down and being exactly who you are and knowing there will be no rejection. Being fully aware of the faults the one you love has, but loving them anyway. Not in spite of the faults, but because of them. It was a wonderful feeling.

The door of the bathroom popped open and into the room bounced a crazy man. He had nothing on but a towel around his neck and a big 'S' drawn with lipstick on his chest. "I'm Superman, here to save the day!" It would have made quite a picture, him bouncing round the bed, her laughing hysterically at his antics. How she loved this man!

33

Bob Farley had boarded the plane in D.C., located his seat, and then leaned back trying to absorb what had happened over the past few months. He had received the letter about three weeks ago. Actually an invitation to a wedding in Belize. All expenses paid! A paid vacation in paradise, he could not have been happier.

It was the first time in all his years of crash reconstruction that something good, had come from a tragedy. He was not about to miss the big event. He was a little surprised when Stony had asked him to be best man, but he had great respect for this man. He was glad when they had wanted him to be a part of the ceremony. Bob was especially excited because he could deliver the good news about the anonymous donor to the hospital department that was taking care of Jerry and Jillian Bradford's daughter. The drugs now paid for by the donor made it possible for the girl to receive the very latest and most effective drugs available. The brain tumor was actually shrinking and prognosis was she would survive this ordeal and be perfectly normal. Bob felt that Stony would like to hear this news, since Bob was almost positive that Stony had been that donor. Nevertheless, even if he wasn't, Bob knew he would appreciate the news about Jerry's family.

He recalled how Jillian Bradford had called and thanked him for sending Stony to see her after the rescue. Bob had put two and two together and come up with four. He had not been the one to send Stony to her, but had been very glad to hear that Stony had made that trip. Bob had kept in touch with Jillian and the girls, at first just checking on their wellbeing. However, he now found himself more involved than was necessary for a person in his position. It began with a phone call about the visit from Stony. Then his phone calls to see how she was getting along and was there anything he could do for her and the girls. Next was the phone call about the anonymous donor, did he know who it could possibly be? As the months passed, he found he was looking forward to hearing her voice. He liked being included in the progress of her child. Now he didn't even think about what anyone would say, he would be there if she needed him. They had become phone friends, they were sharing their lives, becoming more involved each time they talked, and he liked it that way. They had never met personally, but he felt he knew her and he welcomed her calls.

He recalled even through Jerry's funeral, she still could brighten the mood, because she had faith. Times were tough for her and the girls, but you would never know it to hear her talk. 'Things are going well, and getting better each day', it made him ashamed when he caught himself complaining about something that had happened in his day. He lay back in his seat and thought about that voice. Hell, he thought, I have never been in love, or married, nor even interested. I figure if it is meant to be, it will be! Bob's life had always been his job, first and foremost, but now his life has taken a turn. The voice on the phone intrigued him and had become something that filled most of his thoughts these days. He had tried a hundred times to picture her as he listened to her words. Maybe he was missing something important in his life. He would keep an open mind, and this old dog might just get lucky.

Bob's plane landed in Miami and he made his way to his departure gate for the last leg of the trip. Bahama and Beyond Air was to board in about 45 minutes, so he slipped into the lounge and ordered an extra dry martini while he waited.

Elaine had spent several hours on the phone tracking down important people in Stony's life. Most would get an invitation with stipulations not to get in touch with Stony, because she was hoping these particular guests would be a surprise for him. While she had been speaking with Bob Farley, he had told her the story about Jillian and the anonymous donor. They both figured it had been Stony. Elaine thought it sounded exactly like something he would do and never tell anyone. She had gotten Jillian's number from Bob, wished him a safe trip to Belize and that she would talk to him when he got there. After saying their goodbyes, Elaine thought about the Jillian situation for a while. She decided, I will call her and let her make the decision. If she was ready to take on a venture like this, Elaine thought she would be able to tell from the tone of her voice, but I do not want her to feel obligated to us in any way. I will just improvise, she thought.

When Jillian answered the phone and discovered who was calling, she was thrilled to hear the news about her and Stony. They talked about the wedding, and then Belize, and naturally the conversation got back to the crash and all that had transpired to them since it happened. Elaine told her a little bit about what it had been like to be in the desert, about how she and Stony had grown to depend on each other. She talked to her about the promise that Stony had made to Jerry before he died. The conversation turned and Elaine began talking about meeting Bob Farley and what a help he had been to them while they were in the hospital. They had managed to stay in touch and considered him a friend. Elaine noticed that when they were talking about Bob, Jillian became almost eager, telling her about Bob also calling her, checking on her and the girls. Jillian even admitted that she actually looked forward to their conversations, and the fact that Bob was so easy to chat with although they had never met officially, she also felt like Bob was her friend.

The two women became lost to the outside world and began chatting like old friends themselves. Elaine did get the impression that Jillian was ready to meet the world again, so she blurted out, "How would you feel about coming to our wedding?"

"Are you serious?" Jillian sounded very excited at the prospect of meeting new people. "Elaine, are you sure? You're not just asking because you feel like…"

"Absolutely not! I am looking forward to meeting you. I think it will be wonderful." Elaine told her.

"Then consider your invitation accepted. I'm already excited about coming." Jillian sounded like she had a huge smile on her face.

"Good, that's great! Now, can I ask you one other question?" Elaine had not even thought about this question until this very second. "Would you consider being my maid of honor?"

"Elaine, I would be pleased to be your maid of honor. Thank you so much for asking."

Elaine finished all the phone calls, and then hurried out of the hotel lobby and back toward the bungalow. She wanted to tell Stony about all her plans. Before she reached the bungalow though, she spotted Stony down by the oceans' edge with a group of locals. They were all gathered around Stony and excitedly pointing to the small cove off to their right. It looked almost like a cluster of schoolchildren, jumping up and down, slapping each other on the back, each talking so loud, trying to be heard above the crowd. Elaine took a seat on the small swing behind the bungalow to watch as the whole group moved to the cove. Stony baited his line and cast toward where the locals were pointing. It only took a few seconds until Stony set the hook on something big and the fight was on. Immediately the locals were yelling and laughing and waving their hands around in the air, she watched as Stony slowly and carefully pulled the big shark up on the beach. She could hear all the ahhhs and ohhhs as they admired the catch and the angler on his 'great' ability. Elaine could not help but smile as she heard Stony tell them, "Divide it up and take it home with you." Stony turned and saw Elaine and he laughed as he packed up his gear and started toward their little 'home'.

As she watched this deeply tanned man walk slowly to her, she was so thankful in her heart that she had found him. His heart was as big as a greyhound bus. She saw the look of contentment on his face. They both had fallen in love with this country called Belize. They had been here long enough to make friends with locals, and had met other couples that had come, stayed, and now called it home. Stony had made the comment that it might be a good place to settle down. They had talked about it themselves, but for now they were both satisfied with just being together.

Stony reached Elaine, kissing her and animatedly explaining the shark incident. "That shark will feed their families for several days."

He is just like a big kid, thought Elaine. He had been swimming, fishing, driving his golf cart around, and enjoying a beer at the corner pub with people that simply enjoyed his company. "I love this place. I have yet to feel like anyone here is trying to get something from me. Just a little conversation, a few tall tales, I have come to love these people very much. Life is so simple here. Did you get all your phone calls completed?" He asked the last question as he reached out his hand to brush a wisp of hair off her face.

"Would you be happy living here?" She asked seriously.

He leaned over, kissed her lightly, and said, "I would be happy living anywhere as long as I'm with you." He fixed his gaze on Elaine's eyes, kissed her again, more deeply as if putting an exclamation point on the statement.

She felt the strength of his kiss and the warmth of his hand on her back and knew she had her answer. All he had to do was touch her and her body senses heightened automatically. Sometimes these feelings would almost sweep her off her feet. I cannot believe I have never had the chance to experience this intimacy before, she thought smiling up at him. She had built such a wall around her emotions, that never had she felt 'out of control'. Not a single look or simply a touch of a hand had ever affected her this way. Until now! I actually desire him to touch me or look at me so I can feel that electricity feeling. It is exhilarating! "Stony, I just want you to be happy. Please think seriously about the possibility of living here. Will you?"

"I have been for a long time." Stony took her hand and led her into their bungalow.

34

Bob looked at his watch and the drink left in his glass. There was enough for one last gulp and down it went. They should be about ready for the boarding call, he thought, so I had better be on my way to the gate. By the time he reached the check in station, there was only a small line. A pass through the final metal detector and he was walking toward the plane's small door. He did not have any trouble finding his seat. This was a small jet, with an even smaller passenger list. After Bob placed his bag in the overhead compartment, he leaned back and relaxed to wait for the take-off.

He absently started watching the boarding passengers, wondering the reasons they were taking this flight. His eyes fell on a very attractive figure dressed in a casual linen traveling suit that hung gracefully from her curves, a green scarf tied loosely around her neck. She was petite, with strawberry blond hair brushed back off her face. Her face was healthy looking with a smattering of freckles across her tiny nose. Her figure was neither hidden nor exposed, but was alluring somehow. He could instantly picture her with a bathing suit, maybe even a bikini standing on the beach with the breeze softly blowing her hair. Oh, good Lord, what is the matter with me? He thought anyone that beautiful is with someone, engaged to someone, or married. He moved his gaze on purpose to others in the aisle. However, the next thing he realized, she was putting her carry-on in the overhead compartment, right next to Bob's bag.

He immediately sat up straight and pulled his long legs in under his seat to make room for the woman to pass. As she stepped around his knees, he got a whiff of her perfume. She smelled as beautiful as she appeared. As she settled into her seat, Bob tried not to stare at her and began shuffling papers in his brief case to keep his hands and eyes busy. Neither had spoken, only a brief nod in greeting, simply acknowledging each other's presence.

She fastened her seat belt and leaned back with her eyes closed. Well, I guess that means she wants no conversation, he thought.

And indeed, that was exactly what she was thinking.

The small jet finally fired up its engines and sat on the runway while the crewmembers were going through their checklists. It finally began to taxi to the backstretch of the runway.

Bob could not help but feel the presence of the woman next to him, her look, her manner was intriguing. He would have to find a way to get her into some kind of conversation. He wanted her to look at him, to feel his presence. He needed to come up with something clever to get her started talking.

Not long into the flight, he heard the flight attendant coming down the aisle with drinks and snacks. Stopping at their row, she asked both of them, if there anything she could get for them. Bob got a bottle of water, and the woman leaned toward Bob and said to the flight attendant, "Could I have a diet drink, please?"

Bob had just opened his water and had taken a sip. He turned to look at the woman and instantly three things happened. The briefcase that had been on his knees began sliding to the floor, the woman reached to grab for it, and the water spewed out of his mouth in a spray hitting her directly in the side of the head. She turned to him in surprised shock, droplets falling from her chin. Bob began immediately to make an apology, "Oh, I am so sorry, please let me help. Here is a napkin, I am so sorry. Please accept my apology." Her face became serious, her eyes began getting big, and she opened her mouth to say something. Nevertheless, Bob, beat her to it, "Is your name Jillian?" He sputtered excitedly, "I recognize your voice. Jillian, is that you? I would know that voice anywhere."

"Why yes, it is. How did you...? Bob...? Bob Farley...? This is incredible, what are the chances...?" She did a little sputtering herself. Both started laughing at the spectacle they were making of themselves. Bob leaned over to retrieve his briefcase, as Jillian reached to pick up her dropped napkin, halfway down their heads bumped together and the laughter began anew.

"Okay, let's start again." Bob stuck out his beefy hand and said, "Hi, yes, I am Bob Farley. I am very pleased to finally meet you, Jillian."

Jillian smiled and her face lit up like a Christmas tree. "Yes, I have wondered if we would ever meet. I too have been looking forward to putting a face to that voice of yours."

The two travelers finished the rest of the flight into Belize talking about what came to mind, just a pleasant exchange. Bob told Jillian about the two survivors. How he had felt something special about Stony and Elaine from the moment he had met them. Jillian told Bob about the phone call from Elaine. How they had become instant friends and had talked for almost an hour. "She even asked me to be her maid of honor. I was so delighted. I can't wait to meet her."

Bob found himself lost as she spoke. In his mind were visions of a future and something other than his job. He knew a relationship with Jillian was out of the question for now. He could not get personally involved with any person connected with an investigation. However, his final report submitted months ago, and as soon as it was accepted by Washington, D.C., then his job principles would not be broken if he and Jillian decided to get to know each other better. He had already made up his mind to keep in touch with her. She seemed to enjoy his company as well.

Jillian was totally enthralled by Bob's attentiveness and comfortable conversation. She thought back several times about Jerry and their dreams together which now seemed so long ago. She knew Jerry would want her to make a happy life for herself and their girls. These past few months had taken a toll, the needs she and the girls had required her to move on with her life. She was certainly glad that Bob was the voice on the phone and was on the plane with her as she started a new life, one without Jerry.

35

WITH THE WEDDING arrangements finalized Elaine suggested to Stony they take a break and ride down to the boat basin.

"That's a good idea," he replied. "Besides, I have something I wanted to show you." When they reached the basin, he parked the golf cart and they walked around the yachts, the deep sea fishing boats, and finally they reached the sailboats. Stony led Elaine to an old wooden sailboat. The body half sanded, the paint flaking off, and the metal helm tarnished from lack of care. The whole boat was in much disrepair. "What do you think?" He asked, smiling, pleased with himself. He stood looking over the old boat with a far away look in his eyes.

"Will it float?" Elaine asked skeptically.

"Sure, it will float. All she needs is a little loving care. Then some new paint, a little spit and polish, she'll be better than new." Stony looked at the old boat with admiration.

She noticed his enthusiasm as he showed off the old hulk. This did not surprise her in the least. It was exactly what she expected from him. He seemed to find beauty and purpose in all things, from the desert cactus, to this old junker, and even in me. She smiled lovingly at him. Both of them had been tired, worn out from life in general, and fed up with trying to make relationships work. Yet, with them it had not been an effort, it had been an awakening. Together they were energetic, life was fresh again, and they could tackle anything they set their minds on.

"It does have possibilities." She said, "What are we going to do with it in Arizona?"

He stepped back a step and looked at her. "I thought you wanted to live here, in Belize."

Elaine stepped up to Stony and took his face into her hands. "I do. Nevertheless, it is only if you do. When I marry you, it is for more than just to love you for the rest of my life. It is a total commitment and that includes where we decide to live. Do you agree?"

"You're right," said Stony as he picked up Elaine and kissed her on the forehead. "I haven't been very forthcoming on future plans, have I?"

"Maybe it's time we sit down and talk. I mean really talk about our future." Elaine said as she led Stony down to rocks piled by the breakwater. "There are several things we need to get straight. We need to be open and honest about money, where we would like to live, and what we plan to live on after we are married. We need to be on the same page when it comes to any and all plans or dealings with our bank accounts."

Stony was blushing and searching for words, when Elaine placed her fingertips over his lips. "I know that you probably were the anonymous donor for Jillian and her girls. I understand you feeling sorry for their situation and wanting to help with the medical bills. I also know that you have paid for each of the airline tickets for the guests coming to our wedding. Lord knows what else you have paid that I don't know about. That airline settlement will not last forever. Is there anything I need to know?"

Stony listening closely, realized that from now on his decisions would certainly affect not only him but also his bride to be. "I'm so sorry," he spoke softly, "I guess I've been so used to making my own decisions, I never thought about how this might affect you or rather us." His voice trailed off and he looked up at her with such a hangdog look she almost laughed.

She took his face and tenderly kissed him. "Listen, I do not care if you spend every penny. You should spend it on whatever you desire, but I would like to be included in that decision or at least be aware that you are taking into consideration a big purchase. I certainly intend on letting you know of any decision that I am thinking about making, money or anything else. Are you okay with that? Do you think that is asking too much from husband and wife?"

"I had the money and I just wanted to do something good with it, I have never been able to help out as much as I can now." He said, "And you are quite right. As my wife, you should be there when I make every decision. I have just been by myself way too long. I never intended to exclude you in anything. I promise I will always consider us, not just me ever again. I love you and I trust you, I simply was not thinking."

Elaine looked at this teddy bear of a man and was thrilled that he would soon be her husband. "Well, you will be happy to know that the money has allowed the doctors to get an experimental drug and it has been a total success. The little girls' brain tumor is shrinking and the doctors expect her to lead a long and happy life."

"That's wonderful, I did the right thing. I am sure Jerry is watching and understands why I did what I did." Stony's face was radiant with the pleasure of what his money had been able to accomplish.

"Well done, sailor." She was happy for him. She hugged him tight, and said, "I love you very, very much."

Stony took Elaine's hand and led her back past the boat basin, over a small sandy patch of ground, through a little plot of jungle land and into a clearing where a pink and white cottage rested peacefully in front of a private lagoon. Elaine stopped in her tracks and stared at the picturesque scene.

"That is the prettiest little place I've seen since we've been here. Does this belong to one of your local buddies?" She asked. "Do you think they would consider selling it?"

"Oh no, I am quite sure the owner has no intention of selling this property." He answered.

She was absolutely breathless with the beauty of the place. "You can hear the birds of the jungle. The pink and white house positioned by the blue pool, it looks exactly like something you would see on a post card. You would not know anyone was around for miles. Are you sure they won't sell?"

"I am pretty sure, but you can ask if you want." He turned to her and held out his hand. She automatically reached for his hand and her fingers closed around a key chain that held two keys. "It belongs to us. Do you want to sell it?"

Her eyes filled with tears, "Stony this is the most dazzling place on earth I've ever seen. It's really ours?" She held on to Stony's arm as they approached the cottage.

"It may be a little secluded, but there are some locals I wouldn't mind having over once in a while." He said looking over the grounds.

"Stony, I am shocked." She was laughing. "I remember distinctly that someone once told me, in the desert, that they weren't the neighborly type. Who could that have been?"

"I know. There are a few more things I want you to see. Come on." He took her hand again and guided her down the small slope toward the gated drive. Two pillars chiseled out of coral now held an arched sign over the driveway. "Shut your eyes." He told her as they neared the drive. He stopped, and then said, "Okay, you can look now." Elaine opened her eyes and read.

THE PROMISE LAND

"I probably should have checked with you first about the name?"

"No, I think it's perfect. I wouldn't change a thing." She answered quietly.

They spent the afternoon walking around their new home and Elaine did not take long to start telling Stony how she would like to decorate their home. She had never experienced such a happy state as this. "This is like a fairytale." She turned to him and finished her thought. "And I have my Prince Charming and now my castle too."

On the way back to the bungalow, they walked hand in hand along the boat basin. "What are you going to name your boat?" Elaine asked.

"What boat? Stony stammered.

"That boat." She pointed to the old wooden sailboat Stony had shown her earlier.

"I thought that if I bought her, you might come up with a name for her."

"You mean you haven't bought it yet?" Elaine asked.

"I wasn't sure if you would like her or not. But I was considering it." He said.

They arrived back at the bungalow where they showered, dressed for dinner, and then drove the golf cart to the restaurant. Once at their table, they began to discuss their finances. The conversation included future plans, incomes, houses, children and their in-laws. They decided to keep the trailer in Arizona. When they made trips back to the U.S. that would be their home base. Who knew how long they would stay in Belize? Stony received a retirement check from his military service. Elaine had an annuity that she had set up years ago when she was self-employed. They exchanged information about the settlements they had received from the airline. How much had already been spent, what they had remaining and in what accounts the money was invested. They worked out a budget and by the end of the evening; they were both comfortable and fully informed about their financial situation. They agreed that major investments or interests that might involve large sums of money be discussed together.

When they stepped out into the night air, they decided it would be the perfect end for the evening to take a stroll down the beach. With their shoes in hand, they started down the shore.

36

Bob and Jillian had checked into the hotel and each escorted to their rooms. Two of Stony's flight crewmembers, Alex Anderson and Jack Howard-Scott, had arrived earlier and had taken over a table in the hotel bar. It did not take but a few drinks before they began reminiscing about the 'good old days' in the Navy. Some of the other guests had been in the military and just naturally gravitated to the table with old war stories of their own. The hotel staff had pushed all available tables together because the crowd was growing larger as the evening wore on. Everyone in the bar seemed to enjoy the camaraderie between all the service people. Carol Lee's first husband had been in the Air Force and the experience had not endeared her to military personnel. She was not listening to the stories as much as watching the crowd. The taller one of the two friends of Stony was attractive to her. She stood and walked to the duo and introduced herself as the bride's sister. She was an instant celebrity. The two pulled out an extra chair, and then hoisted their glasses for a toast to the bride's sister.

"Carol Lee, my name is Carol Lee." She laughed and felt a little special when the taller one looked at her and said.

"Hell, no wonder Stony's getting married again, if she looks like you. Glad to meet you, Carol Lee, my name is Jack Howard-Scott." He then asked if she would like a drink.

The complimentary comment made Carol Lee's whole day, she found herself enjoying being with the two rowdy men. Drinks passed from hand to hand, the bar was almost full. The party had begun.

Bob arrived in the bar and was right away absorbed into the crowd. Jillian arrived a few minutes later, stood back and observed for a moment the happiness of this moment. Bob appeared at her side, and then they both disappeared into the mass of well-wishers. When Stony and Elaine walked into the lounge, cheers and whistles went through the crowd as everyone there turned to greet the happy couple. The bar was full with what looked to be everyone in the hotel, all of the staff, a few locals, and friends and family. It was a night that most would never forget. Stony and Elaine tried to make it around the room and talk with everyone. There was laughter, tears, hugs and pats on the back, and many, many shared stories from each one about a particular incident in their history.

The headwaiter rang the bar bell to get everyone's attention. "Dinner will be served on the hotel veranda in precisely 15 minutes. Everyone, please find your places at the tables, there should be no one standing when the staff arrive with the trays. Thank you all and enjoy your dinner." The schedule was to be dinner and then dancing until the party broke up. The hotel had made a Belize tradition, a pig roast and barbeque with all the trimmings, and an all-you-could-drink bar.

The pre-wedding party was a great success and before anyone knew it, the time was well past midnight. Jillian approached Elaine and asked permission to dance with Stony.

Elaine pushed Stony gently toward Jillian and told him, 'You need to dance with the maid-of-honor at least once before the night is over. And while you're doing that I may dance with the best man."

Stony led Jillian to the dance floor and thanked her for coming.

"I will never be able to thank you for all you have done for my family. I will forever be in your debt for giving the doctors a chance on a procedure that we would never have been able to afford." Jillian told him.

"You owe me nothing. I did what my heart told me to do and a simple thank you will suffice. You and the girls can consider our place your home away from home, you may visit anytime, and you are always welcome here." Stony said.

"Thank you again," Jillian said as tears filled her eyes. "I am happy for you and Elaine. I think I am going to turn in for the night. I'll see you in the morning." She kissed Stony on the cheek and then left for her room. Stony watched her as she left, that is one classy woman, he thought. It does not surprise me that she and Elaine have become fast friends. They are so much alike.

He turned to walk to the bar for another drink and almost ran over Bob Farley. He stood watching her leave as well. "She is one fine lady." Bob said, watching until she was no longer in sight. Stony agreed, and he and Bob strolled out on the veranda with their drinks and eventually down toward the beach.

Elaine watched as they strolled away, lost in conversation. She was listening to Alex and Jack as they talked about the exploits Stony and his crewmembers had lived through. She noticed Carol Lee was hanging on every word. The two covered every wild and crazy thing that had happened in Viet Nam and the countless flights they had taken together. It was no wonder they seemed more like brothers than just friends. They filled in some of the gaps from the stories Elaine had heard from Stony and managed to entertain the crowd in the process.

Bob and Stony spent the next hour talking about everything from the crash to Stony and Elaine's romance. Bob told Stony about his and Jillian's lengthy phone calls. Stony laughed and said, "Damn, Bob, it sounds to me like you found a lady for your own sorry life."

"Maybe…maybe I have at that!" Bob replied as he joined in laughing too.

37

Early the next morning, Elaine and Jillian left to do some shopping. Stony and Bob met for a late breakfast and many cups of coffee, trying to untangle the cobwebs from the previous night's activities. Bob was sipping on his coffee, looked at Stony, and asked. "What do you want me to wear for the ceremony tonight?"

"Bob! We have to go shopping ourselves! I don't have a wedding ring! I forgot the damn wedding band. Come on, let's go!" Stony yelled as he headed out the door of the restaurant. Just before reaching the parking lot and a rental car, Stony told Bob. "Anything you brought with you will be fine. The whole ceremony is tropic casual. So, come comfortable."

"Good, I think I can handle that." Bob replied as he got in and closed the car door.

Stony knew where the jewelry store was, it took only 10 minutes to get there. He and Elaine had window shopped here many times. For some reason, he never thought about buying bands for their marriage ceremony. Bob began looking in the first counter he came too. "What exactly are you looking for? Do you know?"

"I have a pretty good idea, something with diamonds and emeralds. Did you happen to notice her ring last night?" Stony had started looking in the opposite counter. Meeting in the middle, they came together at the diamond and emerald display case.

"Well, this shouldn't take long." Bob quipped, "There are only about 500 rings in there."

The clerk took out two matching bands, smiled and placed them side by side on the counter top. It did not take Stony long before his eyes fell on the rings. "Here we go." He said, "These look like the sides of Elaine's ring. What do you think, Bob? Look, the diamonds and emeralds alternate across the top. Let's see…one…two…three. Yes, there are six stones. It will fit her ring exactly." He laid the rings on top of the counter and told the clerk, "I'll take these two."

"Yes sir. I'm sure the bride will be very pleased with your choice." The clerk placed the rings in their respective boxes, then into a bag and handed the purchase to Stony.

"Damn," Bob said thinking aloud, "is getting married always this exciting? On the other hand, is this hectic? Which is this, hectic? Or exciting? Whichever, I am not sure I can handle getting married. My life gets pretty hectic and exciting on its own."

"Sounds to me like you've already made up your mind, Bob." Stony answered with a knowing smile on his face. "That's if Jillian would even have the likes of you."

"Oh, you think not? Well, time will tell. I'm kind of hoping she might find something redeemable in me." Bob was still looking over the rings in the display case. "Some of those are really pretty. I wonder what kind she would like."

That 'business only' person that Stony and Elaine was so grateful to looked almost like a kid in a candy store. Stony could not help but hope that things did work out with him and Jillian. He thought they would make a good match. Nevertheless, if not Jillian, then some other woman would get a good man.

Elaine and Jillian completed their selection of accessories for the wedding, and were just stopping for a late lunch. They were surprisingly comfortable with each other, their friendship growing with each passing hour. Jillian had asked some questions about her and Stony's romance. She told Elaine even more of her feelings about Bob and the calls they had exchanged. "I just feel very at ease with him. We have never really discussed anything that would make me think he would even be interested in anything romantic. I must sound like I'm crazy. Tell me the truth. Do you think it is too soon, Elaine?"

"Do you think it is too soon?" Elaine asked.

"I did worry about that when I started looking forward to his calls. Nevertheless, I always feel so much better after I talk with him. He seems to steady me somehow."

Elaine could tell that Jillian was really struggling with her decision. "Jillian, how long has it been since Jerry's death?"

Jillian answered, "Almost a year, eleven months next week."

Elaine was surprised that it had been that long. She and Stony had been in Belize almost eleven months! "Well, I'm not going to tell you yes or no, I'll just tell you a little story. You make up your own mind. Okay?" Jillian shook her head in reply.

"Once upon a time, two unhappy, lost and very lonely people were on an airplane. They were just taking a trip to get on with their individual lives. Never considering for one minute the possibility there could be happiness for them in this world. Then a terrible horrifying thing happened, the plane they were on, crashed in the Arizona desert. They were the only two people to survive. However, because of this terrible occurrence, they found each other." Elaine stopped for a moment and let Jillian comprehend her story. "Does any of this sound familiar? Jillian, no one is guaranteed a tomorrow. And just because a tragic incident happens in your life, it does not mean your life is over. It might be that it's just beginning, anew."

Jillian and Elaine sat with tears in their eyes, knowing they were beginning a new life, together as friends, and separately as individuals, both suddenly grateful for having found the other. "How can I ever thank you? Losing Jerry was the worst thing that ever happened to me, but you are right. I found Bob, you, and Stony. I can go on with my life knowing I am not really ever alone. Thank you so much, I am truly grateful for your friendship."

"Jillian, I don't think there is a right or wrong answer. Just be honest with yourself and those around you. If it is meant to be, you will be the first to know." Elaine finished with, "We had better get going, and maybe we can get in a short nap before the festivities."

After getting back to the bungalow, Elaine brushed out her hair, took a shower then lay down across the bed. Her mind began to drift back to the day of the flight to Phoenix and she remembered the first time she saw Stony. It was still as vivid as when it happened. She wondered why of all the men in the airport in St. Louis she noticed him. Could that have been a premonition? She had asked herself and Stony a hundred times, why were they the only two to survive that horrible crash? She remembered the dream that Stony had in Viet Nam. How he had searched for that person all those years, only to find them because of a devastating situation. Maybe Stony was right, maybe it was Divine Intervention.

She had never been one to depend on anyone else, maybe that situation taught her there were people out there she could believe in and trust. Stony had known love in his life and lost it. She had never experienced love like she and Stony shared. They were individuals, but still they felt combined as of one mind.

Stony had been in the American Dream. Happily married to his high school sweetheart, had children, a home, and a good job with the military, defending his country with his life. If anyone deserved to be where he was, it was he. Then he lost it all, all those things a man needs to make his life worth it. He had been too young, seen atrocities first hand that no one should ever have to see. Too much of life, too tough, too fast, it had made him age well beyond his years. Maybe he had needed those years in between just to catch up. Underneath that rough exterior was compassion, and tenderness, thoughtfulness not often seen in men anymore. She thought about the bravery, his friends had talked about last night. He did not seem to think about what to do he just did it. In addition, when it was all over, it had been the perfect thing to do. That is why they had survived, he did not think about the souls that were lost and the destruction, he knew they would have to survive on their own and so he set about doing it. The same way he had survived that stupid war.

The story she had told Jillian had been in the back of her mind for a long time now. Sometimes life is presented to you under less than ideal circumstances, but if you just take that chance, you find more happiness than you ever thought possible. Letting go of the past had been the easiest thing she had ever done. She did not have peers anymore she had friends. People she could trust and that could be counted on without question. She and Stony had fallen in love with the people of Belize, she laughed aloud as she remembered Stony catching that shark and the young locals patting his back and thanking him for the fish. She would never forget the look in his eye as he showed her that old half-dead sailboat. He was at times like an innocent child, a man-child with whom she would spend the rest of her life.

Elaine did not fool herself into thinking this life they would share would be always fair winds and following seas. She had seen him when his wall of protection surrounded him. She had seen his short fused anger. There would be challenges they both must face with their new beginning.

This was the happiest day of her life. Her wedding day! There would be no doubt in her mind as she walked down the aisle. This was truly the first day of the rest of their lives and she would make sure they would take advantage of every single minute.

38

Tony spent his afternoon sitting by himself above the little house he had bought for Elaine and him. Bob had left him earlier to get some rest before tonight. So he had taken a walk to their new home. He lay back on the grassy incline behind the little house and watched the clouds drift across the sky. The sparkle of the ocean caught his eye as he listened to the boisterous banter of the native parrots in the border of the jungle.

Suddenly his mind filled with the image of a woman standing in the edge of a desert oasis pool. He remembered the firelight flickering on her body from her shoulders to the calves of her legs. It was such a powerful image. He would probably never forget it. He had admired Elaine's body then he turned back into the darkness so she would not find him looking at her. He had tried to remember his late wife, Marilyn. He tried to picture her, he had seen her naked hundreds of times, but he could not bring her likeness back. How she used to look, how they were together, what she smelled like, her smile, and her face.

It would almost appear, but then melt away into nothingness. Since that night he had tried to get her image back in his mind, he had never accomplished it, until today. He had closed his eyes and he could see her face as plain as day. She was smiling, she was happy. She had no doubt that she had been the love of his life then. The loneliness had never left him, those memories that he would not let go, they were what sustained his life all these years. He had loved her for eighteen years after her death, now he could not remember the details that had stayed with him for so long. Nothing… Since that desert night, when he come back to camp and saw Elaine.

Stony began to sob, "Pris, if you are listening, I hope you understand. I have been lonely a hell of a long time, probably longer that I should. I will always have the love I had for you in my heart, but now my heart has made room for another love. It is different from our young love, more like what we might have grown into, but never got the chance. I should have realized when you died how short life can be. It is time to get on with life and live for me now. She has filled the void in my life but I surely do want to feel your blessing in this. I will be checking back with you from time to time. Elaine makes my heart pump with love and excitement. I am going to make her my wife tonight!"

Stony wiped the tears from his eyes, took one last glance toward his new home and then headed back to where he would begin his new life.

He had not gone far when he noticed a sea duck flapping wildly at the edge of the shoreline. It had entangled itself in a fishing line left on the sandy beach. As he walked to the duck, he slowly stooped down and gently picked it up. He learned years before to avoid the serrated beak of any sea bird. Most had a toothy edge that would cut and tear if they got a hold. Stony held the duck loosely in one hand as he unwound the line from its wing, then its leg. After checking for other injuries, he held the bird for a minute thinking it would realize it was free and fly away.

However, the little duck was very relaxed in his hands. He stroked the head and neck of the small bird admiring its beauty. He expected it to take flight at any moment. Finally, he said, "My, my, you are quite pretty, little girl." He still petted her head gently and noticed that she closed her eyes when he stroked her. "Listen, little girl, I do not have much time and you need to be about doing those ducky things you do. So, off you go." He tossed her into the air. The duck flew off down the beach and then out over the boat basin, and then circled back and flew directly over Stony's head. He turned and watched as she flew off in the direction of the setting sun.

A chill came over Stony. It dawned on him this might be a sign from Marilyn. He was free as well to fly into his new life. He closed his eyes again and he could feel her happiness for him, she seemed to say, 'It's okay. I loved you and you loved me, now go on with your life. Be happy with Elaine, she will be good for you. Your life together will be a good life'.

The peace that passed through his body was a physical release. There was no dishonor for Marilyn in his love for Elaine!

Call it the Indian blood that flowed in his veins, but he had learned that animals do communicate with you and they could speak volumes if you paid attention. Stony spoke humbly, "Thank you for allowing me to turn you loose. He was still watching the little spot as it disappeared into the horizon.

He smiled, happy and finally at peace with the past. He was ready to begin his new life and welcome all that would come. Glancing at his watch, he had less than two hours to go.

The entire hotel had turned out for the wedding festivities. Stony and Bob stood at the backdrop of white linen. Tropical flowers surrounded the whole room, brightly colored ribbons hung in a swag on each chair at the end of the rows of seats. When they both turned around to face the crowd, Bob whispered, "Wow, the staff did a beautiful job, looks like someone's getting married here." He glanced at Stony. However, Stony's eyes were fixed on the back of the room.

The music began and Jillian had started down the aisle. She

seemed to float in a pale sea foam green gown layered with rows of eyelet cotton lace from the waist down to the floor. The top had one row of eyelet lace on an elastic ruffled neckline pulled down over her pale shoulders. A single gold choker chain on which hung a simple heart locket encircled her neck. She looked very much the part of a peasant girl on the way to market to sell her wares. It was typical of what the locals wore every market day. The bouquet she carried looked to have one of every flower that grew in the tropics, tied with a ribbon that matched her dress perfectly. Bob was smiling from ear to ear and Stony let out a low whistle. "I hope it works between you two," said Stony, "you are a lucky son of a gun to have found her." Jillian smiled up at both Stony and Bob as she took her place to the left side of the stage. All three turned to look down the aisle toward the back of the room.

Elaine stepped into view. Her gown was a shade or two darker than Jillian's, but was simplicity itself. Her hair piled in curls on top of her head, and cascaded over the back of her pearl and tiny seashell encrusted headband. One lone teardrop pearl hung from the headband exactly in the middle of her forehead. Her strapless silk gown draped her body like a second skin and trailed her with a two-foot long train. She looked exactly what you would picture a mermaid to be if she grew legs. The bouquet she carried was white gardenias and rainbow colored scallop shells tied with a single white ribbon that hung almost to the ground.

She was a truly astonishing beauty. Stony could hardly breath.

Stony was smiling from ear to ear and Bob let out a low whistle. All heads turned and audible gasps were heard throughout the room.

As she approached the step she must make to the stage, Stony took a step down, held out his hand and steadied her as she stepped to his side. Their eyes met and to every eye in the audience that witnessed the event, tears brimmed with the happiness that filled the room.

The minister took over the service, they exchanged the 'I wills' of love, honor and obey. The minister asked if there were rings to be exchanged also. Stony turned to Bob who was gazing at Jillian. The minister asked a second time, and then Stony elbowed Bob, who said. "Yes… yes, sir, there is." He fumbled in his pocket to retrieve first one band and then the other. Looking sheepishly at the minister and then to Jillian, who was almost as embarrassed as he was. Bob could only smile.

Elaine glanced to Stony, they both knew what was about to happen in the future of Jillian and Bob. In conclusion, they got through the ring exchange and the finalizing I Do's, and the minister presented to the audience, Mr. and Mrs. Stony Dawson.

They must have shaken more hands and hugged more people than a presidential candidate on the campaign trail. Stony and Elaine, Bob and Jillian posed for what seemed hundreds of pictures. The band played and as the guests passed through the reception line, they immediately made their way to the dance floor. Bob and Jillian stayed right by Stony and Elaine's side through the hugs, handshakes, and the pictures. Stony finally told them, "You guys have suffered long enough, go and enjoy yourselves. Drink, dance, and be happy."

Bob and Jillian gave their own congratulations to Stony and Elaine and then slowly made their way to the dance floor. The champagne flowed freely from small fountains located throughout the room, Stony and Elaine each took a glass of the bubbly and stood for a minute watching the crowd. Bob and Jillian were talking a mile a minute as they danced. Carol Lee was cheek to cheek with Jack Howard-Scott. It appeared there were only couples in the room and romance was in the air.

The newlyweds were able to slip off to their cabana set on the beach. There was no one around, just the two of them alone with the moon and its reflection on the ocean waves. They made love, they talked love, and love existed with these two as only among those who truly adored each other. The heavens seemed to open and the earth to shake as they consummated their commitment to the other for the rest of their lives. Their commitment would only grow from this night on. They drifted off to sleep in each other's arms, listening to the rhythm of the waves.

Along with the morning, the sounds of the world brought them back to consciousness. Stony opened his eyes and kissed Elaine on the forehead, breathing in her aroma. "Good morning, Mrs. Dawson." He whispered. Elaine snuggled even closer together, so close that the sweat from their bodies mingled together. She took a deep breath and said. "Oh, How I love your smell." She realized she had spoken aloud and chuckled softly, "Good morning to you, Mr. Dawson." She said, "How are you feeling this fine day?"

Stony kissed her deeply and sighed, "I feel like I am on a cloud, drifting through a beautiful and peaceful world, with an angel at my side."

"Happy?" She asked.

"More than I have ever been in my life, I do believe. Why would you ask?" Stony questioned her.

"You just seemed different and so new last night. I felt as though you were entirely mine. Just you, totally here with just me, I liked it! A lot!

"Yes, I've put an end to all the demons of my past. Well, maybe not all, but those that kept me chained. This is a new day, a new life, and I couldn't be more excited. I am yours baby, hook, line, and sinker, for the rest of my life. It is too late to back out now." Stony teased.

Elaine smiled, kissed him on the tip of his nose then bounded out of bed. "Let's just make sure it stays that way, buster!" Finding their swimsuits and towels folded on a stool by the flap of the cabana, she stopped and immediately began putting on her suit. She tossed his to the bed and yelled. "Last one in is a rotten egg!" She whirled and ran out of the cabana straight to the ocean's edge.

For the first time in her life, she possessed a confidence in love and in her lover that made her giddy with exhilaration. "He loves me! I love him! Life is beautiful, exciting, and I will not miss a minute of it!" She turned to see him right behind her just pulling up his swimsuit. He slipped his arms around her, pulled her to him, "I want to feel you." He was gasping for air, he had run so fast to catch up to her. "I want your warmth next to me always. I don't want to ever stop feeling again." He squeezed her tighter, laying his head on her shoulder, "Don't ever let go of me."

The coolness of the water rushed in around them as they parted, "You can believe me, you do not have to worry about that. It took me too long to find you, I will never let go, in fact, I'll probably smother you." Elaine laughed.

Stony buried his face between her breasts and laughed, "Smother away, baby. Smother away."

They walked to the shallower water and sat with their lower bodies submerged. The rhythm of the waves pushed then pulled their bodies under the surface. Stony lay back on his elbow and told Elaine, "This is probably the most relaxed I've been since I was a child."

"Yes, I know what you mean. There is something about being outdoors and away from crowds of people." Turning to look toward the sound of voices, she said. "Speaking of crowds, it seems our time in the cabana has run out. They are taking it down. Come on, let's get our stuff out of there and then we can head back to the bungalow."

They packed their belongings into the decorated golf cart, making sure they did not disturb the "Just Married' sign. "What do you think? Should we take the tin cans off now or later?" Elaine asked.

"Hell no, let them have their fun. We will just join in, too." He replied, climbing behind the wheel.

Everywhere they went in the settlement around the resort, they heard whistles and cheers. They had to stop often to shake hands, get hugs, and then applauded as they drove on. Even the small children were tossing flowers at them. "I'm glad we got married here, these have to be the nicest, most sincere people left on earth." Stony commented as they drove on waving to all they could see.

The locals were enjoying their marriage, and so were they. Elaine laughed until she cried knowing these people were sincerely welcoming them into the family. It took them over two hours to make it around to their bungalow.

39

A FEW DAYS BEFORE the wedding, Elaine had bought furniture and asked that it be delivered today. Not knowing exactly what time the deliverymen would be coming they decided to go on to their house to wait. As they drove noisily down by the boat basin, they stopped and Stony bought the old sailboat with the stipulation that it be brought to the lagoon by their home. The seller readily agreed that would be no problem. They continued down their lane and through the gate to The Promise Land.

Cleaning in the back yard, Stony and Elaine heard the voices and laughter approaching down the lane. As they stepped from behind the corner of the building, there coming toward them looked to be the entire town each carrying a piece of furniture. Here a chair, there a lamp, a small table, there were dishes, pans, linens, a bed, the mattress and springs, all marching down the lane in single file. Stony asked. "Just how many pieces of furniture did you buy? This might take a while."

The first locals to arrive ask Elaine to please go inside and show them where each piece was to be placed. Stony stayed out front and directed each one at a time into the door, trying to give Elaine the time to place the items exactly as she wanted.

The exuberance of the crowd was almost more than they were ready to handle, but soon a cadence began and before they knew it, each large piece was exactly as she had pictured them in her mind. The local women almost had a sixth sense about the kitchen items. They should be within reach, as they were needed. The dishes in the cabinet closest to the table, silverware in the nearest drawer, glasses by the sink, mugs by the coffee maker, and the list went on. Elaine finally threw her hands in the air and said, "Go ahead, you can do it better than I would."

By giving them free rein, they were finished and all back in the front yard celebrating their accomplishment by the time she had made the bed, put the personal items in the bathroom cabinet, and put up the shower curtain. When she came out to join them, the curtains covered the windows, pictures hung on the wall, even Stony's ashtray set on the table by his chair. As she stepped outside to thank them, the crowd was already beginning to disperse. The patio furniture was on the veranda, the umbrella fully opened to provide shade for drinks this afternoon. She turned to Stony in disbelief. "Did I not hear you distinctly say, this might take a while? How in the world did they do all of this?" The group turned as one and waved to Stony and Elaine.

"I think you just got your answer, apparently they work well with others?" Both laughed and waved at the exceptional people whom they had the good fortune to call neighbors. "I know who I'll be calling when I need a boathouse." They stood waving to their new neighbors until they were out of sight. Stony pulled Elaine into his arms and said, "It will be a good life here."

Suddenly there were shouts from behind the house, and they ran to see if there was a problem. There were a dozen or so fishermen winching the old sailboat onto a skid. They had floated the old girl around and were heading into the lagoon. They then ran cables from three palm trees to the boat and were winching her into place on the makeshift skid.

Elaine laughed, "Now I feel like we are home. You have your toy in the backyard. I'll know exactly where you are when I need you."

The men were laughing, pointing, and waving as they clamored aboard the tow vessel to make their way back around to the boat basin.

Suddenly they realized how quiet it was. Everybody was finally going back home and leaving them to theirs. The jungle birds, the frogs, the monkeys, and the sea birds were providing them with beautiful background music for the ending of a perfect day in paradise.

"Well, what do you think, Mrs. Dawson?" Stony asked quietly, not wanting to disturb nature's sonata.

"I could never have dreamed anything this beautiful. But if I had dreamed of it, this would far surpass anything in my imagination."

Stony picked her up and carried her across the threshold of The Promise Land. Because, indeed, it was.

40

One by one, the wedding party departed for the states. Jack had even stayed over a day so he could go back with Carol Lee. She had to get back to work, but Jack lived in central California, so visits between the two made possible the hope for further commitment.

Stony and Elaine moved personal belongings from the bungalow to their new home. The hotel bills, the florist, the wedding planner, the band and the minister, all compensated for their services, with many thanks for a job well done.

Bob and Jillian had grown closer while they had been in Belize, and since both had planned vacations after the festivities, they decided to stay in Belize. Bob began to help Stony repair the old boat, while Elaine and Jillian took long walks and sometimes even longer talks. The boys could not figure how they found so much to talk about. They had just met a few weeks ago! Nevertheless, secretly they were all pleased that they had become best friends. The crash had been an awful thing, but it had made all of them stronger. Ready to take chances with life that a year ago none would have considered. The experience had bonded them together like family. There was no doubt but that they would remain close forever.

One night after Bob and Jillian had left for the hotel, Stony and Elaine went to bed and lay talking in the dark. Stony told her, "Bob is thinking about retiring early. He says he might even retire here to Belize."

"You are kidding! I didn't think the 'career man' would leave his job for any reason. Do you think he is seriously considering it?"

"It seems he has gotten a bit of sand in his shoes while he's been here." Stony laughed. "It would not surprise me to see him very soon. For sure after he and Jillian get married."

"What makes you think that Jillian will marry him?" Elaine rolled toward him and laid her arm across his chest.

"Trust me, I know these things." Stony quipped, "Besides, he will make a good dad for those girls."

Elaine laughed. "Sure, you know all kinds of things. What do you know about women, Mr. Dawson?"

"I know about you. You are longing for a swim. Lagoon? Or ocean? Which will it be?" He asked.

"How did you conclude that?" She said, "You do know I am not wearing my swimsuit, right?"

"I do. I know you are wearing absolutely nothing! That is why I want to get you in the water. Have you ever gone skinny dipping, Mrs. Dawson?"

"No, I haven't, but I might be willing to try it. Do you think it is safe? At night?"

"Sure it is, come on." He rolled out of bed, grabbed her hand and started out the back door. When they reached the sandy beach of the lagoon, he reached to get a hold on her waist to toss her into the water. However, she grabbed hold around his shoulders and the momentum carried them both into the cool blue liquid. They laughed and played in the water like a couple of kids, each trying to out splash the other. Out of breath, arms and legs tired from the exertion, they stumbled to the beach and fell on the warm sand, wrestling each other teasingly for a few minutes and then lay back quietly together, just holding hands.

"Do you really think Bob and Jillian might get married?" Elaine asked thoughtfully.

"He is a good man and there aren't too many of us left, and I know he is crazy about her." Stony responded. "Jillian is a very smart woman, and I know she enjoys his company, you can tell that. So just seems to me, the natural thing to do. Maybe later, maybe sooner, but sometime they'll do it."

The days passed into weeks, weeks into months, Elaine and Stony had become regular visitors at the village market. She had asked for and received numerous recipes for local dishes, and had prepared every one of them. Elaine loved to explore the arts and crafts booths. She spent many hours there as the village women taught her about grasses, seeds, feathers and flowers that would create many items of jewelry or just pieces for the beauty of art. She learned about their families, children and grandchildren were treasures here as well as in the states. She listened as they told the history of their country, the tales of how they met and married their men. They made new friends nearly every day. Captains and crews of the fishing boats would stop by occasionally to see new repairs on the boat. They all had suggestions about style, what was the proper equipment, the number of sails to have and color. Color was very important they told him, you must choose just the right one or the boat would not be complete. Stony listened to all their stories of adventures at sea, the fish they caught and those that got away. They told of crewmembers that lost their fight with the sea and about the new brave men that took their places. Sometimes they would question Stony on the military, about the skirmishes, and different countries he had seen. It was an exchange of knowledge that a classroom would never see.

Stony and Elaine became more familiar with the jungle and the animals that dwelled there. Some were dangerous, some were not, and it had nothing to do with their size. On one excursion, they discovered a waterfall with a small freshwater pool below. They skinny-dipped on occasion there, but their lagoon was the beloved swimming spot. Their favorite past time was bird watching. No matter the time of day or where you were, there were always birds to be seen. All the birds of Belize were colorful, some were rare species, and there were all sizes and all shapes. Both Stony and Elaine had started a bird watchers journal, keeping notes to identify what kind, the site they were on, what season it was and the birds' behavior. It was just one more thing they shared in their lives.

One morning Stony was behind the house working as usual on the boat, when he heard the familiar sound of the bell on the mail carrier's bicycle. He hurried into the kitchen and then out the front door with a tall glass of ice water for the carrier. They sat on the veranda and chatted while the carrier drank his water. "Very good! I look forward to coming to Promise Land." He smiled. Stony smiled back knowing he had started a tradition that would last a long time.

He glanced at the mail as the mail carrier's bicycle went back through the gate and up the lane. "Ta da!" He was holding an envelope from Washington D.C. F.A.A. Headquarters. Normally he let Elaine open the mail, but this one, he was curious about. It was indeed from Bob Farley. They had gotten married eight days ago! In addition, they were on their way to Belize with the girls for their honeymoon. "Hot damn! I knew it." Stony yelled, "Wait until I give Elaine the good news." He read on and found that they would arrive next Saturday. By George, that old dog did it, Stony thought.

He tossed the mail on the table and headed back to work on the boat. The new pier was finished last week. The local laborers had done a great job. He would need it shortly to tie up the boat. He heard Elaine coming down the lane on her new scooter. She had purchased a 49 cc from a female officer in the police department. It sounded like a popcorn popper and smoked like a diesel truck, but it got her where she wanted to go. It never failed to start when she needed to go for supplies. She loved that crazy thing, had even painted it pink. She was quite a sight running down the road popping and smoking. It brought a smile to his face just to picture her on it.

She stuck her head out the back door and yelled, "Honey I'm home. I'll be out in a minute." Putting the fresh supplies away, she headed to the project tent where she knew Stony would be working. Calling out again, "Babe, I'm home." Laughing at the obvious. She knew he could hear the scooter as soon as she reached the boat basin.

"Yes, I thought that would be you coming home, unless there is another one of those in town. God forbid!" Stony answered. He sat down the can of spar varnish and stepped out from the canvas cover. They kissed, and Stony told her, "I've got some good news." He reached for her hand and they walked back through the house and onto the veranda. He pointed to the letter from Bob. Elaine read the letter and began smiling before she was finished. "Well, how about that. You were right, and it appears sooner than later. That is great news."

Stony sucked in his stomach, which made his chest expand, and raised both arms in a mock bodybuilders pose. "See, I told you, I know these things." They both busted out laughing.

"I hate it when you are right." She said mockingly as she slapped at his stomach, making him exhale. "I'm going to fix dinner. See you back here in about 30 minutes."

After dinner, they were having a drink on the veranda and discussing Bob and Jillian. "I am really surprised that they are bringing the girls with them on their honeymoon." Stony said.

"Why?" Elaine asked. However, before he could answer she said. "Maybe they want to see their 'Uncle Stony' again." She smiled at him and continued, "Bob didn't just marry Jillian, the girls are a part of that package. I'm sure it will be fine."

'You are probably right, as I recall they were very well behaved when I was there. I have some more good news! I have finished the boat. I put the last coat of spar varnish this morning. So, after you paint on her name, she can be christened. Have you come up with a name for her?" Stony asked.

"Yes, I do have a name, when can I paint it on?" She asked excitedly.

"The varnish I put on today should be dry by tomorrow morning. You think that will be soon enough?"

Elaine was up early. She poured a cup of coffee, slipped on a pair of cutoff jeans, then headed for the tent. Stony was sound asleep. He had been sleeping longer and deeper than he had for years. His old nightmares were all but gone and the night sweats were a thing of the past.

When he was sleeping so soundly, Elaine let him sleep. She knew he would never catch up to what he had lost, but every little bit helped. After moving here and he started working on the boat, he had become almost as dark as the locals. When she really stopped and looked at him, he acted and appeared much younger than he had in the desert. She thought he was getting more handsome by the day. Of course, she was probably just a wee bit prejudiced. It was amazing, she thought, what the lack of stress and a good dose of sunshine could do for the human body.

After painting the name on the stern of the boat, she moved to the front bow and painted an emblem on each side. She could not see the whole boat, but if the top side looked as good as the bottom, the old girl was going to be a real looker. She had never imagined the old broken boat would be in one piece again, let alone be beautiful. She knew Stony's work ethic. He would not be stopping if it were not perfect.

She stepped out from under the canvas without looking at the rest of the boat. She knew he wanted to keep it a surprise until he was ready to launch her into the water. He is going to be disappointed if it does not cut through the water like a knife. She was just finishing the clean up of her brushes, when Stony came out the back door carrying two cups of hot coffee. As he approached her, he said, "Good morning, love." She loved the sound of his voice, first thing in the morning. It was gravely, rough, and man-sounding. It was music to her ears. "Thank you for the coffee. You timed that just right." She leaned close and kissed his mouth tenderly.

"How long have you been up?" He asked.

"Oh, I don't really know for sure, probably about three hours. But, I am finished. You can launch her when ready, Cap'n," then snapped him a sharp salute.

'Well done, sailor." He was pleased with her playfulness. It just made him adore her even more. "I love you." He kissed her forehead, her eyes, then her cheeks, her neck, and then back to her lips. They kissed deeply, passion rising in them both. He could feel her responsiveness as he heard her breathing heavier and more rapid. He glanced down at her breasts pushing against her tee shirt. "Come on, baby. Let's break her in properly. He climbed the ladder, and then helped Elaine aboard. She followed him into the cabin where they were surrounded by the smell of fresh varnish. They made love for the better part of an hour. Just when they thought it was the last of their passion, the waves would begin again, passion rising higher with each new union, until their bodies could stand no more. Both of them gasping for breath, they still could not let go of each other. They fell together back on the bunk and after several minutes, their breathing was almost back to normal.

"Greek mythology says that when the body has multiple orgasms, that if you look hard enough, right at the height of your passion, you can see the face of God." Elaine spoke ever so softly. They both thought about that for a while.

"Do you think the old girl can live up the 'break in' we just gave her?" She asked.

Stony began laughing, "She might come close, but I don't think anything could live up to that!" They had lain there long enough for Elaine to get a good look at the cabin area.

"I'm impressed." Sitting up to get a better view, "You have done some mighty fine work here, and I'm not talking about just your lovemaking ability."

"Which ever, I am glad you like it. You're not so bad yourself." Stony replied.

"I can't wait to see if she lives up to your expectations. When are you putting her in the water?"

They dressed and climbed down the ladder. Stony jerked the sides of the tent to the ground, and then pulled the top down into a pile at the front of the boat. "We need a drum roll. Tell me what you think."

Elaine just stood with her mouth open, admiring the shiny red and white sailboat. "She looks like a brand new boat. Stony, she is beautiful. I cannot believe it is the same boat. You've done a wonderful job."

Stony was smiling from ear to ear listening to her praise. He told her, "You go in and get yourself all spiffed up and when you are ready, bring the bottle of Champagne with you. I'll have to go get some local help to launch her."

Elaine was making some sandwiches and drinks when Stony left to get the help. She showered and changed into the sailor suit she had made herself. She put on her white shorts and the blue top with a pocket flap on the left upper chest. When she walked out back, it looked as if everyone in the village had come to help with the launching, or just to watch the process. After all, this was an important event.

The men finished placing the skid rollers, and then loosened the lines holding her on land. The only thing left was to christen her and knock out the chock that kept her in place.

Elaine served the refreshments while Stony took his shower and changed into his white trousers and blue striped shirt. Everyone had eaten and then crowded around the boat waiting for the moment of truth.

"Would she float?" "Isn't she beautiful?" "The color is perfect." "Would she be seaworthy?" The questions and comments were flying throughout the crowd. Elaine had gone back in to see if Stony was about ready. He was, and they walked out of the house together.

Stony helped Elaine climb the ladder at the bow of the boat. He gave a short speech, "I want to thank you all for coming. We appreciate each and everyone for helping through the progress of repairs. I think we are ready for the official christening of the boat. Elaine, do your thing!"

Elaine cleared her throat, the crowd quieted to hear every word. "I christen thee, this fine sailing ship, the *DREAMCATCHER*." She swung to bottle of Champagne into the bow of the boat. The bottle shattered and sprayed over those closest in the crowd.

Stony, completely caught off guard by the name she had chosen, walked to the stern to read the name for himself. He looked back to Elaine with his eyes brimming with tears. She smiled and said, "Okay, time to remove the chock, Captain Dawson."

He leaned back and swung the sledgehammer, caught a direct hit on the chock and knocked it free.

The *DREAMCATCHER* did not budge… she just sat there. Someone at the bow of the boat stepped forward put out his hands as if to give her a push. Stony shouted, "No, wait!" Then ever so slowly, she started her slide backward toward the water, gaining speed as she went. A deep V splashed in the water as she hit. The ropes began to tighten as she drifted out into the lagoon. The cheers from the crowd were deafening as each one ran to the water's edge.

Stony helped Elaine down from the ladder and said, "Great name!"

Elaine replied, "I thought it was appropriate." She handed him a present. "Open it!" She said.

As he tore off the wrapping, he recognized a Captain's sailing hat! He looked over at her as she pulled loose a flap over the pocket of her blue sailing blouse. He immediately saw the words in white stitching, 'First Mate'.

"Well, Cap'n Dawson, our chariot awaiteth. Put on your hat, I think we are ready to go sailing." She told him.

They walked down to the pier and climbed aboard the *DREAMCATCHER*, tied by the neighbors to the dock's edge. The red and white boat sat proudly in her new home. Elaine had painted the classic Indian Dream Catcher emblem on either side of the bow in beautiful traditional southwest colors. The name *DREAMCATCHER* was in vivid red across the stern. They walked to the bow and waved to the throng on the beach. Stony kissed Elaine to the cheers of the crowd. He cast off the lines and backed the boat into the lagoon. Raising the sail on the *DREAMCATCHER*, she listed slightly with the wind filling her sail. Heading out and around past the boat basin and into the open water. They cleared the breakwater and turned parallel to the land. The *DREAMCATCHER* heeled over picking up speed. She was slicing through the water like a hot knife through butter.

Elaine glanced over toward the shoreline and yelled for Stony to look. The whole town was watching from the shore of the boat basin, waving and shouting with great delight at the sight of the boat sliding through the ocean with such ease.

The afternoon sailed away, with Stony putting the *DREAMCATCHER* through every maneuver that he could think to perform. When they finally tied her back up to the pier, they stored her sail in the forward hold. After closing her up, they stepped onto the pier. Elaine turned to Stony and saw tears. He was crying tears of pure joy. She stepped forward, took him into her arms, and snuggled to his chest. Holding him tightly she said, "Go ahead, honey. It is okay to cry. You have needed this for a very long time. There is no one around but your *DREAMCATCHER* and me, the dream you caught and we both understand." She went on, "I am here for you, just like you have been there for me." She held him until the sobbing ceased. He bent down and kissed her. "God, how I love you." He said. They walked slowly toward the house arm in arm.

41

Saturday Bob and his new family arrived at the airfield. Stony was there to pick them up in his newly acquired WWII Army jeep. He hugged Jillian, shook Bob's hand, then bent down and picked up the two girls loading them into the jeep. Jillian introduced the two girls, Jessica, the oldest, and then Jennifer, the youngest, formally to their 'Uncle' Stony. The girls hugged 'Uncle' Stony's neck and both talking at once said, "We remember you! You are the man that brought our presents from daddy."

"That's right, Jess and Jenny." Stony answered." Is it okay if I call you that?"

They both smiled and looked at their mother, "Yes."

"Are you girls ready to go to your home away from home?" 'Uncle' Stony asked.

Jenny shook her head yes, and after loading their luggage they headed for Promise Land.

Elaine came running out of the house when they arrived. She

met each and every one with a kiss and a hug. As Jillian and the girls settled into their rooms, Stony took Bob out to see the sailboat.

"Dream Catcher...mmm? Ain't that an Indian name?" Bob asked.

"Sure is." Stony smiled. "I love it! That's something Elaine surprised me with, I told her she could name it whatever she wanted."

"Damn," Bob whistled softly, "man you sure made that old scow look some kinda good."

Just then, Jillian, Elaine and the girls came out of the house into the back yard. The girls came running down to the pier to join 'Uncle' Stony and "Daddy' Bob. Stony looked at Bob and smiled, "Feels good doesn't it? Being a daddy." Bob just smiled and said, "I can't begin to tell you how good."

Stony helped Jess and Jenny onto the boat and told them to look around if they wanted. They were delighted to oblige.

"So, how is married life? Is it different than you expected?" Stony asked. "The girls seem to have accepted you pretty well, how about Jillian?"

"Stony, I hope you don't mind, but I kinda used you as my example. I figured that if a crusty old sailor could make the leap after so many years, surely I could manage it." Bob started laughing. "In the beginning, it was tough for me. The little ones, intimidated me at first, but Jillian has stepped in when she saw I was at a loss for words. We are getting closer every day. It seems like the most natural thing in the world. I love them all, very much. I can not imagine life without them now."

Bob went on to explain, "Jennifer has a clean bill of health and should be fine. Which, by the way, I feel I owe you for what you did for Jillian and the girls."

"You do not owe me anything. You just take care of them. If I'm going to be their 'Uncle', you just need to take care of my interests." Stony told him. "They are pretty cute little critters, if I do say so myself." They both laughed, Stony patted Bob on the back. "Come on I want to show you our boat."

After dinner, they put the girls to bed for the night. The adults moved out onto the veranda for a few drinks and much conversation. Eventually, the topic being discussed was the plane crash that had brought them all together. Bob made the comment that sometimes he really did not understand the way things work out in life. "It was always my responsibility to find the problems and to point fingers to specific things. On the other hand, events are just flawed sometimes. The results that come from them are never good. I think there are some things that might be beyond normal reasoning. Things that man was just never meant to know." Stony thought about what Bob had said, he stood and walked to the edge of the veranda. "You know," he said, "sometimes we are faced with things beyond our control. Then, we do what is necessary to overcome that situation. The Indian knew how to cope with almost any situation that might occur at any given time. I learned early in life from my grandmother, who was half-Indian, about the ways of the Indian people. Probably the most important thing I learned was to observe. Often when I questioned her, Grandma would quote to me words from a Medicine Man. It went something like this. I have noticed in my years that men have a liking for a certain animal, or tree, or even a spot of ground. Men should pay attention to that preference. They should seek diligently what is best to do in order to make themselves worthy of that entity. They might have dreams, which could show how to purify their lives toward that end. Let a man concentrate on that item and make a study of it, learning of its natural innocent ways. Let him understand its sounds and movement, for nature wants to communicate with man. However, God will not allow it directly. Man must do the greater part in trying to understand and secure that communication and connection.

What she taught me has served me well through the years. I pay attention to nature and listen as it speaks. The trouble with man today is that they do not pay attention to anything except to line their pockets.

That, my friends, is why I have lost my self to this country, these people. They do not need the worries of money, or our imagined successes, they have each other. They have their faith in the nature they live in and around everyday. A handshake is still the accepted form of commitment. They have no idea there is a piece of paper that men call contracts. If they commit to you, a piece of paper would make no difference.

Hell, most Americans are too lazy to even welcome a new neighbor next door to them, let alone to the community. They want every one to come to them. 'Call me, come by, do you have something I can borrow? Is there any way I can take advantage of you?'

The freedoms that Americans enjoy were paid by the blood and lives of my ancestors, my pilgrim forefathers, my brethren in uniform. Nevertheless, they will be the first to scream and yell if their children are sent into a conflict somewhere in defense of their way of life. The world has gotten so far away from the ways of nature. I am surprised that humankind has survived at all.

People are so distraught with their very existence, so anguished with their meaningless lives they are almost beside themselves. They are poisoning their own water, polluting the very air they breathe, gorging themselves with food trying to fill that void they feel in their very souls. Parents cannot understand why their children are rebellious, smoking dope, poking holes in their own bodies. Thanks to my Grandmother and her infinite wisdom, I paid attention to nature and I learned her ways so that I could live in harmony with her.

Elaine and I became dependant on nature's idiosyncrasies to survive. In the process, we fell in love and found eternal companionship. We never looked at the desert as a dry, desolate and hostile place. It was vibrant and abundant with life. All we had to do was look and listen to what it whispered. We then adjusted to take full advantage to what nature was putting before us. Was it good? Was it bad? Hell, I cannot answer that. <u>It was just life.</u> We took what was given. We appreciated it and thanked God every day for what was provided.

Bob, I cannot give you an answer. Every man, woman and child, every creature, every living thing has to find their answer. There is just one catch. You have to look, to seek out. You have to let nature show you the way.

Learn to listen to nature and act accordingly. My hope is that you raise your children to watch, pay attention, and respect it. It could be a best friend someday!"

Stony turned to Elaine, she was crying, Jillian was wiping her eyes with Bob's handkerchief. "Whoa, guys, I didn't mean to make you cry. I am sorry. I guess I got on my bandwagon there for a minute. It was supposed to be a good thing!"

"Damn, you would make one hell of a politician! Bob said in amazement. "I would vote for you, by God! I might even run your campaign."

"Hell, Bob, they would have us killed within a week. No thanks! I will just stay here and try to keep this place as pristine as we found it. I like my life, now. We seem to have found the best this world could offer, a nature lover's paradise. I have good friends and the love of my wife. It does not get any better than this. Yep, life is just fine here in The Promise Land."

Morning came and Stony managed to drag himself out of bed and to the kitchen for a cup of coffee. Glancing out the back window, he noticed Bob was already up and down on the dock. He seemed to be watching something very intently. Stony ambled out the back door and down to where Bob stood and joined him. Not wanting to disturb him, Stony stood watching the water with Bob.

Bob said, "Look out there," pointing to a dolphin swimming lazily in the lagoon. "That thing has been up here by the pier at least 10 times. Do you think it is trying to tell us something?"

Stony thought for a second that Bob was joking around, but Bob never took his eyes off the dolphin. "Maybe it is," Stony replied. "What is it doing to make you think that?"

"Well," Bob answered. "It swims out to the breakwater like it is leaving, then it turns and comes straight back to your pier."

Stony told Bob, "Cast off the lines!" They boarded *DREAMCATCHER*, Stony started the motor and backed out into the lagoon and headed out toward the breakwater. The dolphin swam directly in front of the boat, arching in and out of the dark blue water of the lagoon. They followed the dolphin around and out of the boat basin.

Bob yelled. "There, look Stony, it's a boat. It looks as if it has capsized and is floating in the rocks." Stony turned and headed for the boat and the leeside of the rocks. There they found the fisherman alive and well, but very much waterlogged. After loading him onboard, they idled into the area around his boat. Several tries later, Bob snagged the rope of the overturned vessel. Slowly they took the fisherman and his boat back to shore inside the boat basin.

The locals had seen them dragging in the boat and was soon onshore to help get the boat tied to land and turned upright. Stony was always surprised at the number of people that showed up in a crowd. It didn't take them long to get the boat right side up and the fisherman to the beach.

Stony told the Police Chief how Bob had listened to the dolphin, and therefore, had found the fisherman and his overturned boat.

The Chief of Police invited Bob to come to the station with him to file a report. Stony grinned from ear to ear. He waved to Bob and the Chief as they backed out of the lane, turned around and started up the small hill into town. There had been at least fifty locals patting Bob on the back, jabbering away, wanting very much to be associated with the new 'hero'. "See you back at The Promise Land!" Stony yelled at he headed around to take his boat back to its home in the lagoon. Bob waved.

Elaine and Jillian met the boat. "Is Bob alright?" Jillian asked, "I thought he would be with you."

"Oh, he is fine. Right about now he is meeting everyone in the village that was not down here on the shoreline. After all, he was a hero this morning. I imagine he will be home in a while, as soon as the Police Chief tires of showing him off."

The women stood with their mouths open, neither one knew what to say. Finally breaking the silence, Elaine asked, "Okay, what did we miss?"

Stony started laughing, "Come on, I'll tell you over breakfast."

When stony finished his coffee Elaine scolded him, "Shame on you, you knew the Chief would drag Bob to every house in the village."

"Well, it is the best way to get acquainted with the locals. I'll just bet when he comes back he will understand why I like these people so much."

Jillian was giggling. "You mean, Mr. All-Business, may actually let his hair down at little?"

"Yep, I think I can guarantee it!" Stony replied.

Bob arrived back at Promise Land shortly before noon. He walked into the kitchen where Elaine and Jillian were talking.

"Where is that sorry assed husband of yours?" Bob's voice boomed in the small room.

"Why Bob? Is something wrong?" Elaine asked him smiling.

"Oh, nothing! Nothing at all. That is if you like holding every baby in town, shaking every hand in the village, and for all eternity, I will be known as 'The Man Who Talks to Fish!' My life is now complete."

"Sit down, Bob." Jillian spoke softly but firmly. "Think about what really happened today. Now here, drink some coffee." In less than a minute all three were laughing so hard they were wiping tears from their cheeks as Bob told them every detail of his morning experiences.

Stony had taken Jess and Jenny on a short cruise and just returning when he heard the laughter coming from the house. "Well, I reckon your Dad is back from town." The girls ran up the pier together, and then into the house.

Both girls tried to jump into Bob's lap at the same time. "Uncle Stony took us on the boat and we drove!"

"Wow, that's great!" Bob said glowing, "You will really have something to tell all your friends when you get back home."

Stony had slipped in the kitchen door and was pouring himself a cup of coffee when Bob noticed his presence in the room.

"Thanks a lot, old buddy." Bob told him. "You may now refer to me as 'The Man Who Talks to Fish.' I have held more babies than I could count, visited every damned house here, and became close personal friends with the Chief of Police!"

"That's not a bad day for your first day in Paradise." Stony replied smiling from ear to ear.

The next few days were spent exploring the area and the girls loved the jungle. Uncle Stony and Aunt Elaine were now their 'bestus friends in the whole wide world.'

The last night of their stay, Stony and Bob walked the beach and around the boat basin talking about future plans. Bob told Stony he had come to a decision about retirement. He wanted to spend as much time as he could with Jillian and the girls. He and Jillian had chosen to make their home in the States, more for the girls, than for themselves. "But, that doesn't mean we won't be back. We plan to become regular visitors to Paradise."

Stony told Bob how he appreciated his honesty and help back in the Southwest after the crash. "I am proud to be considered your friend."

"It's me who should be thanking you for giving me some insight as to what humanity is doing to itself. It is easy to get caught up in trying to get ahead." Bob stuck out his big hand and as Stony took it, he said, "You will always be my friend." They sat talking late into the night.

They had one last dinner and then one last swim in the sunset before going to the airfield. Uncle Stony and Aunt Elaine were hugged at least a hundred times before the new family finally boarded for the flight home. Stony and Elaine stood and watched as the plane flew out of sight.

On the way home, Stony stopped the jeep at the gate and looked up to the words, The Promise Land. Elaine said, "It really is that and so much more." She looked down the lane to the little pink house trimmed in white, with the blue lagoon providing the backdrop, the green of the jungle off to the right, and every color of the rainbow displayed by the birds that flittered from tree to tree.

"It is that for sure." Stony said as he drove on to the house, "And you, my dear, are the most beautiful of all that surrounds you."

They parked and walked hand in hand down the hill to the pier, untied the red and white sailboat. They had decided on a moonlight cruise. Stony trimmed up the sail and they watched the sun set from the waters far beyond the boat basin and the shoreline. Stony readjusted the course and watched as Elaine slipped off her clothes and lay atop the cabin. He watched as the ocean air and the moonlight danced over her gorgeous body.

Stony smiled, remembering that not long ago, he did not have much of a will to live. He felt as though he had lost every purpose to go on. His children were grown and busy with lives of their own. He was old before his time, aged beyond his years. He thought about the bad dreams, the sleepless nights, the gallons of liquor in which he had tried to drown. Yet, in a moment of unanticipated horridness, he was forced in a unwanted situation. It had changed his perspective on living and therefore, loving again.

He stood at the helm watching the perfect beauty of a creature that only God could have dreamed into existence. The moonlight was dancing over the curves of her breasts and down her thighs. The moon seemed to be highlighting the sensual lines and curves of her body. She was his, the very reason for his desire to live life again to the fullest. She was his and he was hers, a dream come true. He tied off the helm and made his way toward a night to remember aboard the *DREAMCATCHER*!

CPSIA information can be obtained
at www.ICGtesting.com
Printed in the USA
FSOW03n0149160217
30857FS